AN AGE OF HEROES

S. A. Richardson©2020

Other Titles

Tales of Valhanor Series:
The Chalice of Knowledge

The Laurel of Victory

The Mask of Melanthius

The Banner of Stars

The Tall Elf

Copyright

An Age of Heroes

Copyright © S. A. Richardson 2020

The author S. A. Richardson asserts his moral right to be identified as the author of this work. All rights reserved. No part of this publication may be reproduced by any means without prior written permission of the author.

ISBN: 9798638887117

About the Author

S. A. Richardson lives in the historic town of Tutbury in the U.K. with his wife and two children. He graduated from school in 2002 and took a fulltime job at one of the largest poultry suppliers in Britain, where he worked until 2010 when a minor medical problem with his spine forced him to give up the job. Failing to find another job, he took up writing as a pastime and has continued it ever since.

Follow Author S. A. Richardson on:

Twitter @Valhanor

Or

Facebook @s.a.richardsonauthor

An Age of Heroes

Is dedicated to the memory of

Jean Florrie Hadfield

Our Mamma

Table of Contents

Other Titles 5

Copyright 6

About the Author 7

The Lost Isle of Arcanum 12

The Last Dragon 85

The Song of the Lost Prince 113

Trials of a wizard 195

Appendix 315

There was once a time when dragons ruled the sky,

when mythical beasts roamed the wild.

A time of noble men and valiant deeds, a true age.

An Age of Heroes.

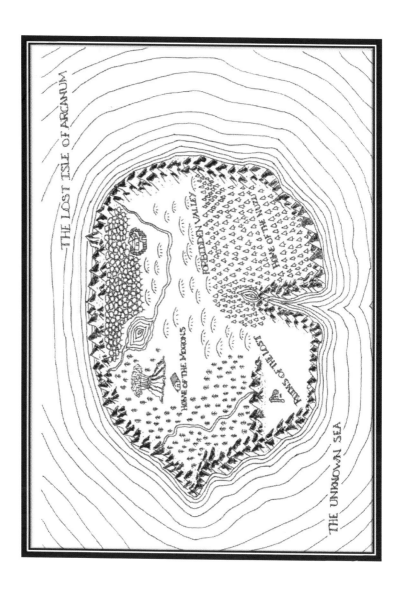

THE LOST ISLE OF ARCANUM

I

The Disappearance of Aetius

From the early kingdoms of men, there are but a few stories that have survived the long decay of time. The few that have echoed down through the ages are stories of brave men who stood for truth and justice, of heroes slaying fierce monsters, and of wise kings that ruled over a golden age. But of all these stories there stands one above all others, for the great courage of those involved; that is the story of the brave men that undertook the quest to the mythical Isle of Arcanum.

The tale begins long-ago with a solitary man standing upon the shore of Thalassa, the cold sea foaming around his bare feet as it surged and then retreated over the sand. The sun had now sunk, and night had swept across the bay, readying the world for slumber. But for hours more did the man wait, his eyes fixed out across the blackened sea and purpled sky dotted with stars. His name was Miltiades, the son of the ill-fated Aetius, and a member of one of the leading families of the town.

Behind Miltiades was the ancient town of Thalassa, built upon the clifftop that overlooked the northern sea in the Bay of Evas. A large columned temple that housed a bronze statue of the Star Goddess Thalassa, the town's namesake, had been built at the highest point alongside the

Assembly House where the members met to debate matters of state. Following a pathed road down from the public buildings were the villas of the wealthy, stone buildings that had been painted white with flat, red tiled rooftops. From there the road narrowed into where those that had money, but were not considered the elite, dwelt. There the houses lessened in size and grandeur from those of the elite but were yet still adorned in comfort. From there the pathed road became a dirt track that wound its way down the cliffs towards the docks. Here the houses were of wood, painted white with a red stripe around their base. This was where most of the people of Thalassa dwelt, cramped around the docks that harboured ships from near and far.

Miltiades was, at this time, believed to be soft. He was short in stature and plump from an easy life. Born into a wealthy family, Miltiades had wanted for nothing, having servants to build his fires, bathe him and prepare his meals. In appearance, he is said to have looked much like his father, having his father's dark hair and brown eyes. But that is where the similarities ended, For Miltiades' father was known to be a great man, a man of the sea, and much loved by the people of Thalassa. Unlike Miltiades, his father Aetius was not gifted with noble birth, and had risen from a humble oarsman to a member of the town's Assembly, a feat never being done before.

It had been during this rise that Aetius had met Thea, the daughter of a leading family and renowned as a beauty. If rumour is to be believed, they had many secret meetings down at the docks where they had declared their love for one another. Whether true or not, none now know. But what is well-known is that when Thea's hand in marriage was announced to some rich man, Aetius donned his best cloak and stormed to Thea's family home. There he declared his undying love for her and demanded that it was he that was betrothed to Thea. But Thea's father had laughed at Aetius and mocked him by setting him an unachievable challenge. In front of members of the Assembly, he told Aetius that if he could offer a gift more pleasing than what had already been offered, then he would grant his daughter's hand. It is said that Aetius set sail at once, being in command of a small fishing boat, to return two weeks later with a golden necklace adorned with black pearls from the furthest shores to the east. This was deemed to be a princely gift, and thus Aetius and Thea were wed.

In the years that followed, Aetius made a name for himself by being the first to circle navigate the entire island of Valhanor, mapping the coast as he went. On his return he gifted the town with exotic goods brought back from his expedition and dedicating the map to the temple where it was to hang many years after. These actions blessed Aetius with fame which he used to aggrandize his position. The Assembly acknowledged his worth and appointed him, and all his kin to follow, a place within the Assembly. But for all Aetius' qualities, he was no politician, and was often said to have fallen asleep during lengthy debates. But it was not for his political promise that the Assembly found him of use, but his reputation and good standing with the neighbouring towns. Many missions did Aetius undertake for the town of Thalassa, securing trade and friendship for its people. Though these dealings brought much fame and wealth on Aetius, he longed ever for the open sea, to sail into the unknown. For at heart, Aetius was an adventurer.

After a late summer's storm had ravaged the town, a man was washed up on the shore, his skin red and cracked from the sun. He was taken in by Aetius and given treatment for his wounds. It was after speaking with this man that Aetius learnt of Arcanum, an island believed to be naught but myth. The man's words of an uncharted island stirred Aetius' spirit, and the next day he sought approval for an expedition from the Assembly. After a debate that lasted an entire day, Aetius was given his leave, and he set sail in the following spring. But Aetius was yet to return.

For ten long years had Miltiades waited; and each night he would stand upon the shore, looking out for his father's return. For hours he waited, until the sea rose to his knees. Then he would give up his watch and began his long walk home, his heart once more disappointed. He had grown up in his father's vast shadow, and he had found it difficult to achieve the high expectancy placed upon him. After Aetius had left, he had felt freed from all the pressure his father had put on him. But now, after ten years, he felt vulnerable.

Miltiades waded out from the cold sea and donned his sandals, walking up the beach and taking the narrow path up towards his home. His thoughts drifted back to the day his father had left. He had been only twelve at the time, but already plump from a soft life, and he remembered vividly the cheering crowds at the docks. Many of the other children had begged with their fathers to go with them, but Miltiades had been relieved that he was to stay at home with his mother. Looking back now, Miltiades had wished that he had at least made a pretence of wanting to go, that maybe it would have somehow given him prestige in the eyes of the people. Each of his father's crew had been draped with a garland of flowers as they boarded a bireme, an ancient warship with two decks of oars. His father's ship was called the Amica, a large vessel with a blue hull and black sail with a white octopus in the centre. Before his father had boarded, he had kissed his mother and promised her that he shall return before the winter. He had then turned to Miltiades, placing his hands upon his shoulder.

"Take good care of your mother Miltiades, do well in your studies and pay heed to counsel." Without another word Aetius had boarded his ship and gave command for the oarsmen to pull away from the dock. Miltiades, along with his mother, had watched until the Amica had sailed out of sight.

Once Miltiades returned home from the shore, he discovered his mother in the company of two members of the Assembly. One was aged and the other much younger, but both were often in opposition to Miltiades. His return had gone unnoticed, and so he listened in on the conversation.

"The Assembly must insist upon you coming to the Assembly House and pronounce that your husband is dead."

"The Assembly has not the power to demand that of me," Miltiades mother replied with confidence. "And nor shall it grant itself the power to allow a woman into the sacred chamber of men."

"Your father has sent us out of respect of Aetius' good name with the people and implores you to come before the Assembly and proclaim your husband dead," the older of the two men said. He was wrinkled with age with a receding hairline and small rodent-like eyes, and he wore the red robes of a member of the Assembly. "Too much time has passed, and your father wishes that you mourn no longer."

"I do not mourn for my husband, for in my heart I know that he still lives." Thea stood from her chair to signal that the meeting was at an end. "No, I shall not act against my heart by proclaiming Aetius dead. While I have hope within me, I shall stay loyal as the Star Gods will a wife to be."

The two members of the Assembly remained seated, their decorum turning serious. The younger of the two leaned forwards in his chair and said, "Then the Assembly has no choice but to convene on the morrow and itself proclaim Aetius dead. Then we shall debate on which of two suitors you should marry." He was a sly looking man with thick lips and short, dark hair, and himself wearing the robes of a member of the Assembly. His voice was self-confident and his face constantly half smiling in a mocking expression.

Miltiades disliked the way they spoke to his mother and entered the room with the intent of driving them away. "Is this what our noble members of the Assembly have become? Mere tyrants that force their will upon women?"

"Miltiades," the younger of the two members greeted, "we are merely doing our duty as the First Citizen has instructed us." He stood from his chair and glared at Miltiades, his hatred evident. "You know the law Miltiades, that all women must be married."

"My father is not dead," Miltiades replied, "and my mother is not free to remarry."

"If you will not proclaim Aetius dead, then the Assembly will convene on the morrow, and itself pronounce that Aetius is dead." It had been the elder of the two that had spoken. Seeing that there was no more to be said, he stood and politely bid Miltiades and his mother a goodnight, before taking his leave with the younger member.

"They cannot do this!" Miltiades said, his anger forcing tears to well in the corner of his eyes. "What right do they think they have?"

"There is little choice now my son," Thea said as she slumped back down in her chair, feeling defeated. "The Assembly will convene and vote a motion declaring your father dead and forcing me to remarry."

"I'm a member of the Assembly," Miltiades said as though he had real power to stop the motion, "I will speak against it and have it vetoed like before."

"You cannot veto the motion again; it is against the law." Thea said, having a sound knowledge of the proceedings of the Assembly. "Nor have you the support of enough members to stop it."

"But those that loved my father shall back me," Miltiades answered in hope.

"Your father has been gone for too long," Thea explained, "his power has faded, and his supporters have turned to others in hope of aggrandizing their own position."

"Then I shall not attend, and the Assembly will be forced to adjourn."

Thea shook her head. "They will simply just vote in your absence. It is better that you are there to speak against it."

"Then what must we do mother?"

"Prey to Thalassa that your father returns or offers up some proof that he yet lives."

"You sound as though you have given up hope mother."

Thea stood and walked over to Miltiades, kissing his forehead. "Get some rest, you will need all your wit for the Assembly tomorrow."

That night Miltiades found little rest as his mind was filled by the daunting task of swaying the Assembly not to pronounce his father dead. There had been two votes before, the first coming five years after Aetius' departure. That vote had been easily defeated as Aetius still had many supporters within the Assembly, but the second had been a much closer contest, and Miltiades had been forced to use his veto over the motion. But tomorrow, he would have no such right, and his only hope was to persuade enough members not to back the motion.

II

The Assembly of Thalassa

The Assembly House was an old building, said to have been built upon the spot where the first people of Thalassa settled. It was a rectangular building with six marble columns on both sides and four on the front and rear. The roof was a sloped pediment, red tiled and decorated with small statues of sea creatures around the edge. Thick wooden doors reinforced with bronze barred the only entrance to the inner chamber where the Assembly met to debate and vote on matters of state. The rectangular chamber inside was lit by many braziers, their smoke staining the white walls they were placed against. The floor was a colourful mosaic of the sea and marine life, and the stepped seats were cushioned to offer a little comfort for the members. A throne-like chair was opposite, and unlike the stepped seats, this chair was far more grandeur, being decorated in golden leaf and silk cushions with a matching footrest. This was the seat of the First Citizen of Thalassa.

The Assembly was made up of two hundred men from the leading families; and from these men one was elected as the First Citizen. The First Citizen held the power of a dictator and served for a term of two years. At the end of this term, the First Citizen would then be called before the members of the Assembly and be judged on whether he had abused his power while in office. Any one of the members could bring a charge of misconduct against the First Citizen, and should that charge be proven, then the First Citizen would be exiled for ten years.

In times of a state emergency, the Assembly could extend the First Citizen's term of office for an unlimited period. One such period had been during the war with the Cremetis, a southern tribe renowned for their burning of towns. At this time, a man called Bellerophon had been the First Citizen. When the Cremetis had invaded territory belonging to Thalassa, Bellerophon had been at the end of his term. The Assembly recognised that he was the leading man of the state, and had the love of the citizens, so they granted him an extension of two more years to deal with the threat. Thalassa went on to win the war, but on the appointed day that Bellerophon was expected to yield his power, he refused and proclaimed himself king. But the Assembly would suffer no king, and a month later they assassinated Bellerophon on the steps of the Assembly House and threw his blooded corpse off the cliffs that overlooked the sea.

On the morning appointed, Miltiades took his seat in the Assembly House along with the other members. All had been told of the purpose of the meeting and there was much talk on how it was necessary for the state to move past the matter of Aetius.

As the First Citizen entered, the chamber fell silent and all stood in a show of respect. He was an older man with short grey hair and knowledgeable eyes that scanned the chamber to be sure all were present. Like all the members, he was dressed in a red toga. His name was Erastus, a wealthy man with strict traditionalist views, and the father of Thea.

"Esteemed members of the Assembly," Erastus said as he raised his arms, "Be seated and let us begin."

Sat on a stool beside the First Citizen was an ancient looking man, heavily wrinkled and toothless with age. In his hands he held a heavy looking staff with a bronze tip at the base which he used to bang on the floor to bring the members to order. He was known as the Father of the House, and his duty was to ensure that the laws were upheld. "I hereby proclaim this session of the Assembly now open." His voice was croaky and horse. "I invite the First Citizen to the floor."

Erastus rose from his chair and placed one hand across his chest and the other held out in front of him with his fingers curled up as was the fashion for when making a motion. "Esteemed members of the Assembly, I called forth this session to propose a motion of marriage between my noble daughter Thea, and our most trusted colleague Orpheus."

"You overstep your right First Citizen." It was the Father of the House that had spoken. He banged the bronze tip of his staff on the floor and called, "Order dictates that we must first vote on whether this session is indeed valid."

"Then let us vote," Erastus replied as he went and sat back in his chair, wanting to get on with business.

The Father of the House shakily stood from his chair. "Is there agreement to the validity of this session?" His eyes narrowed as he scanned across the chamber, watching as many of the members stood in favour of the session's validity. "A majority has been reached, and I therefore proclaim this session valid. All motions put before the members this day are therefore lawful." He once more banged his staff on the floor before sitting back on his stool.

Erastus now stood and addressed the Assembly. "Esteemed members, as you are aware there is a great matter that divides us. For too long have we argued over the fate of our most honoured citizen. I therefore put forward that we vote in favour of the marriage of Thea and Orpheus to end this division."

The Father of the House banged the tip of his staff on the floor to silence the muttering amongst the members. "The motion is heard, and I now invite any to speak against it."

Miltiades shot up onto his feet and angrily pointed down at his grandfather, the First Citizen. "You seek only to aggrandize your position with this motion, for all in this sacred chamber knows that Orpheus is your puppet, and through him you would take my father's wealth from its rightful belonging."

"You speak not as a member of this Assembly, but as an angered child." Erastus replied in a calm tone as though he were in the right. "Every member within this chamber knows the law, that all women of child birthing age should be married to produce children and secure Thalassa's future."

At this point, a man sat close to Miltiades stood. His name was Aegidius, a middle-aged man with short grey hair and thick arms from his years of seamanship. "Miltiades does indeed speak as an angered child, but he has every right to do so. Aetius was beloved by many here, and more so by the people we serve. Should one so revered be simply cast aside, his great deeds forgotten?"

"I seek not for banishment of Aetius' deeds," the First Citizen answered, "But to proceed forward from this impasse."

"This motion put before us, if passed, would render Aetius and all his crew dead. For I hear two motions merged into one. The First Citizen asks that we vote in favour of his arranged marriage, but by doing so we would also proclaim Aetius and his crew dead. I therefore put to the Assembly that we should vote to separate the two motions."

The chamber erupted into arguments and counter arguments, and the Father of the House was forced to bang on the floor with his staff to restore order. "In agreement with Aegidius is the law, the Assembly cannot pass two motions with only the one vote."

Erastus' face reddened with frustration, though he had expected such a move against him. "I concede to the law in which I serve, and therefore retract my motion and put forward another, that Aetius and his crew are pronounced dead so that their families may have closure."

"The motion is heard." The Father of the House once again banged the tip of his staff on the floor, "does any wish to speak against it?"

"I reject this motion," Miltiades stood, "and so should all within this sacred chamber. Esteemed members of the Assembly, my father undertook many diplomatic missions on behalf of the people of Thalassa. Successful missions that brought much trade to our ports, missions that made our enemies our friends. No one man has ever served Thalassa like my father has, tirelessly working in securing years of peace and friendship. It was this Assembly that appointed him to these quests, would the same Assembly now vote him dead with not one shred of proof of his failure?"

"It has been ten long years since Aetius departed on his quest to find the lost isle of Arcanum," Erastus replied in a confident tone that he hoped would sway the vote in his favour. "And it grapples with my heart, for Aetius was a son by law to me. But my duty as First Citizen forces me to ask why it is that he has failed to return, for we all know that Aetius was at his greatest when sailing upon the sea and was considered the best amongst us. If this Assembly votes against this motion, it will give false hope to the families of that ill-fated crew, families that look to us for leadership and closure. Esteemed members, for too long has this matter tormented us, and it was out of honour for Aetius and his crew that we have not given up hope. But now our hearts must give way to the reason of our minds. I ask that you vote in favour of this motion so that the families may end their lamentation, and that the names of that ill-fated crew can be carved into the walls of the temple."

"To vote in favour of this motion," Miltiades warned, "is to vote in favour of creating a tyrant. For if this motion is passed the motion of my mother's marriage shall swiftly follow. I accuse the First Citizen of abusing his power to pass motions that will aggrandise his own position!"

Erastus' face reddened with anger, and his earlier calm began to crack. "Esteemed members, Miltiades' grief has clouded his better judgement. He stands there and accuses me of ambitions of becoming a tyrant, but was it not I that rejected this Assembly's call to grant me longer powers beyond that of what our laws grant?"

Many of the members were swayed by the First Citizen's argument and believed that he was simply trying to do his duty; and so, they heckled Miltiades until he slumped back in his seat, defeated.

"Division is heard," the Father of the House banged on the floor with the tip of his staff, "does any wish to propose a counter motion?"

At this point Aegidius stood and raised his hands in the formal fashion for addressing the Assembly. "In an unknown limbo we find ourselves, for both Miltiades and Erastus have fine points. What folly it would be if we were to do nothing as Miltiades would have us, and how untrustworthy we would be perceived to foreign powers if we were not to honour our own laws. But what folly it would look also if we esteemed members were to proclaim Aetius and his crew dead, only for them to return."

"So, what motion do you propose?" Erastus said as he sat back in his throne-like chair. "What does the great mind of Aegidius will us to do?"

"I propose that we send another expedition to Arcanum, with the quest of discovering the fate of Aetius and his crew."

Erastus at first shook his head, unseeing of how another expedition would help. But then dark thoughts swept into his mind, and a plan was quickly formed. "In agreement am I with Aegidius, for his proposal is one of worth. I therefore propose that Miltiades lead the quest to find the answers he so sorely seeks."

For the remainder of that day did the Assembly debate, with Miltiades arguing that he was not experienced enough to lead the expedition. But Erastus had swayed the members that it was most befitting to the Gods for the son to seek the father. So, it was passed by a majority that Miltiades was to lead a crew of volunteers into the unknown. But Erastus, fearing that Miltiades would simply just sail to some safe port to leave the Assembly in limbo, imposed a time condition. Miltiades was given one year to find his father and return home; if he did not return in the allotted time, or returned without a trace of Aetius, then both he and his father would be proclaimed dead. To further hinder Miltiades, Erastus had a motion passed that forbade the state from intervening. From his own purse would Miltiades have to find a ship and provisions; and his crew were not to be commanded by law or oaths to go further than their will would take them.

III

The Crew of the Oculus

So it was that Miltiades reluctantly took to his task, first securing weapons, and armour, then a ship, a bireme with two decks of oars that could employ 120 rowers. It was 80 feet long with a beam width of 10 feet and a flat keel so that it could be easily beached. A tall mast rose above the deck to which was fitted a yellow and black striped sail. A bronze figurehead of a woman with her arm outstretched as if pointing out to sea was attached to the bow, and painted on the blue hull below the figurehead was a pair of white eyes, from which the bireme took her name, the Oculus. But securing a ship worthy for the quest was the simple part, as he had the money to afford such things; now he needed the men to crew it.

So, Miltiades sent one of his most trusted servants down to the docks, where he tried to recruit the best men available. But none were willing. News of Miltiades quest had quickly travelled and was much talked about in the taverns. Miltiades was no captain went the talk, a dangerous undertaking that only a fool would agree to. If the great sea master Aetius himself had not returned from Arcanum, what chance did a milksop like Miltiades stand? So low was the reputation of Miltiades, that the rowers' benches of the Oculus remained empty.

Days passed with little joy for Miltiades, and he was forced to offer one hundred gold rings to any that would take up the quest. But this attracted the most untrustworthy men, debtors and desperate men that insisted upon half of the sum being paid upfront. By the week's end, Miltiades had filled the rowers' benches and began buying salted meats and other supplies that would be needed, all from his own coffers as the Assembly had instructed.

One morning while Miltiades supervised the loading of the ship, he was approached by a tall, slim woman with the pointed ears of an elf. She wore a long, dark green tunic covered over by a grey cloak that was tied in place with golden lace. At her waist was scabbarded two fine looking daggers, and in a brown leather case strapped across her back was an unstrung bow.

"I seek the captain of this vessel, a man who goes by the name of Miltiades." The woman's voice was soft and alluring, her hazel eyes knowledgeable in the lore of the forests.

"Seek no more," Miltiades answered, "for I am he."

"I am Lagina from the woodland realm to the south." Lagina bowed and presented Miltiades with a gift of silver rope that was said to be enchanted. "I have come to join your crew for the voyage to Arcanum."

"Blessed am I to have my quest spoken of far and wide," Miltiades replied as he inspected the rope, "but to enlist a woman is to turn aside our customs and invoke misfortune upon our voyage." He handed back the rope and began to walk away as though that was the end of the matter. But the half-elf would not be turned away so simply.

"This is not payment for my passage," Lagina said as she walked up beside Miltiades, "but a gift of friendship from my people."

"Out of friendship I accept this gift and can offer you safe lodgings in my villa while you remain in Thalassa. But, alas, I cannot accept you into my crew."

"My eyes are gifted with long sight, my feet light and silent. My skills with a bow are yet to be surpassed by any, and to think of me as a feeble woman is your folly. For I challenge any man here to best me."

Miltiades rubbed at his jaw, unsure whether to believe the half-elf's claims or not. So, to find the truth in the matter, he arranged his crew in a line upon the shore. From among their number he picked out the swiftest of foot and challenged Lagina to a footrace. The route was agreed, to run the length of the shore and scale the cliffs at the far end. The winner would be the first to reach the top.

The man Miltiades choose stripped off to his waist, but Lagina refused to even remove her cloak. The race began and it became evident from the start that the half-elf would win. So light were her feet that they left no marks upon the sand, and rapidly she reached the cliff where she climbed as swiftly as a spider. There upon the clifftop, Lagina was proclaimed the winner.

Next, Miltiades offered Lagina a competition of archery to prove her claims. From among his crew, Miltiades chose his champion, a man named Isadore. He was a short man with thick arms and a barrelled chest from his years of using a bow. His skills were renowned, and people would pay to watch as he practiced each morning by shooting down birds from the clifftops. Miltiades took both out on a small boat into the bay so that they were a good distance from the Oculus, the crew stood upon the deck watching. There Miltiades stopped and pointed up at the distant mast, declaring that the winner would be the one to hit it nearest the top. Isadore invited Lagina to shoot first, but she refused. So, Isadore strung his bow and carefully selected the finest arrow from his quiver. He looked up at the mast, measuring the distance and considering the swell of the sea before taking his shot. Once happy, Isadore drew back on the bowstring and let loose his arrow. True was its flight, striking the mast at the very top. Impressed with the shot, Miltiades offered Lagina the chance to forfeit; but she simply complimented Isadore for such a fine shot, before taking out her own bow. It was the finest bow both Miltiades and Isadore had ever seen, white with black carvings of trees on it. The bowstring was silver and seemed to glow in the sunlight, the arrows of equal elegance with white shafts and black feathers. Lagina drew back her bowstring and pointed up into the air, loosing the arrow high into the sky. For a moment, the crew wondered if she had missed and were about to cheer Isadore's victory, before the arrow arched down and struck the mast on its flat top. All who witnessed stood silent in awe of such a feat. Thus, Lagina was declared the winner and deemed worthy of a place amongst the crew.

With the Oculus well supplied, and a crew to man her, Miltiades announced his departure. The town's elite gathered in the temple which housed the bronze image of the goddess Thalassa and made offerings for a favourable outcome for their town. The priestesses that served there were renowned for their beauty and singing voices. There Miltiades was given the blessing of Thalassa, a ritual of anointing his skin in holy oil. It is believed that Miltiades stayed alone in the temple after the ceremony, where he spoke with the goddess Thalassa. It is also claimed by some that he fell to his knees before the statue and asked, "Now that I have undertaken this quest on behalf of my people, going against my natural comfort, should I find that of what I seek?" Three times Miltiades asked this, imploring for divine intervention; and on the third time of asking he was given his answer.

"What is lost may be found, but what is found may be lost." Those were the words that the goddess Thalassa had given him, and those were the words that troubled his heart.

Miltiades had returned home after the ceremony and sat in his father's office, pouring over his notes on the passage to Arcanum. He was unable to find sleep as he feared the morrow, questioning everything, from the loyalty of his crew, to the amount of supplies being enough, and whether the goddess Thalassa really would bless his passage. Finely, in the early hours, Thea gave to him a tonic which helped Miltiades find slumber, and until the morrow his grief was no more.

That night was said to have been strange, the sea fell calm and the world fell silent. Many claimed to see shadows, a vail of black mist that crept from house to house causing terror. Cattle were unsettled and dogs were said to have refused to go outside. An ill omen for the looming voyage of Miltiades.

But that same night brought a visitor to Thalassa, a small creature seldom seen in this part of the world. An Imp was found dancing in the temple, merry from the wine that had been gifted as an offering. His tunic was made of leaves, his boots of tree bark, and around his waist was tied a vine with a small bag of stones hanging from it. When apprehended, the Imp revealed that his name was Lasus the Wanderer and that he had roamed the wild for years since he had been expelled by his tribe for his misuse of magic. To steal offerings from the temple would normally mean death, but the High Priestess said that the offerings were given for the blessings of Miltiades on his quest, and that it was from he that the Imp had stolen. So Lasus was given a straight choice, to find death for his crime, or place his fate into the hands of the gods and join Miltiades' crew. Lasus feared death the same as any man, and so chose to become part of Miltiades' crew.

The next morning dawned and the people of Thalassa gathered at the docks where the Oculus was moored. Members of the crew were bid farewell by their wives and loved ones, their cheeks dampened by tears, and as they boarded, each were given a garland of flowers that was placed on their heads.

As Miltiades watched his men board, he was approached by Erastus.

"I bid thee the blessings of Thalassa," Erastus said loud enough so that all nearby could hear him, "and with the blessings of a grandfather."

Miltiades knew that his words were naught but niceties, an act to the citizens to enhance is image. "I find myself blessed to have been chosen to serve our state," Miltiades replied with every bit of graciousness that was expected from him.

Walking up behind Erastus were two of the Town's Watch, their bronze armour and blue plumed helms catching the morning sun. They escorted a small childlike creature with greenish skin, an Imp.

"This is Lasus the Wanderer," Erastus said with a wry smile. "By order of the High Priestess, he will be joining your crew.

Miltiades looked at Lasus and feared what trickery he intended, as Imps were renowned for their mischief. But as much as Miltiades wanted to turn him away, he knew he could not, for to disobey an order from the High Priestess meant death.

"Remember Miltiades," Erastus said in a lower manner, a more warning tone, "if you do not return by the passing of a year, both you and your father shall be proclaimed dead. And should you return having no news of Aetius, then my motion of your mother's marriage shall pass into law."

It has long been known that Erastus had no love for Aetius, and since the day he had won his daughter's hand, he had worked to limit his fame. The charge was that Erastus was jealous of Aetius' rise from a humble oarsman to a member of the Assembly. But what Erastus was most envious of was Aetius' wealth. Though Erastus himself was a wealthy man, it was nothing when compared with the lavish gifts Aetius had received from foreign emissaries. With so much wealth, Aetius had dedicated many fine jewels unto the temple, and had paid for public works out of his own coffers. This had enhanced his prestige with the people but had also made him enemies in the Assembly. It had been Erastus himself that had led a faction against Aetius, secretly hoarding ambitions of securing Aetius' wealth for himself. For if both Aetius and Miltiades were proclaimed dead, the law would grant him all that had once belonged to Aetius.

So it was that Miltiades bid his mother a farewell on the dockside, his heart both anxious and determined to find his father. His eyes were welling with tears, but Thea bid him to not let one drop fall, for it would be seen as a weakness.

"Follow your heart my son, for it shall lead to your father," Thea said as she undid the necklace of black pearls that Aetius had gifted her all those years ago. "Give him this and tell him to return it to me."

Miltiades took the pearls and bid his mother a final goodbye before walking up the boarding plank onto the Oculus' deck. There he stayed as the men rowed out of the bay, and there he remained as the Oculus sailed out of the bay, towards an empty northern horizon.

It was later said that Miltiades uncontrollably wept as the sight of Thalassa lessened behind them, and that he refused to move until it had completely disappeared. But other storytellers say that he simply took to his cabin, ill from the gravitas of his quest. The truth of it may never be known for sure, but what can be diverged from the tales, was that Miltiades was no seafaring captain.

IV

The Fury of Cetus

The first few days of the voyage were heartening as the Oculus sailed familiar waters. The crew were in good spirits as a fair wind blew up from the south, catching the sail. They each took their share of work and relaxed by playing dice and singing. But Miltiades was seldom seen from his cabin and was suffering from seasickness. In Miltiades' place, a First Mate was elected to run the day-to-day handling of the ship. From among the crew's number, a man named Obelius was chosen, a former pirate that had been given a pardon in return for his service during the war with the nomad raiders that had sailed up the eastern shore seven summers ago.

Obelius was known to be an able man and was believed to have joined the crew of the Oculus after receiving a huge bribe by Miltiades. He was tall and well-built with a head of dark, curly hair and a tanned face that gave him a dark hew. His years at sea had made him naturally superstitious, so much so that he refused a new blue tunic in favour of his old, red threadbare one that had faded pink. His claims were that it was lucky, having worn it on all his sea battles and was yet to receive a single wound.

For two weeks did the Oculus sail north as Miltiades had commanded, and by the end of the third, the crew had grown uneasy. They were surrounded by nothing other than the endless great green of the sea, and the daunting sight disheartened them. They began speaking out against Miltiades, saying that the goddess Thalassa had deserted him, and that he would lead them to their deaths. Obelius tried to reason with the ringleaders, but madness clouded their minds. A fight broke out between those that supported Miltiades and those that did not. Miltiades' supporters were too few and were apprehended. Miltiades himself was dragged from his cabin and tied up against the mast, along with Lagina, Lasus and Obelius.

Unbeknown to the crew, was that they had entered enchanted waters, cursed long-ago by unknown entities. It was this enchantment that drove the crew the madness of taking the ship. There the quest could have failed had it not been for Lasus, who began singing of the stars and moon. Lasus' soft verses dispersed the enchantment and the crew fell back to their senses, all begging the pardon of Miltiades. But Miltiades was in no mood for forgiveness and forbade all from their games of dice and singing, saying that they would have to answer for their crime. It was his damaged pride that angered Miltiades, as he believed that his noble birth gave him the right to his crew's loyalty. Walking amongst them, Miltiades demanded to know whom had first spoken against him, who it was that gave spark to the fire of their rebellion. But the crew remained silent and yielded nothing.

It was Obelius that stepped forward and said, "Miltiades, it is you that was made captain of this ship. And from Thalassa you have remained parted from your crew, remaining in your cabin claiming illness and pouring over your charts."

"I am the captain," Miltiades had angrily replied, "and as captain you are owing to me your allegiance, as the laws of Thalassa demand."

"We are far from Thalassa, and the only laws that shall keep us among the living are those of the sea." Obelius strode over to Miltiades, looking him straight in the eye. "A good captain will know that he needs his crew as much as the crew needs their captain. Your father, Aetius, understood this."

Miltiades was said to have stormed back to his cabin where he wept for the remainder of the day. But the morning after, he emerged early, his sickness gone. He assembled all upon deck where he addressed them, giving his pardon on condition that they give theirs also. So, a reconciliation was made, and for the next few days all was at ease. But then, from the northeast came a storm, violent and merciless. It began to rain as dark clouds blotted out the sun, softly at first and then heavy and unrelenting.

Miltiades, now acknowledging that he was no seaman, gave command to Obelius. Obelius ordered the sail hoisted and for the men to strap themselves to their benches. The storm swept over them stirring the sea to great waves the Oculus was forced to ride. From the helm did Obelius call to the crew to row for their lives as great flashes of lightning forked across the blackened sky above.

"The fury of Cetus!" Yelled some of the crew. "The great serpent swims!" Yelled others.

Cetus was an ancient sea monster believed to have been the creation of the goddess Thalassa to guard the entrance to the underworld, and to stop any evil from coming forth from it. But if the ancient myth is to be believed, then it was said that the goddess Fornax released Cetus into the sea, and Cetus began pulling souls down into the depths of the oceans. Many sailors claim to have seen Cetus, their accounts differing over the years. But all describe a creature larger than the biggest ships built, a creature that was said to swallow ships whole.

But there was no serpent, just high waves driven by a violent wind. The sea smashed over the hull and sprayed into the faces of the crew as they desperately rowed. A man by the name of Oran was swept overboard, his pleas for help drowned out by the rain and thunder. For hours did the storm rage, lasting well into the night and the early hours. By the time the sun rose the next day, the sea had calmed, and the crew were exhausted. The deck was silent as the men rested, but Miltiades knew that they must go on with their quest and ordered them to set the sail.

All that day there was a fair wind that blew them ever further to the north, where the air began to cool. After another week of sailing, the Oculus entered Icey waters and land was spotted on the northern horizon. The charts Miltiades possessed, had called it the land of Gelu, which in the ancient tongue meant ice. Miltiades had studied his father's notes on the passage to Arcanum, and in his writings, he had written that he would explore the island should the place exist. Miltiades was overcome with relief that it did exist, for it gave him hope that he was indeed on the right trail to find his father. Now Miltiades gave orders that they should sail along the coast and look for signs of the Amica and her crew. After a day of sailing the coastline, Lagina, who was stood by the figurehead, called out that there was a large cairn made of loose stone close to the shore. Miltiades knowing in his heart that it must be of some meaning, ordered the Oculus to make for shore.

Obelius was ordered to remain with the ship while Miltiades went ashore with a handful of men. By now each was dressed in thick woollen garments to protect them from the cold and armed with their short swords and spears. Snowdrifts partially covered the cairn and the men were forced to use their hands to pull away the stones. Hidden inside was a small bronze chest, now blackened by the passing of time. Inside was a leather case that contained a scroll with words written in a hand Miltiades recognised.

"My father was here!" Miltiades almost leapt for joy as he read the hastily written words of his father. But Miltiades joy was not felt by his men who were now wet and cold from the scraping away of snow and stones.

The message was a log detailing Aetius' voyage from Thalassa and his plotted route on his next stage to Arcanum. But the message also contained a darker tone, a warning to any that follow of the stalkers of the night. Miltiades stowed this message in his bag and wrote his own report, which he placed in the leather case and stowed back in the cairn. By the time his men finished replacing the stones, night was drawing in. The days at Gelu were said to be short, and unease swept through the men, as they knew that it should not yet be night.

The wind suddenly whipped up, blowing a blizzard that threatened to bury Miltiades and his men. They tried to reach the safety of the ship, but so thick and fast did the snow come, that they became stuck. All around them came unsettling noises that sounded like stags calling to each other. The distant glow from one of the ships lanterns tormented Miltiades of how close to safety they were. The noises took a sinister turn and shadows were seen darting back and forth in the blizzard.

"We need to keep moving," Miltiades urged his men on. "If we stay here, we shall all find our end!" Most of his men were now waist deep in the snow and had to dig their way forward using their bare hands. But their going was slow, and they became easy prey.

From the darkness of the blizzard came the Cervos, a race of most foul beasts that were half man and half elk. Their eyes were yellow and full of malice, their breath hot with the desire of feasting on man-flesh. From unknown origins they came, feasting upon the flesh of any that were washed up on the island's shore. So fearful was the Cervos' appearance, that one look from their yellow eyes could instil terror in to the greatest of champion's heart. They were an ancient evil with an insatiable greed for devouring men.

"Take out your swords!" Miltiades yelled above the wind. Though all tried, the cold had frozen their swords in their scabbards. Helplessly did Miltiades watch as two of his men were dragged off, their screams a haunting sound that would not be forgotten. One man close to Miltiades made a desperate attempt to escape but was hacked to pieces by the bone weapons of the Cervos. Miltiades tried to crawl towards the light of the ship, shouting for help as he went. But his legs were grabbed, and he was forced onto his back. Standing above him, readying to strike with its bone club, was a Cervos. Its head and legs were that of an elk, but its torso and arms were that of a man. It snorted wildly, its hot breath misting in the cold air, and there Miltiades should have met his end. From out of the darkness of the storm came a white arrow with black feathers. Its flight was true and unaffected by the wind, striking the Cervos stood above Miltiades in its right eye. Backwards fell the beast as Lagina and Lasus came to Miltiades' aid.

Three more arrows did Lagina loose from her bow, all striking their intended mark. But it was Lasus that caused the rout of the Cervos. From his bag hanging from his belt, he took out a stone that he tossed up into the air. The stone suddenly burst into a bright white light that blinded the Cervos and caused them to flee in terror. Thus, Miltiades was saved, and the remainder of his men hastily boarded the Oculus and set sail at once, leaving the ill island of Gelu behind them.

Miltiades was said to have proclaimed both Lagina and Lasus heroes to the crew and promised each a princely reward once they had returned to Thalassa. But Lagina refused this promise, saying that the laws of her people had prompted her actions. For it is said that the half elves swear an oath to the stars that they shall share all perils of the road with their traveling companions, and never abandon them to death. Lasus then too was said to have refused the promise, though bound by no law like Lagina, Lasus claimed it to be unjust to do so when he had been at the same risk as Lagina.

From Gelu the Oculus sailed east, towards warmer air. From the reports taken from the cairn at Gelu, Miltiades knew that his father had taken this same route, and Miltiades' hope was that Aetius had left further clues on his voyage upon the island he now sailed towards. For three weeks did the Oculus sail before the island appeared upon the horizon, an island Aetius' reports called the Fingers of Nereides.

V

The Cave of Urania

The Fingers of Nereides is recorded to be a barren place full of toxic vapours. The ancient sources say that Nereides was once a Star God that had led a rebellion in the heavens. For his actions, Nereides was cast down upon the earth where he formed a vast pillar of fire and smoke. But Nereides' power diminished with time and the sea claimed him. All that remained of Nereides was his hand that he outstretched from the sea.

For the most part, the island was flat with five finger-like heights rising above bubbling springs. A mist rose from the crags that fell in to dark, unknown depths. By the time of Miltiades' coming, the cliffs had eroded with one of the fingers partially falling into the sea. It was not a welcoming sight, and no man would needlessly step ashore. But beyond this island, Miltiades knew nothing of the way to Arcanum, and his hopes of finding any clue were dashed further by no sight of a cairn containing some message.

Miltiades ordered the Oculus beached, and for the men to make camp ashore. That night they took a light meal of salted fish and water mixed with vinegar, as now their rations were becoming low. Some of the men reasoned that Aetius could not have made it to the island, or that he must have taken a different route. But Miltiades was said to have taken angrily to their words, reminding them of how fine a seaman was Aetius, and that he would not leave an account on his planned passage only then to take another. It was during that night that the long sight of Lagina spotted the flickering light of a fire close to the top of the highest finger.

So, at the first break of day on the morrow, Miltiades took a small company towards the height that formed the middle finger. Lagina lead the way, often scouting ahead to search out any dangers. The rocks there were rough and sharp, and the climbing steep. It took most of the day to reach the point where Lagina had seen the light, and their hopes were not snuffed out by the sight that greeted them. There in the mountainside was the mouth to a cave with signs of life strewn before it.

"Only one may enter, one that goes by the name of Miltiades!" The voice was high pitched and croaky, friendly, and yet sinister.

Miltiades pulled his sword from his scabbard, but Lagina stayed his hand and said that there was no evil to fear. Miltiades reluctantly slid his sword into its scabbard before cautiously peering through the mouth of the cave. There was a long tunnel lit by the careful alignment of mirrors that reflected the light of the sun, but beyond that Miltiades could see nothing.

"I am Miltiades, Captain of the Oculus!" Miltiades crept down the passage, fearing some evil trickery. "How is it you have come to know my name?" The tunnel led to an empty cavern with a shaft that let in the light. There sat upon the floor with crossed legs, was the witch Urania.

Urania was said to be a hideous enchantress with the gift of foresight. Her skin was pale and covered with black spots, her eyes white from being blind, and her clothes naught but soiled rags. For a hundred years Urania had dwelt in the cave, growing a deep dislike for the world that had cast her out. For there was once a time when Urania had been beautiful and desired by many kings. War had broken out over her hand in marriage, a long terrible war where many were killed, and great cities destroyed. After many years of bloodshed and turmoil, and with no victor, a peace treaty was made. The kings proclaimed that Urania had bewitched them, and for her crime she was made to drink a potion that made her ugly. Then they had placed her in a wooden box and cast her out to sea. The Star Gods watched down from the heavens and were aggrieved by Urania's mistreatment. Taking pity on her, they manipulated the sea's current to guide Urania to the Fingers of Nereides, where they gifted her with foresight and long-life. As for the kings that had cast Urania out, their kingdoms were punished by a terrible plague that killed half of their people, and then seven years of famine.

"You have come seeking the passage to Arcanum?" Urania stood and walked closer to Miltiades, her bare feet slapping against the stone. "And your heart knows that you are not the first."

"You have news of my father, Aetius?" Miltiades took a step back, fearful that Urania would somehow bewitch him.

"A hero of Thalassa came by way of this passage," Urania said as she took another step closer to Miltiades, holding up her hands to feel his face. "A fine man of noble spirit, if not his birth."

"I ask that you reveal to me what passage Aetius took hereafter, to grant me that kind mercy so that a son can find his long-lost father." Miltiades trembled with fear as Urania's hands stroked his face.

"You are indeed the son of Aetius," Urania said as she removed her hands and began sniffing at the air. "His strength flows through your blood, though you have yet to show it."

"Speak not to me of my failings witch!" Miltiades' anger grew and his hand fell around the hilt of his sword, warning Urania.

"The hero of Thalassa entered here as a humble traveller, armed not with a bronze sword or threatening manner. He acknowledged the custom of one visiting another's home by waiting at the cave's entrance until I welcomed him in. There at the entrance he left his sword upon the ground and carried only gifts of friendship into my dwelling. The gods bid me to aid in his quest, and I obliged them by revealing the passage he must take and gifting him with an enchanted medal that would protect him on his voyage." Urania turned away from Miltiades and sat back on the floor. "Aid you I shall son of Aetius, but I ask for a gift in return."

"Name it," Miltiades replied, "if it be in my power to grant, you shall have it."

Urania revealed to Miltiades that she wanted a member of his crew to spend the night with her so that she could conceive a child. Miltiades refused at first and offered for his crew to build her a lavish home instead so that she would no longer have to dwell in this grim cave. But Urania would not yield and made clear her terms. So, it was agreed, and Miltiades sent his men in groups of four to the cave where Urania inspected each by rubbing her hands over their faces. She chose the youngest member of the crew, a man that was yet to grow a beard and went by the name of Adonis. His face was said to have been pleasing with youthful blue eyes, a slender nose, and thin lips. Never before had Adonis lay with a woman, and it was not pleasing to him now. He beseeched Miltiades to break this agreement, that they could discover some other passage to Arcanum. But Miltiades was not inclined to relent to his pleas. Leaving Adonis in the cave of Urania, Miltiades retired back to camp where he and his men rested until the morning.

The agreement with Urania had given new flame to the crew's dislike of Miltiades. For they saw the agreement as a detestable thing, and they charged Miltiades with treating them as harlots. So angered by this treatment, the crew refused to continue with their quest until Miltiades had answered for his crime. So, the crew convened a trial, for if Miltiades should be found guilty, he would be removed from office and taken back to Thalassa, his quest deemed to have failed.

As Miltiades addressed his crew, desperately defending his decision, Adonis returned. His face was ashen, and his eyes lowered with self-sorrow. Adonis himself addressed the crew, saying, "I hath returned, knowing that my duty as commanded by Miltiades has been done. Though against my will I did as commanded for the necessity of the quest. Here lies the passage to Arcanum." Adonis held up a scroll and a clay token with the image of an octopus stamped on to it. "I know now that this was the only path to gain this knowledge, and I lay no charge at Miltiades' feet."

The crew were surprised to hear Adonis say such words. But unbeknown to them was what Urania had prophesied for the child of Adonis. She had told Adonis that the gods had willed this union, and that from it shall be born a son who shall unite a broken people and restore balance between the gods and men. When Adonis revealed this to the crew, it was decided that it was a divine hand of the gods that had caused the agreement, and thus Miltiades was exonerated from his crime.

The Oculus set sail as soon as she was readied, and Miltiades took to his cabin where he studied the scroll that Urania had given to Adonis. It told them to sail towards the rising sun for seventeen days where they were to make their offerings to the sea. Then if they were deemed worthy, the way to Arcanum would be shown to them.

VI

The Passage to Arcanum

So, the Oculus sailed to the east, with each passing day becoming more tedious for the crew. On the seventeenth day, Miltiades ordered the sail hoisted. The sea was calm and the sky above clear, with no clue of what they must now do. Miltiades, along with Lagina, stood by the figurehead looking out across the sea.

"Tell me," Miltiades asked Lagina, "what do your eyes see?"

"An endless ocean that plummets down to dark, unknown depths," came Lagina's response. "And yet I sense that some answer is near."

"A curse upon my quest have the gods given! Do they not know that I am the son of Aetius?" In Miltiades' hand was the clay token that Urania had gifted, and out of frustration and anger he tossed it out into the sea.

The sea began to bubble, and the Oculus rocked violently from side-to-side. From the depths came a giant octopus, black in colour, with its eight arms wrapping around the ship. The crew took up their bows and began shooting arrows at the great arms in a desperate attempt to break the ship free. But the octopus' grip would not yield, and from its glands seeped out a black ink. Soon the Oculus was covered, and all the crew fell into a slumber. Miltiades was said to have been one of the last to fall under the enchantment of the octopus, but it was Lasus that the enchantment did not effect, and it was he alone that saw the passage.

When the crew awoke, they found themselves in a dense fog so thick that one stood at the stern could not see the figurehead on the bow. Lasus had lit the lanterns and cleansed the ship of the black toxic and was greatly questioned by Miltiades. But each time Lasus was asked on which passage they had taken, he would only reply that the way had been shown to them, and he would say no more.

There was no wind, and the sail hung limp, the sea eerily still as though the Oculus were gliding upon a mirror.

"Lagina!" Miltiades called out, "What do your elf eyes see?"

Lagina looked out over the bow, but even her gifted sight could not penetrate the mist. "I see only this shroud, an evil resides in these waters, their shadows I do see."

From beneath came a soft humming that was alluring and beautiful to hear, and the crew of the Oculus fell silent. Distant splashes were heard all around them, and all looked over the sides to catch a glimpse of what wonder made the sounds. The names of the crew were sung in soft verses that reduced them to tears as they began thinking of home and their families. But Lasus, being wise in the lore of magic, urged them to cover their ears. Heartache now befell the crew, and many fell to their knees in despair of never seeing their homes nor families again.

Like fish jumping up out of the water, came mermaids, but not like the ones told in tales to children. These mermaids were grotesque in sight and filled with an evil malice for all men. Their skin was like that of a rotten corpse, discoloured and stinking, their eyes black and full of ancient hatred. They were each armed with a bow, and they now rained down arrows upon the deck. Few were wounded and dragged to cover by their comrades, others taking up their own bows to fend off the vile creatures. The Oculus now had come to a complete stop, the crew becoming easy prey for the mermaids. A few more men took wounds, and there they might have found defeat had it not been for Lagina and Lasus.

Lagina danced across the deck, weaving around arrows, and loosing her own, singing of the warming rays of the sun as she went. Many of the mermaids were felled by her arrows, their screeches fading down to the depths of the sea. While Lagina led the defence of the Oculus, it was Lasus that saved it. From his bag hanging from his belt, he took out a small stone that he placed in an empty clay pot that had been used for storing water. Lasus whispered into the pot and tilted it towards the sail. From the pot came a wind that filled the sail and took the Oculus to safety.

For hours did they sail before the mist thinned to reveal land upon the distant horizon. As the Oculus neared the island, details were slowly revealed to them. The coast was a sheer wall of unclimbable mountains haloed by a vail of mist that concealed their peaks. For nine days did the Oculus sail along the coast before a passage was revealed to them. As the sun rose to its height on that ninth day, the Oculus came before a tunnel where a wide river of fresh water flowed out into the sea. Hewn into the rock around the entrance of the tunnel was faces of woe that were meant as a warning to the dangers that lay ahead. Many of the crew were said to have been unnerved by these faces, and many claimed to have seen their eyes blink. But Miltiades would not be swayed to turn back by the crew that now fell to fear and refused to go any further.

It was now that Miltiades gave his impassioned speech, jumping up onto a rowers' bench he addressed his crew. "Hear me o' brave men of the Oculus! Let me begin, as is proper, with my father. Aetius was born with no silver, nor of any noble blood; but was born upon the docks where most of you were. Many fine deeds did he do on behalf of the people of Thalassa, for you. The raiders from across the sea once pillaged our villages, and thanks to Aetius they are now nothing other than bad memories, and the very same villages that once burned now prosper. Our neighbours once took money from our temple as payment for their protection, and through my father's efforts, they now gift us with gold and seek protection from our ships.

And did Aetius keep all his well earnt spoils for himself? For if any of you lay this charge at his feet, then I say go, return to Thalassa at once, and there look upon the public buildings that he paid for out of his own purse! Eleven winters' ago, would many of your families have perished in the winter snow had it not been for my father opening his own home, warming you by his own fire and feeding your empty stomachs from his own stores! All this was done for you, for our beloved Thalassa. Would you now forget these deeds because of your fears! Or is it because you hold his son in disdain? Because you think me a coward and unworthy of Aetius' good name? It is true that my father's shadow blocks out the light of my own deeds. But was it not I that secured a most worthy ship for this quest? Was it not I that made sure you had armour and weapons to defend yourselves on this voyage, food, and wine? And what fine things do I hold back for myself? I share the same meals as you and drink no finer wine then what you do. I know that I am not of great renown like Aetius, nor do I share in his bravery or abilities! But whom amongst you does? Who here can claim to stand equal to my father? I shall go on alone, and not command you to join me, nor does any oath or law oblige you to. You may all return home and collect your generous pay that was promised by me! And there you shall receive a hero's welcome. Your tales shall echo down the ages and pass into legend, your names etched into the walls of the temple alongside that of other heroes. Your actions against me here may be received well by the people, or by the goddess Thalassa herself. But before you go, you should know that I understand your fear, and that I too share in it. But consider what fear must lay beyond these faces, knowing that it is the brave men of the Oculus that comes to their shore. For you have already overcome great evils upon this quest, and to turn back now would be your shame! I shall go on and earn my name in the annals of history, and in those scrolls it shall say that the unworthy son of Aetius went on, that on the shore of Arcanum did the crew of the Oculus leave their captain and give up on Aetius! Go home then knowing that I hold no grudge against you for the way you have behaved against me, and that my words are to make known how you have treated me, the son of Aetius!"

The crew lowered their heads in shame, for many amongst them believed Miltiades an incompetent captain and a lesser man then them. But now he endured to go on where they feared, and for the first time, they felt admiration for Miltiades. Shamed by Miltiades' words, they took to their benches and urged Miltiades to command them on. That day a bond was formed between Miltiades and his crew, a bond that would strengthen more as their quest continued.

VII

The Nuzu

So, Miltiades gave the order for the crew to row into the tunnel, Obelius leaning over the bow with a plum line to measure the river's depth. All were silent as the sunlight faded behind them. There were torches fixed on the rockface, illuminating crude paintings of woodlands and hunters. For the remainder of that day did they pass under the mountains before the tunnel ended and they sailed out into a vast lake. All around the lake was tall redwood trees, a dense forest that concealed the land beyond. Miltiades ordered the ship beached, and upon the sandy shore did they make their camp.

That night was to pass with some unease amongst the crew as argument broke out over their next move. Some pointed out that if Aetius had passed this way, he must have beached his ship also. But others spoke that they were in foreign lands unknown to them, and that they should erect a palisade and dig trenches to secure a foothold while others returned to Thalassa to gather reinforcements. But Miltiades rebuked the later plan, stating that they had not come as conquerors. So, at the break of day Miltiades took a company of men and began searching the lake's shore in hope of finding some clue of Aetius' ship, the Amica. For eight days did they search, but they returned each night with no news. It was on that last night of the search that sightings of people were seen at the forest's edge. There was no clear sight and the crew were unsure whether they had seen people or monsters. All night the men took turns keeping watch, donned in their bronze armour and helms with thick blue plumes that lined from their brows to the back of their necks.

Miltiades rose with the sun, himself donning his armour and blue cloak that marked him as a man of rank. As the crew broke their fast, he revealed to them that he intended to go into the forest and seek out any dwelling there. Obelius was ordered to remain with the ship to secure an escape should they need it, But Miltiades would take a company and enter the forest. Lasus stepped forward at this point and said that he would travel with Miltiades as his lore of magic may be of use. Lagina also stepped forward, saying that she had been raised in forests and her hunting skills and lore would be greatly needed. Miltiades welcomed them both to his company, recognising that their skills would be needed. But the remainder of the crew were more reluctant, and so lots were drawn to see who would accompany Miltiades.

So it was that Miltiades and his small company entered the forest, walking for hours and finding nothing. The trees of that forest were said to have been of wonder to the company, and none amongst them could help staring up at the majesty of the light filtering through the treetops. Soft voices were heard all around them and Lasus revealed that the trees were speaking with one another. There was an ancient beauty about the forest, a still wisdom that lingered on the tranquil air. Whenever the company stopped to rest, Lasus would place a hand upon a tree trunk and speak in a long-forgotten tongue. Lasus claimed that the trees were watching them with fear, unsure if they were friend or foe, and soon learnt that the forest was called the Whispering woods. Each time Lasus had spoken with the trees, he had reassured them that they willed no harm upon their ancient trunks or branches. It was revealed through Lasus that the trees were over a thousand years old and were free from the corruption of wickedness. They were mistrusting of the company and refused to answer many of Lasus' questions, but they revealed that other men had passed the forest's paths. When Lasus pressed them for answers as to what happened to these men, they answered only that they passed through.

Onwards Miltiades led them, with each direction looking the same as the other. After days of hopelessly wandering the forest's paths, they became lost, so lost that even Lagina could not trace which path they had trodden. From the concealment of the undergrowth, they were being watched and listened to. That night as the company slept, all were captured bound and blindfolded. They were carried off deeper into the forest where they were then placed down a deep pit dugout into the ground. After many hours of being left to fear their fate, all were pulled out and taken to a clearing with a tall totem hewn with four faces of long-haired women. Stood all around them was a tribe of women known as the Nuzu.

They were barbaric to look at, a far cry from the civilised women of Thalassa. Their skin was tattooed and pierced with decorative bones. Their clothes were of deer hides and rabbit furs, and each carried weapons of flint. From amongst them stepped forwards a tall slender woman with long braided hair, her skin a dark hue.

"Why have you come to the land of the Nuzu?" The woman cut free Miltiades blindfold with her stone dagger.

Miltiades was shocked to hear her speak in the same tongue as him, and his hope was lifted by the thought that she must have had contact with Aetius and his crew. "Fear us not, for we come not as conquerors."

"Why do you carry weapons if not to kill?" The woman's eyes were dark, hard staring as she weighed up Miltiades. Other women carried in the company's weapons and piled them before the totem.

"For many leagues have we sailed, facing many dangers, dangers that were overcome by these weapons," Miltiades answered. "Our mission was not one of subjecting unknown people, but of rescuing my father, Aetius."

The woman warrior bent down and tilted her head as she looked at Miltiades' face, and there saw a recognition.

"Others like you came and felled trees. Now we and the trees are one with mistrust towards your likes."

"Others," Miltiades said with renewed hope, "Tell me what you know of these men."

"They came like you on a giant floating log," the woman replied. "Like you also they were lost in the forest. Not wanting them in the forest, I led them north, to a hostile place."

"Take me and my men there," Miltiades pleaded, "I beg you to show me the path my father has taken."

"Not safe," the woman replied with a shake of her head, "Grunts dwell in the valley to the north, and they are flesh eaters."

Miltiades is said to have wept on hearing of such savage beasts and feared that his father had succumb to such a fate. But his heart told him that his father still lived, and so his wit returned to him. "Why spare us from this path, and yet willingly lead my father to it?"

"The others like you came and felled many trees, burning and hunting without our leave." It was now that the woman turned to Lasus, her eye filled with curiosity. "This small man speaks with the trees like we, and it is for his sake that we now spare you."

The Nuzu would hear nothing of Miltiades' pleas, and he and his men were taken back to the pit. Both Lasus and Lagina were spared this treatment as they were beheld to be unlike men and given a hut high in the treetops. Each day for two months did Lasus and Lagina speak with the foremost women of the Nuzu, stating that Miltiades' quest was one of great importance. Still unsure of these men's motives, the Nuzu decided to give a hut to Miltiades and his men, and had women warriors keep a careful watch over them. Their weapons were kept by the Nuzu, but taken care of, along with their armour. Miltiades then spent another month exploring the village and took the time to learn of the Nuzu. All were women with not a man in sight, and that posed questions in Miltiades' mind. Whoever he asked as to why this was, all would answer the same, the Mogons.

The Mogons were another tribe to the west, past the borders of the Whispering Woods and the Forbidden Valley of the Grunts. The land there is said to be barren, a wasteland of woe and misery. They dwelt in the shadow of a mountain that spewed out fire from its peak, in huts made from bones and skin. Once a year, the Mogons would venture into the forest to hunt the women of the Nuzu. Those that were caught were never to be seen again. Then on the first day of spring, the forest would be awoken by the sound of babies crying, females that the Nuzu took in as their own. The boys were kept by the Mogons.

Miltiades earned a measure of respect from the Nuzu for taking the time to learn of their lore. So, it was decided by the leaders that they should tell him of the bronze men that came before him. It was now that Miltiades learnt of the settlement to the north, a place the Nuzu called the Dwelling of the Bronze Men. They spoke with Miltiades, telling him how they had seen men wearing skins of bronze battling with the warriors of the Mogons. Seeing that Miltiades was saddened by this news, they agreed to take his company to the northern edge of the forest.

So, the day after, Miltiades and his company were given their weapons and armour and led from the village by four warriors of the Nuzu. For Many days did they travel before they came to the edge of the forest. There the women warriors bid Miltiades and his company a farewell, saying that they would go no further. Miltiades personally thanked each of the warriors and announced that the Nuzu were his friend. So, they parted company, with Lasus taking the lead as he had learnt of the passage from the Nuzu.

VIII

The Forbidden Valley

The land before them was harsh, a rocky valley with snow-capped mountains in the far distance to the north. Lasus led them down a narrow passage with steep stony hills rising on each side. After a full day's walking, they came across a red stream that trickled down the rocks and pooled beside a small cave. Lasus said that they should rest there until morning but warned them not to make a fire nor drink from the water as it was poisoned. So, the company settled in the cave, taking a meal of green bread that the Nuzu had supplied them with and then began taking turns at keeping watch. It was a man named Timon, a known poacher, which disobeyed and first drank from the water. The water was enchanted long ago by ancient ancestors of the Grunts, used to ensnare their victims. Timon was allured over by a sweet smell that plucked at his curiosity. He went and knelt beside the pool, staring down at his reflection. There he felt something urge him to drink, that there would be no consequence. And so, he cupped his hands and drank a mouthful of the water. To his surprise it tasted of sweet wine, by far the finest he had ever tasted. He drank so deeply and swiftly that he became recklessly drunk, and he woke his companions to share in his disobedience. All partook, except for Miltiades, Lasus and Lagina who were awoken later by the loud singing of the drunken men.

"What new disobedience is this?!" Miltiades looming with anger began snatching away their waterskins and pouring out the contents on to the ground. "What madness has driven this insolence?"

"Miltiades," Timon drunkenly staggered over to him, "Come join us o' glorious captain. Be free from the laws of home and your rigid commands."

"You dare to break my commands and endanger us all?!" Miltiades' anger took control and he drew his sword, holding it posed to strike. But his men were lessened in their senses and drew out their own swords.

"What dangers are there to threaten us," Timon replied, "For did you not yourself say that whatever dwells in this cursed place shall fear us?"

There by the enchanted pool would the company have fought amongst themselves and met its end. But echoing from the hills was a grunting sound. On hearing it, those that had drank from the pool fell to the ground and were unable to move. Lasus Spoke a few words of protection, but even his lore of magic was weak compared to the enchantment.

Standing midway down the opposite hill was a Grunt, carrying a club in one hand and a horn in the other. The Grunt stood nine feet tall with thin arms longer than its body and a round swollen belly. Its skin was grey and oily, its fingernails and teeth yellow, its eyes as black as night. Painful sores cracked the Grunts' face which pained the creature as it sniffed at the air.

Had Miltiades' men been free from the enchantment, they would have fled in fear at the sight of a Grunt. But helplessly they lay, unable to even scream. Lagina notched an arrow and took aim at the Grunt. Seeing the danger, the Grunt blew into his horn. The sound caused great distress to Lagina, Lasus and Miltiades, causing them to blackout. When they awoke, they found themselves in a wooden cage deep in a dark cave. There was a distant glow from a fire and a lingering smell of rotten fish and filth. It was Timon that revealed that they had been taken further into the valley and then down into the belly of the world. Bones littered the ground around the cage and a constant drip of water fell from above, adding to the company's misery. The orange glow from a torch suddenly grew brighter as the Grunt walked over to the cage and plucked out one of the men. Anais was his name, a man of little standing to any except his wife and two children. The grunt took him over to the fire where he was chained to a spit and placed over the heat of the flames. His screams filled the cave and were horrifying to hear, instilling fear into Miltiades and his company as they knew they too would share Anais' fate. The torment of Anais' screams faded as his flesh blistered and his life parted from this world. Miltiades and his men turned away from the sight of the Grunt devouring their comrade's flesh, no words were spoken as each gave in to despair.

After taking its meal, the Grunt laydown and slept, its vile snoring causing the cave to shudder. For Miltiades and his company there would be no rest as each feared the morrow, and whom would be devoured next. But fortune was smiling upon Miltiades that night, for the Star Gods would not abandon him to such a cruel fate. From the shadow of night crept a ghostly figure that snuck past the sleeping Grunt and walked over to the cage. It was upon closer inspection that Miltiades noticed that the shadow was a mere man with a white sheet covering him. Attached onto the sheet was slow burning wicks that wisps of smoke emanated from, giving a ghostly illusion.

"Who are you," Miltiades asked, fearing some sort of evil trickery.

"No time for such answers," the man answered in an irritated tone. "We need to get out of here." From under his sheet, he pulled out a wooden rod with a hooked end which he used to pick open the lock. Pulling open the door, he told Miltiades and his company to remain silent, and with each person treading carefully, he led them out of the cave. They kept moving until the first rays of light peeked over the eastern horizon, whence they came to a small camp upon a hilltop. There was three other men awaiting them, all were men of Thalassa with long beards and dressed in hides.

Miltiades' spirit was lifted by the sight of these men and he immediately began questioning them. But he was only answered with that they were still in danger as they were many Grunts dwelling in the valley. It was explained to Miltiades that though the Grunts were a fearful sight and wielded great strength, they were easily fooled and nervy of spirits. They were no lovers of the sun and mainly remained in their caves during the day, but by nightfall many would roam the valley in search of food. So, the company took a small meal of nuts and berries as they were led north to where the valley met with a wide river.

The water there was dark and fast flowing, but the men that had rescued Miltiades knew where best to cross. After following the river to the east for hours, they came to a ford where they crossed. The water, though cold, rose only to their knees and they soon crossed on to the northern bank. There they were permitted to rest for a little while before continuing.

By the onset of night, they came to a settlement protected by a wooden palisade. They passed through a small gate that was opened by another man and taken to a large roundhouse in the centre of the settlement. Sat around a fire inside was twelve other men who all stared at Miltiades and his company as they entered.

"You are from Thalassa?" One of the men said as he stood. He was tall with a grey beard and narrow eyes that saw recognition in Miltiades. "Do you not recognise me?"

Miltiades took a closer look at the aged face that was staring at him but could not place it.

"Lysander is my name, first mate to your father Aetius." Lysander bid Miltiades and his company to sit around the fire and offered each a bowl of warm stew."

It was here that Miltiades learned of his father's fate. Lysander spoke at length of how the Amica had been critically damaged when passing through the tunnel that led under the mountains, and that she had sunk in the lake soon after, the crew having to swim to the shore. After a few weeks of lolling around the beach, the crew became restless and began fighting with each other. So, Aetius had led them through the forest, where they became lost and were guided out by the Nuzu. Lysander's voice then turned sorrowful as he spoke of how men were taken by the Grunts as they passed through the Forbidden Valley. He then explained how Aetius led them to the site where they now dwelt and founded the settlement. The next few years, Lysander revealed, were a desperate struggle with little enough food to fill their bellies. More had died from illness during the winters and Aetius sent out messengers in every direction to plead for aid. The Nuzu refused them any answer, but from the west came a reply of death. Each night for a month came the birdmen, bringing with them fire and death. Each night the crew of the Amica defended themselves, until finally Aetius was struck down by a stone from a sling. A ferocious fight broke out over possession of his body, but it was the birdmen that secured it and dragged it off to the unknown regions of the west. Since then they had seen little of these strange men and had continued in their struggle for survival in hope of rescue.

The news of his father's death aroused Miltiades' anger, and he refused to accept his fate. Something deep within his soul still grasped on to the hope that Aetius was alive, and Miltiades pressed Lysander for the whereabouts of the dwelling of the birdmen. A heated argument was said to have broken out, with Lysander urging Miltiades to accept the fate of his father, and to return home. But Miltiades was in no mind to listen and announced that he and his company would go on. None among the company shared Miltiades' willingness to continue, and they too urged for their return home. With no oath binding them to go further than their will, the company, except for Lasus and Lagina, refused to go any further. They accepted Aetius' fate and in a show of respect of his many good deeds, they said they would wait with the Oculus for a month. They then warned Miltiades that they would wait no longer than the month they had given, for they were longing for their homes.

IX

The Mogons

So there the company parted ways, with Miltiades, Lagina and Lasus continuing alone towards the west. For many days they journeyed, passing over hills and crossing streams until the lush woodlands ended by a vast lake, a lake so vast that the western shore could not be seen from the eastern bank. The light of the sun glistened from the water and for a time, Miltiades rested upon the sand and found comfort in the scenery. Lagina walked the shoreline in search of a boat that the survivors of Aetius' crew had used for fishing. Lasus waded into the lake until he was waist deep in the cold water, where he dropped a few crumbs of bread and stood as still as a statue. Fish took the bait, and with lightening quick reactions, Lasus caught a large fish with his bare hands. Miltiades was too tired to continue that day and decided to rest where he lay until the morrow. Lasus made a small fire and cooked the fish which they all ate to quell their hunger. That night, Lagina took watch while Miltiades and Lasus slept. She saw orbs of white and blue lights gracefully dancing below the water's surface, as well as hearing soft humming. So moved by this experience, that it is said that Lagina sang back, and together the lake and Lagina formed a verse of blessed water that is now lost to us. So it was that the next morning they climbed into the boat and began their crossing. The water was calm, silent, and as the sun reached its height, they came to the banks of a small island within the lake.

The island was a bleak place when compared with the lake, and Lasus said that it was forebode of what was to come. There they rested until the following morning, the night passing cool with a sinister aura that troubled Miltiades sleep. During the few hours he found sleep, he dreamt of his father standing at the water's edge as he looked out across the lake. Miltiades had walked up beside Aetius, tears falling from his cheeks.

"Father," Miltiades said as he stood beside Aetius.

"Glory and woe to my name," Aetius had replied, his eyes fixed out across to the southwest towards a mountain spewing out fire. A vast column of smoke rose above the fire and blotted out the light of both moon and stars.

"I have come to take you home father," Miltiades had said as the ground beneath his feet began to tremble. "Come now father." The smoke from the mountain reached out across the lake, But Aetius remained still and braced for the violence that now surrounded them. Miltiades fearing the smoke grabbed Aetius' shoulder and spun him around. His face was disfigured and his eyes empty sockets. Suddenly Aetius burst in to flames and held out his arms as if wanting to embrace Miltiades. Flashes of lightning lit up the black sky above and from the west came a long sigh. The column rising from the mountain suddenly collapsed and rolled across the water, consuming all. Miltiades woke at that point and is believed to have wept as a veil of despair hung over him.

With the rising of the sun, they continued, rowing their small fishing boat towards the distant shore. The shore there was an opposite when compared with the east where Miltiades had found some comfort. Gone was the shore of soft sands to one of sharp stones. Patches of dead trees were scattered across a desolate plain that led to a lonely mountain that marked the location to the dwelling of the Mogons. To the southeast were the distant hills that formed the Forbidden Valley, and beyond that the Whispering Woods where the Nuzu dwelt. It was the bleak sight before Miltiades that gave him doubts and questioned his decision to go on. But that sense of his father being alive had never abandoned him, and it now drove him on to the conclusion of his quest.

The next few days were spent silently walking towards the mountain, with an aura of unease surrounding them. The air now hinted of the summer's passing and the days suddenly became shorter and cooler. The leaves on the few living trees they passed were turning amber and already falling to blanket the earth, the early air dampening the ground with silver dew. The mountain grew as they drew near, and the land became shrouded by a veil of low-lying mist. Lagina would often run in advance and scout what lay ahead. Evil, she said, lurked in such a place, and the mountain would be unwelcoming to them.

The ground began to rise as they reached the foot of the mountain, and for a full day did they climb. As the shade of night swept over from the east, they found rest on a crag that overlooked the land to the south. A forest of dead trees ran from the western side of the mountain and towards the south where it met with another mountain range. To the east were high hills shrouded by a veil of mist that concealed what lay beyond. Close to the foot of the mountain, nestled in a cleft between the forest and hills, was a village. It was a dull place made up of huts that cloistered around a large hall made of blackened stone and a roof of feathers from giant birds that nested in the mountains to the south. But it was the huge effigy of a man crossed with a ram that caught Miltiades' eye.

It was made from wicker and stood taller than the trees, its all-seeing eyes being of red stone and painted with a blue circle for pupils. All around it were the Birdlike people, known to the Nuzu as the Mogons. They were all dressed in a cape of feathers, their bodies painted red with blue symbols on their arms and legs. Their heads were covered over by sinister bird masks with long beaks and black beady eyes.

From the crag, Miltiades watched as the distant figures of the Mogons danced around the wicker man to the rhythmic sound of the drums and horns. It was a disturbing sight to behold this pagan ritual, and yet Miltiades could not cast his eyes aside and was drawn to it like a moth to a flame. Unbeknown to Miltiades, was that they had been seen, and a patrol of the Mogons were now moving to take them.

So it was that Miltiades was captured, along with Lasus and Lagina they were stripped of their weapons and armour and taken down into the village. There they were cast into a pit and closely guarded until the morning. That night passed slowly and was the coldest that Miltiades had ever experienced, finding no rest. The morning after they were pulled up from the pit and taken to the hall where a masked man sitting on a throne-like chair was awaiting them.

The hall was rectangular in shape with wooden carvings of birdlike men placed along the bare walls. In the centre was a squared fire pit, where tall flames flickered. Above, hanging from the rafters, was stuffed birds in flight.

"From where hath you come?" The masked man asked. He was withered up heavily with age and wore a robe of red feathers with a collar that stood colourful like a peacock's plume. In his right hand was a staff made of bones and crowned with the skull of a raven. He was the king of the Mogons, and he was guarded always by men clad in black feathers and raven masks, hence where they took their name as the Ravens.

"I have travelled far," Miltiades answered, "and I have not come seeking quarrel, nor with intent of subjecting your realm. But with the quest of finding my long-lost father, Aetius." Miltiades was suspicious how the man knew their language, and his hope began to flare once more. "From the distant shores of Thalassa have we come, overcoming many perils, and I now beseech your mercy to grant us leave of your friendship and reveal to me any news you might have of my father."

"Your words speak of friendship and of you traveling in peace, yet you crossed into the boarders of my realm armed as if for war, uninvited and unknown to us." The king of the Mogons twice banged his staff on the floor and two of the Ravens rushed out of the entrance. They quickly returned, holding between them a withered man which they unceremoniously dropped to the ground before the king's feet.

Recognition of his father struck Miltiades like a spear thrust to his chest, filling his heart with both joy and sorrow. For his quest had not been in vain as many believed it would. Yet Aetius was but a pale reflection of his former self. Gone now was his heroic image of strength, giving way to a much-thinned body and a weakened face with sunken eyes. He wore a tattered tunic of blue cloth, much faded and soiled with age.

"Father," Miltiades wept, "father it is me."

Aetius looked towards Miltiades and forced a weary smile, but he was far too weak to reply.

The king of the Mogons then turned his attention towards Lasus, never having seen an imp before he was most intrigued. "You are of a different tribe to these, tell me from whence you came."

Lasus stood from the floor and answered, "I am Lasus the Wanderer, and I hath no tribe that calls me kin. From place to place I do travel, gifting unto those I deem worthy my lore of magic."

"In my realm you now find yourself, seeking leave of my friendship, and what is it you offer unto the king of the Mogons?"

"Deep is my lore of magic, crafted by years of training. For the safe release of my companions and Aetius, I shall grant you the skills to turn stones in to gold."

Lasus had once belonged to a tribe of imps called the Vagor, a tribe that wondered the wild in search of ancient magic. From infancy, Lasus had showed great promise and ambitions. But in his quest to become the greatest in the lore of magic, he found himself experimenting in forbidden alchemy. He began to read from ancient scrolls that revealed how to raise the dead, and how to turn objects to gold. It was forbidden to even read these texts, and to put them to practice was the most heinous crime. Once discovered, Lasus was put to trial where the charges for misusing magic were laid upon him. After a valiant defence of himself, Lasus was found guilty and exiled from the tribe, never to return on penalty of death.

"What use have I of gold, and you offer me nothing that is not within my hands." The king banged his staff again, and Lasus was taken away by two of the Ravens.

It was then that the ground began to violently tremble, and the Ravens fell to their knees and began hooting like birds in an effort to soothe the tremors. After a few minutes, the tremors passed, and the Ravens returned to their feet.

"Grannus awakens and demands a sacrifice," the king said as he wearily rose from his seat. He banged twice on the floor with his staff, and the Ravens carried off Miltiades, Lagina and Aetius, throwing them back into the pit.

There Miltiades rushed to take his father in his arms, but Aetius was too weakened to even open his eyes. Lagina then placed her healing hands upon Aetius' brow and spoke a few words in a tongue far too ancient to now decipher.

Aetius, now gifted with a little strength, opened his eyes, and looked upon the face of Miltiades. "My son," he said as Miltiades helped him to sit back against the wall of the pit. "How can this be?"

Miltiades revealed to Aetius of his quest, and of the politics back home. He also spoke of Thea's longing for his return and that she had given her black pearl necklace to him, though now it was taken along with his weapons. But as Miltiades urged their escape, Aetius replied that there was no escape. Indeed, this was true as four of the Ravens stood guard over the pit, rigid they stood with their eyes cast down at Miltiades like birds watches over their prey.

"I was told by Lysander that you had been killed during a battle with these Birdmen," Miltiades said in want of answers. "How is it you have survived?"

Aetius revealed to Miltiades that he had been wounded during the battle and dragged back to the dwelling of the Mogons, where they had healed his wounds. But this nurturing had not been out of kindness, for the Mogons wanted supremacy over all races, and they saw Aetius as a way of obtaining it. Once Aetius' wounds healed, he was questioned and given a role as a tutor. From Aetius the Mogons learnt much of the ways of war, seamanship, and governance. In his years of captivity, Aetius had watched the Mogons grow in strength, and his guilt had plagued him. For it was Aetius' lore that had given the Mogons their supremacy. It is believed that the Mogons were once nothing more than a primitive tribe, their warriors armed with crude stone weapons, and their people living in fear of their god, Grannus.

The story of Grannus says that he once ruled over the world, his reign begotten the world to a thousand years of darkness. But the goddess of ice, Khione, led a rebellion that overthrew the wicked reign of Grannus. As punishment, Grannus was exiled to the underworld where his molten fury still dwells. The fire mountain where the Mogons dwelt was believed to be a gateway to the underworld, and many times Grannus had banged his fists upon the underside of the world, causing great tremors. His toxic breath rose up from deep fractures that scarred the land, and the mountainside swelled from Grannus' fury.

The Mogons claimed heritage from Grannus, and still honoured him as ruler of the world. Aetius had quickly learnt of their plans to subject all to Grannus, and so begin the second darkness that was said would last forever. The first to fall was a tribe to the south, an unknown people that had lived peacefully for an eon of time. Their dwelling had been of stone with step pyramids built to honour the Star Gods. Now their civilisation is gone, lost to the destruction of war with the Mogons. And now the Mogons turned their attention towards the east, to the Whispering Woods where the Nuzu dwelt. To conquer that forest meant to gain control of the only passage in and out of Arcanum, and that passage meant access to the world beyond the Unknown Sea. A passage that would need to be held against the Mogon threat if the world was to endure its freedom.

All this Aetius warned Miltiades, that the Nuzu were now the only people guarding the world from the second darkness. He also warned Miltiades of how futile it was to try and escape as he had once tried to warn the Nuzu of the Mogon threat. But he had been quickly recaptured and closely guarded ever since.

As the sun sank below the distant western peaks, they were all dragged out of the pit and taken before the giant wicker man. The Mogons were stood in a large circle around their effigy, each holding a torch out in front of them. All were clad in robes of feathers and masks with long beaks and dark eyes. Drums beat and horns blew as the Mogons began chanting and hooting as they jumped up and down in time with the beat. Miltiades, Lagina and Aetius were all tied to a stake and inspected by an old hag with a withered right arm and bent legs. Her eyes were colourless, and her head scraped free of any hair, her skin grey from being anointed with ash. She worn no garments and was an ominous sight to behold. In her left hand she held a wooden bowl filled with red powder that she blew into the face of Miltiades and Lagina. Aetius, however, was untied from his stake and dragged to the feet of the wicker man where he was tied between the ankles of the effigy, his arms stretched out like a bird in flight. As an offering of gold, the necklace taken from Miltiades was place around Aetius' neck, the same black pearl necklace that he had gifted Thea all those years ago.

The drums struck up a more vigorous beat as dry wood and pots of pig fat was placed all around the wicker man's feet, blocking sight of Aetius. Most men now would have shouted for mercy, fearing death. But Aetius was no ordinary man who succumbs to fears of the flesh, but was a hero of Thalassa, and so no sound of mercy passed his lips, and he welcomed his fate.

Miltiades was distraught by the sight, and desperately tried to free himself from his bonds, but all was to no avail. The effects of the red powder now dulled his senses and blurred his vision, yet he could still make out the Mogons as they chanted and danced, the light of their flickering torches arching through the air as flame was given to the wicker man. Slow at first were the flames before the pots of pig fat burst from the heat, giving the flames a ferocity unmatched by even the fires of the underworld. On went the chanting as flames consumed the wicker man and flickered high into the air, incinerating both the flesh and soul of Aetius, the hero of Thalassa.

X

The Battle of Arcanum

That night passed both slow and full of sorrow for Miltiades, his heart tormented at the cruel fate of his father. Dark thoughts entered his mind, thoughts of those back home that had spoken against Aetius, claiming that his lowly birth was unworthy for a place in the Assembly and that Miltiades should resign his position. The memory of their faces angered him further, and he wanted nothing more now than to sail home and kill those vile men, men that had sat growing plump while his father had forged a most worthy state for Thalassa.

All night had Miltiades and Lagina remained tied to the stake, hopelessly watching as the flames slowly weakened and died down. By the rising of the sun, nothing remained of the wicker man other than smouldering embers. War drums stirred the polluted air as the Mogon Warriors mustered, each armoured by breastplates of bone decorated with blooded handprints and armed with newly forged bronze swords, their heads crowned with a plume of green and white feathers. Without any explanation, both Miltiades and Lagina were untied and placed into a wooden cage that could be lifted by poles. From their dwelling the Mogon warriors ran south-east, four warriors carrying the cage as they went. Towards the forest were they heading, passing through a valley of high hills. The wildlife here fled to safety as the ground vibrated from the warriors' bare feet as they passed through. For hours did the warriors keep up this pace as if some evil spirit gave air to their lungs and strength to their legs.

As the forest came in to sight the hills gently sloped down to a wide plain that was flanked by more hills to the north and south. There in the east, formed up for battle before the forest's edge, were the female warriors of the Nuzu. Their armour was simple tree bark, their weapons fashioned from flint. The Mogons halted and fanned out to form a battle line that ran from the northern edge of the battlefield to the southern edge, matching the Nuzu line. Then the drums and horns fell silent, the world falling eerily still as if pausing to take breath before unleashing carnage.

Miltiades and Lagina were left in the cage and were being guarded by four grim looking warriors. The ground that their cage had been placed upon was higher up, and their view of the gathered armies was a worthy place for any commander. From this vantage point, Miltiades cast his eyes over the battlefield and quickly saw that the Mogons had the greater numbers and were better armed. Folly Miltiades believed it to be for the Nuzu to leave the forest, where they could move undetected and would surely win by wearing the Mogons down in guerrilla warfare. But some madness brought them out of the forest and to a battlefield where there was no hope of winning.

The Mogons' drums broke the silence, and their warriors ran forwards to within range of the Nuzu. Each warrior carried a sling and bag of small stones that they used to pepper the Nuzu line. So great was this barrage, that the Nuzu retreated into the forest where the trees sheltered them. The Mogons, now seeing that their slings were having little effect, took out their bronze swords from their sheaths and charged the Nuzu.

The Nuzu charged out from the treeline and clashed with the Mogons upon the plain. There was fought a most desperate battle, where the numbers slain were beyond count. Valiantly did the women warriors of the Nuzu fight, holding out against the greater numbers of the Mogons. But those greater numbers were edging the Mogons to victory. The Nuzu were pushed back to the forest's edge where they planned on making a last stand to the death. But in that moment of defeat came the men of the Oculus, clad in their bronze armour, and armed with long spears. They came not owing any allegiance to the Nuzu, nor out of any hatred for the Mogons, but for the shame of leaving their captain, the shame of fear. For at the beginning of their voyage, they had disliked Miltiades and believed him to be foolish and soft. But his determination for finding Aetius and his lost crew had won them over, his resilience of abandoning hope had shamed them.

Upon the left flank of the Mogons did the crew of the Oculus form their phalanx, locking together their round shields and lowering their bronze tipped spears. Like a solid mass of bronze and muscle advanced the phalanx, smashing the Mogons in the flank and causing much slaughter. To the Nuzu this was a godlike sight which renewed their spirits and caused them to fight with all the vigour they could muster.

The Mogons were now hard-pressed and began to falter. The phalanx of the Oculus pushed deep into the Mogons' ranks where they broke formation and dropped their spears in favour of their swords. Many more of the Mogon warriors now fell as their courage faded and they began to flee back towards the hills. The Nuzu halted their warriors, refusing to pursue the Mogons as they believed that too much blood had already been spilt that day. Obelius, who had led the men of the Oculus, urged the Nuzu to pursue the Mogons and complete their victory. But still the Nuzu refused, claiming that it was unjust to wipe-out another people. So there upon the plain did the crew of the Oculus and the Nuzu come together in victory.

Miltiades and Lagina had watched the battle from the cage, fearing what fate would hand them should the Mogons win the day. But when defeated, the warriors guarding them turned their weapons and went to kill their prisoners. Miltiades, sickened by grief, refused to even try and defend himself and was dragged out from the cage. His life would have ended there had it not been for the timely arrival of Lasus.

Wrapped in a cloak of leaves that made him invisible to the eyes of the Mogon warriors, Lasus plucked out a pebble from the bag hanging from the vine tied around his waist and threw it at the Mogon warrior posed to kill Miltiades. The pebble had struck the warrior between his shoulders on his back and instantly turned him to stone. The other three seeing the fate of their companion fled in terror, believing that some sorcery was protecting Miltiades. There Lasus removed his cloak and revealed himself to Miltiades and Lagina.

"Lasus," Miltiades weakly spoke, "Do my eyes deceive me?"

"If so Miltiades," Lagina said as she crawled out from the cage, "then my eye share in this trickery."

"This is no trickery," Lasus replied, "for it is truly my good self." He then revealed how he had managed to escape the Mogons. As the ground began to tremor, his captors had lost their footing and their grip of him, and with his lore of dark magic, he had been able to conceal himself as he made good his escape. From there he ran the many miles to the dwelling of the Nuzu, and there warned them of the Mogons' preparations for war. With the Nuzu warriors now mustering, he had swiftly run back to the lake where the Oculus was beached, and there informed Obelius of all that had happened. Dishonour had been felt by the crew, and they had donned their bronze armour for the rescue of their captain.

In the days after the battle, the weather turned wet and wild. Storms swayed the trees of the forest and rivers swelled from the heavy downpours. To honour the victory over the Mogons, each of the crew was gifted with the title of Friend and given leave to settle on Arcanum if they so chose to. But all were now longing for home, to see their wives and families. Upon the battlefield, the dead were given full honours as a warrior's death deserved. A vast mound was built and each of the fallen warriors was placed inside, their weapons laid besides them. The twelve men of the Oculus that had fallen were each placed upon their own pyre as was the custom of Thalassa, their souls to rise to the starry heavens where they would live for eternity.

Winter had now come, and the sea was too dangerous to sail upon. So, for four months did the crew rest, gathering supplies and making any repairs needed to the Oculus for their journey home. In that time, Miltiades was often seen sitting on his cloak beside the lake, scratching a face into the sand to try and capture the image of Aetius.

The cold months gradually passed and gave way to the warmer days of spring. At the appointed day, the crew boarded, along with the survivors of the Amica, all in deep longing for the sight of Thalassa. Lasus, however, did not board as he wished not to return. He had been exiled from his tribe and had wandered the wilderness alone, homeless, and unwanted. Now he had built himself a hut deep in the forest where he spoke daily with the trees, learning much of ancient lore and gifting them with the lore of his people. As a parting gift, Lasus gave to Miltiades an arrow and a cauldron that he had fashioned out of a tree stump, having it placed by the steering oar and filling it with water.

"These items I now gift to you Miltiades," Lasus said as he dropped the arrow into the filled cauldron, its shaft turning so that the bronze head pointed south towards the tunnel. "Follow the head as it shall safely guide you home."

"I thank you with all the love of friendship Lasus," Miltiades replied, "for where many abandoned me to an unknown fate, you remained at my side to share in it."

So it was that on the shore of Arcanum Lasus parted company with Miltiades, both filled with tears as their fellowship came to an end. In his later years, Lasus planted an acorn which grew into a mighty oak tree that was considered to be the finest tree in all Arcanum. The name Lasus gifted this tree was Miltiades, and the wisdom It held was beyond that which men could even know.

The Nuzu gathered by the lake and sang as the Oculus was rowed towards the mountain underpass, parting and never to return.

XI

The return to Thalassa

For many days did the Oculus sail to the south, entering the dense fog. Miltiades steered his ship as he had been instructed by Lasus, and no harm befell them. For the Nuzu had carved runes on to the hull that gifted them with protection from the mermaids. After many more days of easy sailing, the fog gradually thinned and the arrow guiding them shifted towards the southwest. Miltiades altered course and followed as Lasus had bid him. Their journey home went on for two more months, unhindered and blessed by a constant wind that blew from the east.

When sight of Thalassa was seen on the horizon, all the crew were said to have fallen to their knees and wept. News of the Oculus' return quickly spread throughout the town, and the docks became crowded. Miltiades and his crew were given a hero's welcome, and each given a cup of wine and adorned with a cloak of purple silk. But amidst the joy of home, they learned that the allotted year had passed by a month, and that the Assembly had passed a decree that they were dead. Thea had been forced to remarry, the wealth of Aetius being taken by the First Citizen, Erastus. The crew were also dishonoured by the First Citizen as he had refused to pay their families the remainder of what was owed to them for joining Miltiades' quest, and were also proclaimed dead.

Many of the members had received news of the Oculus' return and had rushed to the Assembly House for an emergency sitting. There they berated Erastus for his greed and ambitions that had now made them look foolish, and they demanded that he act to find some solution.

To learn that all had been taken from him, Miltiades was rightfully enraged. He strode back on the Oculus and donned his armour, declaring to the people that he would march upon the Assembly House and free Thalassa from the poison that corrupted it. But Miltiades would not go alone, for all his crew took up their weapons and donned their armour and followed him up to the Assembly House.

There the doors were closed and being guarded by four of Erastus' men, who were under orders to turn all away. But they saw the anger in the eyes of the crew and the prestige of Miltiades, and so stood aside. The crew stormed inside the Assembly House and stood before the members with their hands wrapped around the hilts of their swords. Miltiades entered last; his eyes fixed upon Erastus who was sat in his chair.

"Treason," Erastus called as he stood and pointed a finger toward Miltiades. For to enter the Assembly House under armed guard was a most vile offense. "You shall pay with your life for this crime!" The appearance of Miltiades had unsettled him, for he was much changed. Gone was the plump boy of little reputation to a man of a slimmer physique, his skin darkened and toughened by the salt of the sea. A heroic aura surrounded him, and behind his eyes was a soundness of mind that drove his determination.

Miltiades answered Erastus by hitting him in the face and sending him crashing onto the floor, the members' faces ashen with shock. A few supporters of Erastus called Miltiades a tyrant for his unlawful actions. But the Father of the House banged his staff on the floor to restore order, and reminded the members that it was they which had decreed Miltiades and his crew dead, and was thus under no law until the decree of death was withdrawn.

"Esteemed members," Miltiades now addressed the Assembly, "let us first address the decree of death that you have placed upon me and my crew. For now, you see that we did not find death, but were blessed with success."

It was Aegidius that put forward a motion to withdraw the decree of death, himself having been opposed to it from the beginning. The supporters of Erastus saw the seriousness of Miltiades and his men and feared to speak against it, thus it was passed with no division.

With all that was taken from him now restored, Miltiades revealed all his quest to the members, and after seeing the faces of the surviving members of Aetius' crew, their minds were swayed to support Miltiades. He then charged Erastus with misusing his power as first citizen to steal the riches from greater men. Thus, Erastus was exiled and in the days that followed, votes were cast over his replacement. So great was Miltiades standing with the people, that he won the First Citizenship. His first action was to gift the title of Hero upon all his and Aetius' crew, and paid them all that was owed to them. When he tried to give them double the money what had been agreed, the crew refused to take it. Instead that money was used to erect a statue of Aetius upon the shore, looking out across the distant horizon.

In the passing years, the crew were famed for their quest and many stories of Arcanum spread far and wide. Miltiades was greatly honoured and visited by emissaries from all the neighbouring states, being lavished with fine gifts that were befitting for a king. Many times, he was offered great wealth to lead another expedition to Arcanum, but each time he had refused. Many of the crew had received the same offer, but like Miltiades, who they forevermore called their captain, they too had refused.

Lagina had stayed in Miltiades' home as an honoured guest until his untimely passing some seventeen years later. She was said to have sung a chilling lamentation of Arcanum as Miltiades' body was placed on the deck of the Oculus. Before the fire was lit, she placed her hand upon Miltiades' body and bid him farewell before taking her leave to an unknown fate. Some say that she returned to her people and led them to Arcanum where their ancestors' dwell to this day. But later tales tell of a witch that stalked the southern woodland, a witch that was a half-elf who had a deep dislike of men. The truth may never be known, but those that travel the path of the southern woodland speak of a crying upon the wind, a deep sorrow that plucks at the very souls of those that tread that path.

Thalassa went on, growing greater in power. But the corruption of Assembly members grew ever darker. Never again would there be heroes like Aetius and Miltiades in Thalassa, no champion of the people. The divide between rich and poor widened as rich merchants flocked to Thalassa's docks, and for a century more Thalassa was honoured as the greatest. But empires rise and fall, like heroes come and go. Thalassa was no different. Eventually the harbour would silt up and merchant ships began taking their wares elsewhere. Thus, began the decline of Thalassa.

Now there is little to see of this once great town, for its once magnificent buildings are now naught but crumbled foundations. Many of the buildings, including the temple and Assembly House, fell into the sea as the cliffs crumbled away long-ago. Many travellers still flock to the sight in search of relics, many of which still fetch a worthy price. But there upon the shore is a wonder left untouched, a golden statue of Miltiades, with so fine a craftsmanship that it captured his likeness as though it was the man himself. It still stands in the place where it had been first erected, upon the old docks now claimed by the sea. It is a marvel to behold, partially buried by the silt and covered over by the tide as it sweeps inland. All agree that the statue of Miltiades stands testament to his greatness, and that he did indeed surpass his father's vast shadow. For even now after the passing of an eon, all have heard of Miltiades, the hero that found the lost Isle of Arcanum.

The End

THE LAST DRAGON

I

A Dragon's Wrath

Long ago, before the coming of the great King Elnar, the world was full of many mythical creatures. Giants, known as the Gigantes, still dwelt in the Great Mountains, their smithies producing some of their finest craftsmanship. The forests and woodlands hummed from the dwelling of Imps and Elves as they sang to give life to the ancient trees. Many strange and wonderful creatures roamed the wilderness, creatures that are now lost to us. Men were yet to be united in the west and were a collection of city states still to grow in power. An age after the Beginning, a time now known to us as the Age of Heroes. It was during this time that men were often at war with each other, squabbling over land and the right to say their town was the most splendid in all the west. Though a great mistrust lay between the western states, they had once united to repel an eastern army sent by the King of Balharoth, and thus kept their freedom from the east.

Heath Hollow, at this time, was known to rear the finest of cattle and crops in all the western realms. The castle was yet to be built, and the village was spread over the lush plains below a sacred hilltop. For an eon of time had men dwelt in the shadow of that hill, never building there as it was believed to be a holy place where the Star Goddess Hegemone once danced and sang life into the world. Each year on the first day of summer, Heath Hollow would celebrate the festival of Hegemone the Life Bringer, the

Goddess of earth and rivers; and in the year of the last dragon it was no different.

As the sun rose for the first time that summer, the town's people amassed at the entrance of the Elder's palace in the centre of town. All were robed in white cloth and crowned with a wreath of ivy and white flowers. The village Elder came forth from the entrance, himself garbed in a white robe and head crowned with an ivy wreath. There on the steps of his palace, he proclaimed the beginning of the festival.

"Good citizens of Heath Hollow, let us rejoice in the blessings of Hegemone!" The Elder was the best the village had ever had. His money driven attitude had brought much wealth to the village, and his prestige had put Heath Hollow on good terms with its surrounding neighbours. He was attentive to detail and religious customs but was known to have a short temper. It was that short temper that kept his council in their place and gave the Elder an aura of powerfulness, despite him being small of stature.

The day began with a dance performed by the children. In the centre of a cobbled courtyard, before the palace, was a young sapling. Here the children held hands to form a circle around the tree, where they danced and sang an ancient verse of growth, a blessing taught to them long ago by the Elves. Next the Elder would lead his people up to the hilltop where a squared off section had been fenced off the day before. The people gathered around the arena and watched as the cattle farmers paraded their prime heifers. The Elder would inspect each in turn and pass his judgement on which would be chosen as the prize heifer. But it was in this year that all were equal with little between them, and a decision difficult. After consulting with the head of the leading families, three heifers that were most worthy were chosen for a second inspection. The three chosen cattle were once more walked around the arena, one stumbled and one became spooked and refused to move. This, the Elder proclaimed, was an ill omen and rendered the two heifers unworthy. Thus, the remaining heifer was chosen and led away to be washed and prepared.

With the prize heifer chosen, the people then walked down to the banks of the river Tostig where they washed their hands, face and feet in the cool water. On the plain beside the river were rows of tables laid out in preparation for a morning meal. There the people breakfasted on a meal of fresh bread and fish caught from the river. After each had drank and ate their fill, the people gathered once more upon the hilltop, around the arena where the Elder announced the beginning of the games.

"Good people of the Hollow," the Elder shouted as he walked to the centre of the arena. "This day we do gather to give honour to the Star Goddess Hegemone, and to ask her blessings for the growth of our crops! In the beginning of days, Hegemone raced across the world, crying as she went; and her tears gifted the world with green. Today let us honour that gift! Come forth those who wish to compete!"

Eleven men entered the arena, where they stripped down to their loincloth. They each jogged around the edge of the arena to warm their muscles and stir the crowd. Flags were stuck into the ground to mark out a circuit and the competitors lined at the starting position. The footrace was an age-old tradition, held on this day since the time of the

Beginning. Any were permitted to enter, but only one would be proclaimed the victor and claim the prize of a year with no labour. Instead his fields would be worked by the men he had beat.

"Each man knows the rules! You must run and not stop until exhaustion claims you. To the last man upon his feet shall go the victory!" The Elder walked out and took his seat which was in the prime position to see the race. "Begin!"

The crowd cheered as the men dashed off into a steady pace. Around and around the circuit they ran, as swift as a flock of birds in flight, but as the laps passed, men began to fall. One by one they fell until only two remained. They ran side by side, looking at each other in hope of seeing the other weakening, but neither did and the footrace went on for many laps more. Both were now red in the face and blowing for air, but neither wanted to yield. One man broke away from the other, a hand holding his side as he began to limp. This man fell, crying out in pain as his legs gave way.

The Elder stood from his chair and entered the arena, announcing, "We have our victor!"

The victor was crowned with a silver wreath of flowers, around his shoulders was placed a red cloak of velvet. Attendants to the Elder carried the victor off, as he was now too weak to walk away unaided.

With the footrace now at an end, the arena was cleared of the flags and readied for the bull leaping. This event was most favoured with the people, and they cheered loudly as the five leapers sprang into the arena. Each leaper wore a loincloth of a different colour and had their bodies oiled. There were five in all, all of which were slender and athletic of build. The crowd waved flags and cheered to show their support of their preferred colour as the leapers danced around. The Elder rang a bell and six bulls dashed into the arena, whipping the crowd into a frenzy.

The acrobatics were said to be of great renown, and people would travel many leagues to see the spectacle. But on the festival of Hegemone, a grander feast for the eyes was performed. The leapers would juggle with flamed torches while standing upon a bucking bull and then cartwheel off on to another's back. To add to the atmosphere, musicians would play, and drummers beat to stir the emotions of the crowd. This spectacle would go on for the remainder of the afternoon, when a long horn blast called it to an end. Now the crowd calmed, and the mood became solemn, for now came the serious demeanour of the festival. The bulls were lassoed and led out, followed by the five leapers.

As the western sun sank below the horizon, the sky turning a red purple, the priestesses of the temple ceremonially entered the arena. Their robes were long and white, each of their faces painted red, and in their hands, they carried torches that's flames illuminated the priestesses. Softy they sang as they paraded around the arena and stood in a circle, their soft verses sending a chill down the spine of each of the on looking crowd. The bull that had been earlier chosen as the prize was now led in by two more priestesses, and twice walked around the arena. In accordance with ancient customs, it had been washed and decorated with a garland of flowers draped over its back. The people tossed flowers into the arena and softly said, *flay*, an ancient word for gratitude. It was at this moment that the Elder entered the arena and led prayers.

"Hear us O' Hegemone! Hear our prayers! We humble servants of yours ask thy blessings! Dance upon our soil once more and gift us with a plentiful harvest, let our crops grow bountiful and our cattle suffer from no ailment! As the ancient law dictates, we offer up to you, O' Hegemone the goddess of earth and rivers, our prize heifer!" A priestess then stepped forward and handed the Elder a sacrificial dagger of bronze. "With this dagger I do give to you our offering!"

So, the sacrifice was made and the goddess Hegemone was appeased. The heifer's blood poured out from its neck and collected in a large wooden bowl that a priestess held under it. Then in the dark of night, the priestesses led the people down to the fields. There they would walk the sown soil, dipping their fingertips in the blood and flickering it over the soil. A last prayer was said before the priestesses broke into chorus, singing soft verses of the stars.

With the religious rites now at an end, the people gathered back on the hilltop. The arena was now gone, replaced by tables piled with salted meats, cheeses, bread, and casks of dark ale. Musicians took up their instruments and filled the night with a jaunty tune, and the people made merry, for the night was young and the morrow was a day of rest.

Joining in with the festivities that year was a prominent lore giver that travelled the towns and cities to teach and gain knowledge. Merek was his name, an old man who relied on a staff to aid him as he walked. He wore white robes like the people and was himself crowned with a wreath of ivy and white flowers. Such was his renown, that the Elder invited him to share his lore. The music ceased and all fell silent to hear his wisdom.

So Merek began, "Dragons once lived in the age before time, a time when the world was young and on fire." Merek stood on a table so that he could be seen by all. "Mountains of fire towered over vast plains of molten rock, hot ash falling from the red sky above. The air was toxic, hot, and foul smelling, suffocating any chance of life. But from the great unknown spawned a dragon, the first of its kind. Drakon was its name, a creature of pure evil and torment. From the ashes it ate, and from the lava it drank, growing mighty. In flight its wings would beat a hurricane and its roar would cause the world to shudder in fear. For thousands of years did Drakon rule the world, until its black heart yearned for a mate to share in its evil. Drakon poured his malice and yearning into the ash, and there arose the second dragon, Drakaina. The she-dragon was said to be as ferocious as Drakon, with thick scales just as black, with claws and fangs just as sharp. From these dragon lords are all dragons descended. As more dragons entered the world, gorging themselves on the ash and lava, the world began to cool and the air purified. With the passing of an eon of time, the dragons became lesser in size and numbers until they faded from the memory of the world and spoken only in lore."

"I wish not to doubt your words lore master," the Elder interrupted, "but if the dragons were forgotten, how is it you have come to learn of their lore?"

To this Merek answered, "The Gigantes are an ancient race, spanning back to the time soon after Hegemone danced upon the earth and gifted it with life. There are some among the Gigantes that are well versed in the histories of the world and gifted me with their lore. So unbelieved by such tales was I, that I demanded proof. I was then taken to a cave where they housed a collection of bones, skulls as big as a house with sharp teeth as tall as a man. They were the bones of dragons."

The Elder smiled and stood from his cushioned chair. "I must confess that I have heard tales of such creatures before. But I must also convey my disappointment in your lore, for of such a great renown are you that I expected to be gifted with some great and useful wisdom that you teach in the halls of kings. But instead to speak of mighty dragons, a creature most learned men believe a fable."

"Forgive if I hath offended thee," Merek bowed, "but the lore of dragons is a kingly gift. In many fine halls hath I spoke of the dragon fury that shaped the world."

The Elder yawned and an aura of unease swept through the people, as being seen to yawn in front of a lore giver was a great offence.

Seeing the rudeness of the Elder, Merek climbed down from the table and replied, "Dragons were once lords of the skies, their fire could turn mountains to rivers of lava; their wings could block out the sun and cover the world in darkness. For there are none that can withstand the might of a dragon!"

"Mighty indeed," the Elder gave reply, "so mighty that they could not spare themselves from their own demise. Lords of the skies they may have been, but now is the time of men's rising, a time of champions that fear no creature. Fallen have these terrors of the skies to the mastery of men."

Merek's face paled from the Elder's arrogant words. "Demised have the dragons, yet there is word of one that is seldom seen in the east, one that terrors the lowlands and scourges the cattle."

"Your words are formed to frighten us, to make us yield our cattle of great renown." The Elder pointed towards Merek; his eyes narrow with anger. "A small village we may be, but you should know that we are well connected. No tales of a dragon taking cattle has reached us, and why would a dragon not come hither for such fine cattle?"

"Your words are arrogant for inviting such evil upon yourself. For not a month ago was I in the city of Arnon where they spoke of a winged terror. I saw the horror on their faces and smelt the fear that lingered over the city."

"To the east men lessen in valour, but here we shall not tremble to a mere fable." The Elder clapped his hands twice. "For we have a mighty champion to defend us."

From the crowd stepped forward Sir Borin the Brave. His very image was that of a true champion, tall with a muscular physique and oiled hair. He wore a tightly woven green tunic with a fine red cloak that was held in place at his shoulders by a silver brooch.

"Sir Borin has defeated many heroes, broken many shields, and fears nothing. So confident am I of our hero that I dare any dragon to challenge him." The Elder's words were ignorant of the true might of a dragon. Had he have ever set eyes upon one in person, he would not have made such a challenge. But unbeknown to the Elder, his words were heard.

From the edge of the world did Szar listen, for a dragon was keen of hearing once they were evoked. The Elder's words had stirred it from slumber, and on hearing such a boastful challenge, it took flight.

It began with a gentle stirring to the west, a warm breeze that warned of the dragon's coming, and an impending doom. As Szar neared, a great aura of despair befell over the village. Dogs began whimpering, birds took flight, the cattle lowing in fear. People fell to their knees in woe. It came like a vast black cloud on the horizon, blocking out the light of both the moon and stars.

"From the fringes of the world have I come, fear me and my malice, my might. For I am Szar the biggest and mightiest of my kind." Szar descended and breathed fire down upon the village, incinerating the houses in an instant. His scales were black with a grey underside, its eyes narrow and green, its neck and tail forebodingly long and spiked.

Mothers snatched up their children and fled from the hilltop, hiding wherever they could find cover on the slopes. Men rushed to gather whatever they could use as a weapon and turned tables onto their sides to use as cover. Those that had bows took aim, but what few arrows hit their target bounced harmlessly off the dragon's thick scales. For unbeknown to them was that dragons' scales were far stronger than any armour men could forge, or even the Gigantes.

Twice Szar circled the hilltop, speaking words of doom that filled the people with despair. For a dragon's speech was venomous to the soul, and those that heard it were often grief-stricken. The Elder fell to his knees, laden with grief and regret for his boasts, for now he knew his words had brought the wrath of Szar upon his village.

"O' mighty gods of the stars, deliver unto us salvation from the dragon's wrath!" But the Elder's words were not received well by the gods, for they had long deemed that men had grown too proud, arrogant, and so they remained silent. With no divine intervention, the Elder turned to his champion and said, "A champion you are, and much bravery you have. Stand now against the dragon, teach it to fear men and gift it with the bitter taste of defeat."

Sir Borin, armed only with a dagger he had used to cut his meat, bravely stepped forth from behind an overturned table. "A mighty beast you may be, I, Sir Boring, known as the brave doth challenge thee!"

Szar, still circling the hilltop, bent its long neck and gazed down at its challenger. Its laughter was long, wicked, and cruel. "Foolish man, doth he does not know his death. For I am the evil of the world, the ferocity of fire and architect of doom. For I, Szar, am the lord of blackness, the biggest and greatest of my kind."

The dragon's words filled Sir Borin with terror of his impending doom, shaking his bravery. He froze upon the spot he was stood, battling within himself to find his courage. Szar landed before him, its green eyes fixed upon the champion and peering deep into his soul. For a dragon's gaze was said to be a terrible thing, a thing where one would see their own death and deepest fears. So distraught would the victims become that it was not unknown for them to drop dead on the spot. There Sir Borin saw terror, a nameless evil that tormented his soul, there he saw the dragon's true malice. So ended Sir Borin, consumed by the evil of a dragon's gaze.

Szar then took flight and set aflame to the plains all around the hill, turning it to an ocean of fire. The cattle he plucked out from the flames and devoured with greed, but still he was yet to be appeased. It landed upon the hilltop once more, none daring to challenge its might.

"Mercy o' dragon lord, mercy!" The Elder fell on his knees before Szar, his arms outstretched in plea. "I now bear witness to your mightiness and yield to your malice. Should you gift us with mercy, I shall gift to thee all our finest jewels."

"Fine words you now speak foolish man," Szar answered, "words in which you hope will soothe my wrath. Your cattle I hath taken, their flesh short of what you claim. Yet more would I now claim."

"Mighty lord of the skies," the Elder pled, "you hath taken all but our jewels. Our village is now nothing more than ruins and we have nothing left to offer one so mighty."

In the time of the Beginning, the dragons had demanded offerings from the Gigantes. Each year the Gigantes would choose from among them a woman of virtue and untouched by any male. These offerings went on for thousands of years, until the dragons ceased to claim them. Unbeknown to the Elder, Szar had took flight with the intention of fating men to such customs.

"Late is the hour of men's coming, and many ancient customs it has yet to learn." Szar cast his eyes down upon the Elder, searching deep into his soul and seeing his fondness for his daughter. "Hear this people of the Hollow, feeble men. You shall deliver unto me your most beloved daughter, unspoiled by any man. On this day every year until the ending of the world shall you appease my might by offering unto me your daughters. The first shall be his that spoke and evoked my wrath, my might, my terror."

The Elder pled to the dragon's mercy, offering all the prize cattle from that day forward, as well as treasures enough to have swayed the mind of a king. But a dragon's mind was as solid as stone and firmly rooted to its desires.

Szar's eyes began to glow as its voice took an alluring tone. "Deliver unto me your daughter. Appease my wrath and live on. To deny me will deliver your doom."

The Elder fell victim to the dragon's allure and called forth his daughter. From the crowd huddled together on the south slope of the hill came a slender girl yet to reach womanhood. Tears fell like waterfalls from her pale eyes as she was led to her father. Her straw-coloured hair was long, loose, her feet bare, with the hem of her white robe brushing along the ground as she strode before the dragon. There she looked into the dragon's eyes, and saw something that no man would ever see, the beauty within.

"I gift to thee, O' dragon lord," the Elder said as he pushed forward his daughter. "I gift unto thee Igraine, my most beloved daughter."

More honourable men may have perhaps chosen death over handing over a loved one to an unknown fate. But those men have not stood before a dragon, nor fell victim to its allure. For a Dragon's words were a spell on those of a weak mind, a spell that would force its will upon any it fixed its eyes upon.

So it was that Igraine became the first offering to the mighty Szar. In its claws did it take her, flying back into the west to the edge of the world, to the unknown regions where men have yet to travel. It is not known what fate befell poor Igraine after she was taken. Some believe that the dragons were merely monstrous and ate their offerings. But there are ancient writings that come from the Gigantes that tell of the dragons being of a more tender nature. The writings say that the dragons would gift their offerings with jewels and sing to them the verses of fire and mist. Over time the offerings would come to love the dragons and worship them as gods. For that was a dragon's true desire, as well as being feared.

Thus, the exile of the people of Heath Hollow began. The fire around the hill was extinguished by a sudden heavy downpour that turned the world to a woeful misery of despair. The Elder led his people down to the swollen river, and there they made a camp from whatever they could selvage from their ruined village. In the days that passed, the Elder sent out heralds to all the nearby villages to plead for aid. His appeals were answered as carts of food and tools were delivered, and soon there came to be a makeshift village upon the banks of the river Tostig. This village came to be known as Elder Pride.

II

The Fall of a Hero

News of the dragon had quickly spread far and wide, heroes from all over flocked to Elder Pride to hear tales of the dragon's coming. One such hero was Eneas, a colossal of a man with a squared face and hands twice the size of an ordinary man. Word had reached his ear a month after the dragon's coming and he immediately mounted his steed and took to the road. Many leagues had he travelled from the eastern city of Balharoth, a place that held him in great renown as a true champion of the people. When he arrived at Elder Pride, he saw fear in the faces of the people, remnants of the dragon's malice. He spoke to many of the people, and all spoke of a winged terror that breathed fire and had reduced their former village to smouldering ruins. A vast terror that filled the sky and blotted out the light of the stars. Though the dragon sounded mighty, to defeat it was to gain a name that would echo down the many ages of this world, and above all other things, that is what Eneas wanted.

So came the first anniversary, and the second coming of the dragon Szar.

The morning dawned dull with little hope. Women wailed and dogs howled with woe. That morning the heroes trained together to hone their skills and win the right to challenge the dragon. From among them, Eneas was considered the greatest warrior, and was thus given the title of Dragon's Bane. So full of confidence were these heroes that they deemed it unnecessary to gift offerings to the Star Gods for their blessings. Eneas, like the other heroes, believed the tale of the dragon to be an exaggerated anecdote. But they were yet to cast eye upon Szar and hear its allure.

The Elder readied his people and made a small offering of fish and wildflowers to Hegemone. Then the priestesses led a procession to the hilltop where they gave a lament of sorrow and chose an offering from the gathered noble daughters. Circling around the ridge of the hilltop were torches, that's flickering flames danced with the breeze.

Dressed in a white robe, the Elder led Eneas to the centre. "Doth thee still wish to challenge the dragon? Knowing of its might and malice?"

Most men would not dare, but Eneas was a champion whose bravery stood above all normal men's. "I shall free you and all your kin of this winged terror. On the morrow shall it be no more, and that you may reclaim your homeland and build anew." He wore his famed breastplate made up of interlocking bronze scales, grieves and vambraces. His helm was plumed and shaped like the head of a snake, in his hands a tall double headed axe.

Though Eneas' words were full of confidence, and his very image was that of a true hero. There was doubt in the Elder's mind, doubt that even the mightiest of men could stand against the dragon.

"So be it o' champion of Balharoth." The Elder inclined his head to show his respect and walked back to the ridge where his people had gathered.

So Eneas came to be the second hero to challenge Szar.

As a vast shadow upon the western sky did the dragon come, its words of a coming doom drifting before it and filling the people with despair.

"On Szar, the mightiest of dragons, second coming, lest not you forget thy offerings." Szar twice circled the hilltop, seeing all. "I smell thee and thy fears."

Eneas on first seeing the dragon was filled with a sense of dread and hopelessness of his task. Any normal man might have fled in the face of such terror, but Eneas was a hero, and heroes did not flee. Summoning up all the courage he could muster, Eneas stepped forward to make his challenge.

"Tales of your might has travelled many leagues dragon lord; and now that my eyes gaze upon you, I see that these tales were not unfounded."

Szar landed and bent its long neck so that its eyes were fixed upon Eneas. "I smell your fear feeble man. To stand between a dragon and its offerings is doom."

Eneas was cold with fear, and stood rooted to the spot, his eyes cast up into the dragon's. There they began to glow as images of a blue flame engulfing the world entered his mind. Then he saw himself as an old man begging in the streets, people pointing and laughing at him. Next came an image of a tomb overgrown with weeds and crumbling with neglect and decay. No name was carved into the stone and no gifts of flowers graced the marble base. Then came a voice more wicked than what he had ever heard before, telling him of his fate and the doom of men yet to come. Eneas removed his helm and fell to his knees in despair, dropping his axe at the dragon's feet. Tears rolled down his cheeks and his bravery gave way to torment and dread.

Szar gave an almighty roar that shook the world and reared up on its back legs, spreading its mighty wings. "Flee now or face thy death."

Eneas had awoken that morning as a true champion with great courage and desires of gaining a name that would be spoken of long after his death. But gone now was his valour and thoughts of glory. Now he rose to his feet and fled in a blind panic, causing much distress among the watching people of Elder Pride.

Little is known of what became of Eneas as his name disappears from the pages of history, but in later years men from the east spoke of a beggar that claimed to have seen a dragon, a man that had fallen from pride and was fearful of everything, even his own shadow. From the few coins he was given out as charity, he brought strong drink. So helplessly drunk had he become one night, that the next morning his body was found lying face down in a dung heap. The people each gave a copper coin to bury him and was given an unmarked grave on the outskirts of Elon Dor. To this day one may visit the tomb of the nameless man, and there gain a sense of dread and sorrow.

So, the second coming of Szar ended with the taking of the offering. Snatched up in its claws was the daughter of one of the leading families. Aldith was her name, a fair maiden of renowned beauty, sworn to serve as a temple maid.

Szar took flight, the wind of its wings flattening the bushes upon the slopes of the hill. "My wrath you hath appeased, and on the third annual shall I come once more for my offering."

Back into the west did Szar return, leaving the people of Elder Pride in woe. In the days after the dragon's second coming, the Elder convened a council of the leading families and what heroes remained in their makeshift village. At this council the Elder tried to speak of hope, that another hero might yet overcome the dragon. But many of the councillors believed that they should simply scatter and make anew in another town or village. But the heroes stood at this point and protested, claiming that the dragon would then search them out and destroy wherever they dwelt, and to make other people suffer their fate was unjust. The reign of the dragon would have to end where it first came. The hilltop of Heath Hollow.

III

A Prophecy of hope

After much debate, it was decided that the Elder should travel to the temple at Lhanwick, and there seek out the oracle's advice. So it was that the Elder undertook this quest for the sake of his people, setting out at the conclusion of the council.

The temple at Lhanwick was then newly built, founded only a few years before, and was yet to become the splendour it would later become. During the Age of Heroes, the temple was a simple squared building upon a hilltop that overlooked vast plains, unpainted and unadorned.

Upon arriving, the Elder was made to wait in a long line of people that had travelled far and wide to seek guidance from the gods. For hours did he patiently wait until finally his turn came. As the Elder entered, he was met by the heavy scent of incense that burned in the braziers that lined around the walls. Standing beside a large bronze brazier was the Oracle, a young girl no older than ten. She wore a plain white robe and a vail covering her head.

"What doth thee ask the servant of the gods?" The Oracle's voice was soft, her eyes cast down into the glowing coals of the brazier.

"Tell me o' servant of the gods, how one might defeat the dragon that terrors my people?" The Elder said as he knelt of the cold stone floor.

"At the world's beginning they were," the Oracle replied, "and at its ending shall they be. For their mind is of stone and their mercy death to the pleas of men. Mighty are the dragon lords whose breath is of fire, and words are of malice. Such is the power of their sight, they see all within men, all secrets hidden deep within souls."

"I beseech thee," the Elder outstretched his arms, "tell me not what I know, but what may bring salvation unto my people."

The Oracle began dancing, her bare feet slapping against the stone floor. "The dragon's fire and fury you did evoke." She stopped dancing and lifted her vail to look at the Elder, her eyes turning black as night. "Woe for you and your words that stirred the dragon's wrath. No weapons forged by men may harm the dragon, for it scales are stronger than the finest armour men have ever produced."

"I implore you once more O' servant of the gods, give an answer to this peril."

The Oracle covered her face and began dancing, spiralling around as a mist emanated up through the cracks in the floor. "One cannot fight a flame with yet more fire. Look not to the arms of great men, but for a hero of no renown and might. For a river can but flow in one direction, and yet be tamed by men."

After this, the Oracle would say no more, and the Elder was bid his leave.

On returning home, the Elder reviled the Oracle's words to his council. For weeks after there was a great debate as none could decipher the Oracle's meaning. That year became known as the great tribulation, a year of woe and despair for an answer to their peril.

IV

An Unlikely Hero

In the weeks leading up to the dragon's third coming, the village prepared for a tournament of champions. The people built a squared arena and sent out word for heroes to enlist. But few came, and those that did refused to enlist through fear of the dragon. They came solely so that they could boast of seeing a dragon, taking their stories back to their hometown, for to see a dragon was a great renown of its own. That year there was but one hero that enlisted and won by default. Sir Arnoldus was his name, the champion of a small village to the south of the mountains of Azaroth, a village called *Pago Lapis*, which in the ancient tongue means village of stone. It was called this because of the stone quarry there, and the fact that each citizen lived in a house made purely of stone. The stone from their quarry was once transported all over the island and was considered the best. But as the years passed it waned in favour and the workload lessened. The citizens left their village to find work elsewhere, and now their once vibrant village is nothing more than an empty pit long overgrown with weeds.

Sir Arnoldus was a short, slender man with blond hair and bronze armour that shone like gold, looking lesser in might than all the heroes that came before him. He had ridden into Elder Pride mounted on his steed, Cornu the swift. As he splashed through the river ford, he noticed a woman, long in years and dressed in a simple woollen gown. Beside the river she sang of the dragon's wrath and fire. Sir Arnoldus reined his horse to a stop and listened to the lament. So moved by her soft verses was he, that he gifted the woman with his last golden coin.

In the days after his arrival, he enquired about the dragon, learning all he could. For Sir Arnoldus' strength lay not in his skill with arms, but with the swiftness of his mind. He learnt also of the Oracle's words, *for a river can but flow in one direction, and yet be tamed by men.* As the days passed, he learnt that he was the victor of the tournament by default and was summoned to the Elders hut.

"Many greetings most worthy champion of Pago Lapis." The Elder greeted Sir Arnoldus with a bow and a gift of a silver cup. He was dressed in a dark-green robe with a red sash tied around his waist. "Hath you the bravery and skill to rid us of Szar the Mighty?"

To this Sir Arnoldus answered, "Many I have spoken to, each telling of the dragon's mastery over the arms of men. And I have learnt that to make a challenge of arms to a beast of great might is folly, foolishness that shall send me to doom."

"Hero of the south," the Elder fell to his knees in fear that there was no hope. "I beseech you not to abandon us through fear of the dragon's might, for the Oracle has given words of hope, words that must be unravelled if the dragon is to be defeated."

"These words your people hath spoken to me, words of ravelled mystery gifted by the gods." Sir Arnoldus knelt and helped the Elder to his feet. "But an answer I have found."

Tears welled in the Elder's eyes as he rose back to his feet. "Truly, you have an end to the dragon?"

"A dragon's mind is of stone once set to its cruel purpose. Though this great strength shall become its weakness. For its mind is the river that flows only to its desire of thy offering."

"Tell me O' most worthy champion, tell me how you shall defeat the dragon." The Elder's hands shook through fear that Szar would hear and descend upon them with all his malice. "Whisper unto me thy deed that shall defeat the dragon."

So it was that Sir Arnoldus revealed his plan, and work began at once. For a week did the populace tirelessly work both day and night, hewing deep down into the side of the hill. There they carved out a vast cave in which the dragon would fit. They worked in silence, the Elder forbidding any to speak aloud in fear that the dragon would hear their plan. But it was later believed that Szar heard the constant scraping and banging of pickaxes against the stone but paid no heed as it simply dismissed men as being feeble when compared to its own might. Thus, Szar waited.

V

The Trapping of a Dragon

The morning of the dragon's third coming, the religious rites were observed, offerings were made to Hegemone and laments given. From the daughters of the leading families was one chosen, one most fair and renowned. Celestria was her name, a pale skinned woman with long dark hair and eyes the colour of ice. Sir Arnoldus had any being kept in the dungeon taken to the cave. There the prisoners were chained to the rock and gagged. By the sun's setting, the people of Elder Pride were ready and full of hope. But as the shade of night rolled across the plains, and the western winds stirred, doubt crept in and hope once more gave way for despair.

"I smell thy fear of my wrath." Szar swooped down from the heavens, its mighty wings blocking out the light of both moon and stars. "Who doth challenge thee?"

Sir Arnoldus, alone stood upon the hilltop, clad in his bronze armour and armed with a spear. In his left arm he held a round shield three feet wide and scabbarded at his waist was a short sword of bronze. He called up to Szar, "I challenge thee!"

Szar landed upon the hilltop and menacingly strode up to Sir Arnoldus, bending its long neck and looking down upon him. "Stand aside feeble man or know thy doom."

"Be gone dragon, demon of the sky, trouble us no more, or know thy doom." Sir Arnoldus levelled his spear towards Szar, readying for battle.

Szar's laughter was long and wicked. "Then know thy doom."

Fire spewed out from the dragon's mouth, but Sir Arnoldus had anticipated this and was able to swiftly move, holding up his shield to block the heat. But dragon's fire was a furious thing, and his shield was consumed by the flames, causing wounds to his left arm.

"We shall suffer you no longer," Sir Arnoldus shouted through gritted teeth. "No more shall we give offerings. No more shall we fear thy wrath! The people that you plague hath taken flight to a place where you shall not find them!"

Szar's nostrils flared as they sucked in the air. "Your words are lies, for they hide beneath my feet. Now know this feeble man, know that to deny a dragon its offering is to evoke my wrath. Thy words hath insulted me and now I shall hath my reparation."

In the cave under the hill, Celestria began to softly sing. Her soft verses reached Szar's ears and he immediately rushed down the tunnel to the cave, forgetting Sir Arnoldus. It could smell the flesh of men and suspected that they had laid a trap. But men had no weapons that could penetrate its thick scales, so it did not fear the trap. The screams that came from the cave were horrific and would be remembered by all that heard them until their dying days.

Unbeknown to the dragon as he devoured each of the prisoners in turn, was that Sir Arnoldus had sealed the entrance by releasing a wooden wedge from under a huge boulder, which then rolled over the entrance and a little down the tunnel where it became stuck, thus trapping the dragon. Fearful that the dragon would simply pushout the boulder, the people rushed to fill-in the remainder of the tunnel.

As a new day dawned, the people rejoiced and hailed Sir Arnoldus. They gifted him with many fine jewels and the title of Dragon Slayer, as well as naming him as their champion and permitting him to take up residence in their reclaimed homeland. But Sir Arnoldus refused, whether by humility or by fear of the dragon no one knows. So, in the days after the trapping of the dragon, Sir Arnoldus left. His left arm scarred from the dragon's fire and his manner never being the same again. Little is known of his adventures after; but a merchant said that he had shared drinks with him years after. This merchant spoke of a man still suffering the torment of Szar, a man that claimed to see the dragon in the moon and still heard its voice on the western wind.

So it was that the blackened ruins of Heath Hollow were reclaimed. Atop of the hill was built a castle to guard against the dragon's escape, wooden at first, and then in later years of stone. The Elder became the first king of Heath Hollow which kept its liberation until the conquest of Elnar the Great many years after. For decades after did people hear the dragon scratching against the rocks, and see its smoke rising through the cracks. A woman's voice was often heard coming from below, and it was believed to be the voice of Celestria who sang to send the dragon into slumber. But as the hundreds of years passed, the soft verses of Celestria became silent and the dragon forgotten, dismissed as a myth. But to this day there are a few, said to be the descendants of the people that saw the dragon, that still hear the scratching and claim that one day Szar shall escape and bring an end to men that dwell in the castle.

The End

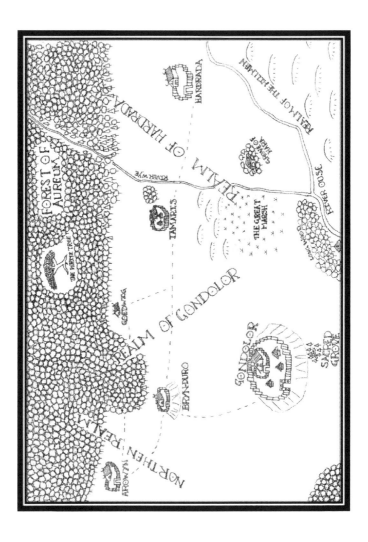

THE SONG OF THE LOST PRINCE

I

The Night of the Hallows

At the height of the Age of Heroes, the town of Gondolor flourished with both power and wealth. It had been founded long-ago by a warrior called Barca the Brave and had long after his death been famed for its horsemen. Built upon a strategic hilltop that dominated the lush grasslands below, Gondolor had grown from a minor settlement into a mighty hillfort that had subjected all the villages as far north as the Forest of Aureum and the river Wye to the east. A long list of kings had reigned over Gondolor and their bones were now entombed in the chambers dug out into the side of the hill below the town.

The town itself was made up of two quarters, the outer bailey, and the inner bailey, both of which were protected by a tall wooden stockade. The warrior class lived in roundhouses in the outer bailey, while the king's family along with the Companions and men of rank dwelt in the inner bailey. There within a hall of stone would the king sit with his Thegns in council of state, and the hall was protected day and night by the King's Companions, an elite unit of horsemen. As well as priding themselves on the strength of their warriors, the people of Gondolor were superstitious and celebrated many religious festivals. The one most important to them was the night of the Hallows, a night where the gateway between the worlds of the living and the dead were open.

The night of the Hallows was a sacred night, long in ancient traditions and ritual. On the mid-autumn day, the people of Gondolor would rise before the sun and break their fast as it was forbidden to eat and drink during the sunlight hours of that day. Then they would hollow out pumpkins and carve sinister faces into their flesh before placing candles inside to turn them into lanterns. Once ready these lanterns would then be placed by the door of their roundhouses. It was believed by all that these lanterns would ward off malicious spirits that were said to freely roam between the worlds of the living and the dead. But the lanterns alone were not enough for protection from the spirits; so, the people would don the skins of animals marked with runes of protection and cover their faces with skulls. As the sun reached its height, the people would gather upon the mustering field where they poured out offerings of strong ale to Dagda, the Star God that pulled the sun across the sky with his chariot. Lamentations of deeds of old kings were sang to the blue heavens until Dagda pulled the sun into the underworld. It was now that the king of Gondolor would come forth from his great hall and lead his people out of the town and down to the Sacred Grove. Since the time of unknown had this tradition been upheld, but in the year 4747 of the cycle of the sun, or on the thirteenth year of the reign of King Corraidin as the people of Gondolor counted, all was to change.

This year the king of Gondolor was gravely ill, weakened by an unknown sickness that had robbed him of his great strength. Unable to rise from his bed, King Corraidin commanded his favoured son, Cingetorix, to take lead of the ritual. So Cingetorix donned the bearskin of the king and led the people down towards the sacred grove, whit face painted white with a red stripe which ran from his forehead down to his chin. The night was clear and cold, a foreboding omen of the harsh winter to come, and the air was scented by the sweet smell of pumpkins.

The narrow road from the king's hall led through the inner gate and straight to the Gate of Peleus, named after the horse of Gondolor's first king. From there the road slopped downhill to where it met with grasslands, an ocean of grey in the moonlight that stretched far to the south into the unknown regions. There Cingetorix led his father's people east across the fields to where there was a pool of water hidden by tall and ancient trees. The whole route was lined with torches and skulls of animals that were illuminated by candles, and all were silent as they trod that path. The people gathered around the dark water and watched as Cingetorix made the offerings to Elaina, the goddess said to guard the grove. Into the depths of the water did Cingetorix toss a fine sword and shield, a silver cup and a woman's belt inlaid with precious stones. He then took a dagger and cut the palm of his left hand, dribbling his blood into the water as a final offering. For it was believed that the water was a gateway used by spirits to enter the realm of the living, and if the goddess Elaina was made offerings, she would again close it.

"Take unto your possession our humble offerings o' watcher of the door to the underworld," Cingetorix said in a solemn tone that echoed around the grove. "Heed mercy upon our pleas and let not the spirits of the underworld walk amongst us."

All were silent and cast their eyes upon the waters, hoping to see a sign that their offerings were acceptable. After a few minutes of anguish, a soft white light was seen in the depths of the waters and the people began to chant a verse of thankful mercy.

With the offerings now made, and the goddess Elaina appeased, the celebrations were to begin. In the king's hall the Thegns gathered for a feast of roasted meats and dark ale drank from curved horns. The hall was large, rectangular in shape and filled with comforts. The flames of a welcoming fire flickered up from the pit in the centre where a large boar was being roasted on a spit, its dripping fat hissing in the flames. Shields and banners hung from the walls, and the spears of a thousand slain warriors supported the thatched roof. The mood was joyous with little concern for the dying king, for all the Thegns knew that their next king was more favoured by the gods.

Cingetorix was born into war, having been born on the blooded ground of a battlefield. He was tall with the muscled physique of a warrior and a handsome face that was flanked by golden hair plaited in the warriors' fashion. Around his wrists he wore bronze bracelets that glimmered like gold when they caught the light. But Cingetorix did not just simply look the part of a warrior, for his skills with both sword and spear were yet to be bested. During the war with Gondolor's troublesome neighbour, Hardrada, Cingetorix had charged with the king's companions in battle and had himself captured the King of Hardrada. Such was his fame amongst the warriors, that King Corraidin named him his heir, even though he was only the second son. Breaking the age-old tradition of the crown passing down to the oldest son would have normally upset the Thegns. But King Carraidin's eldest son was by no means judged kingly by Gondolor's standards.

Brooding in the shadows was Viridomarus, the brother of Cingetorix and firstborn son of King Corraidin. Born with a lameness, Viridomarus would have been left in the wild for the wolves had he not been of royal blood. Having to depend on a stick to aid him walking, the warriors had seen him as weak and unfavoured by the gods. Disease had flailed his body, giving him a permanent sickly look. But behind his shallow eyes lay a sharp mind hungry for kingship. Knowing that he would never be a warrior, Viridomarus spent most of his boyhood lurking in the shadows, watching others and learning their behaviour, and it became easy for him to predict people's actions. As he reached adulthood, this talent gave him prestige and he began sitting in council with the Thegns. This position made him friends with many disgruntled people that disliked King Carraidin, and now he used these connections to his advantage.

Rising from his seat in the corner of the hall, Viridomarus walked over to the empty chair of the king and placed his hand upon it, signalling that he wished to speak.

"My dearest brother," Cingetorix said in a loud tone to hush the hall, "you wish to address us warriors?"

"A fine brother you are Cingetorix, mighty in strength and skill with sword and spear," Viridomarus answered. "Indeed, our father's hall is filled with many fine warriors of great renown."

"You may not drink with us brother," Cingetorix quickly replied, knowing what he wanted. "For you are not our equal; nor are you even a warrior. You are tolerated amongst us men because of your birth. Now sit back in the corner, like a spider, where you belong."

"This I know brother as it has been made clear to me. Since childhood have many here scorned me for my lameness. But have I not served Gondolor like you also?"

"Tell me brother," Cingetorix said as he stood upon his chair so that all could see him. "How many charges have you made with spear in hand? How many men in battle have you slain? None, and yet you speak as though you were our equal."

The warriors in the hall were all loyal to Cingetorix and their faces showed their disgust with Viridomarus.

"If you will not let me share ale with you brother, at least allow me to offer you wine from my personal stores."

"Wine!" Cingetorix face scrunched up with dissatisfaction with the offering. "Your words speak of us as fine warriors, and yet you offer us insult by gifting us with drink made for women and boy lovers!"

The warriors around Cingetorix cheered his words and called for better offerings to be made to them.

"From your stores I shall accept an offering of that fine ale brewed in Hardrada that you keep only for yourself." Cingetorix ordered two warriors to fetch the barrel. "But you brother may take your offering of wine to our women and the men lesser in might then us here. Now begone spider and fall from the sight of better men!"

Viridomarus inclined his head to show respect and walked out of the hall through a door that led to the king's quarters, his face cast with a wry smile, for all was as he expected. From the hall he walked down a corridor towards the king's private chamber. There, stood either side of a doorway were two of the king's Companions, wearing coats of mail the length of their thighs, iron helms with a wide nose guard, and long cloaks of green. In their right hands was a spear and in the other a round shield quartered green and yellow.

"Who approaches the king's chamber," one of the Companions said, though both recognised the distinctive *clack* sound of Viridomarus' stick as he approached.

"I wish to speak with my father," Viridomarus answered, not stopping to receive leave to enter as was the custom. He opened the door to a dark room that was dimly lit by a single candle placed on a small table alongside a jug of water. There laying upon a bed of animal skins in the centre was King Corraidin.

"What brings you here to disturb my slumber?" The king's voice was weak and his face pale as though he were marked for death. "What ill news does Viridomarus the Lame bring his king?"

"I have discovered treason my king, O' mighty Horse Lord." Viridomarus said as he stood beside the bed. "A devious plot to overthrow your kingship."

"Give name to the traitor and have Cingetorix deal with him," the king weakly answered, his shallow eyes looking straight up at Viridomarus' deceitful face leering over him.

Leaning heavily upon his stick, Viridomarus painfully bent down to the king's ear and whispered, "Viridomarus."

The king's eyes widened, and he called for his Companions, but his feeble pleas were met with thuds and groans from outside his chamber door.

"Cingetorix!" the king called with all the force he could muster. "Cingetorix!"

"Fear not father," Viridomarus said with a sly smile, "for he shall join you upon the golden fields shortly." He drew the small dagger hanging at his waist and plunged it down into his father's heart. There he remained still, hand gripped tightly around the hilt, ensuring that he had achieved his purpose. The door opened behind him and he released his grip upon the hilt and turned to meet his co-conspirator. "Is all in place?"

"The men are now entering the town," the man replied. He was short and dressed in a knee length tunic of green cloth, a tunic that signified him as one of the king's grooms. His hair was short, dark, and his eyes a pale blue, his lips thick and his nose wide and flat.

"Good," Viridomarus replied as he walked out of the room. "Spare none that will not pay fealty to me." Satisfied that all was going to plan, Viridomarus walked back to the hall where his brother and his warriors were drinking. There he walked over to the king's chair where he sat, a grotesque action punishable by death.

The warriors fell silent and turned to Viridomarus, few shouting insults and calling for his head.

"You have gone too far now brother," Cingetorix said as he stood from his own chair and approached the throne, his hand gripping the handle of his sword. "Not even your royal blood shall spare you for this outrage."

The warriors began coughing up blood and falling to their knees, many dying quickly, others slower owing to their strength. For unbeknown to them was that the ale taken from Viridomarus' store had been poisoned.

"What have you done?" Cingetorix asked, blood dribbling from the corner of his mouth. A burning wave swept up from his stomach and forced him down on to his knees, his face twisting with deepening pain.

"Great bravery and strength you have been blessed with, yet your mind is as sharp as a blunted sword brother," Viridomarus answered as he stood and watched his brother's life waning.

Though the poison was strong, it would not completely rob Cingetorix of his great strength. His anger now forced him back onto his feet and he staggered closer to Viridomarus, wrapping his hands around his slender neck and squeezing with all the force he could muster.

For a moment Viridomarus gasped for breath and fear took hold of him. But Cingetorix's grasp suddenly weakened and he slipped to the floor as the poison claimed him. The hall only moments ago had been lively with cheer and song but was now silent and still with death. From outside came the distinctive sound of screams and shouts as men fought and died. Viridomarus slowly stooped down and removed the golden horse ring from his brother's finger, and unremorsefully stepped over his body that lay face down and lifeless before the throne. Viridomarus walked out of the hall knowing that his victory was not yet complete; for Cingetorix had an infant son named Orgetorix.

The wife of Cingetorix was Arawn, a shield maiden of equal bravery and fame as her husband. Her fiery coloured hair matched her spirit and her green eyes were pools of desire where many warriors had drowned in lustful want. Hearing the commotion of foreign voices rushing through the royal apartments next to the king's hall, she instantly snatched up Orgetorix from his crib and ran. Rushing down a corridor lit by torches fixed to the stone walls, she was met by two warriors of Viridomarus, their bodies and faces covered with blue woad. They made a challenge and rushed to seize her, and though each were skilled none were the equal to Arawn. With Orgetorix still wrapped in her arm, she swiftly disarmed one warrior and killed the other, and without hesitation killed the remaining one and rushed out, blooded sword still in hand.

Warriors were fighting with the king's Companions in the courtyard before the King's hall, the air ringing from the sound of battle and the ground blooded and strewn with bodies and broken shields. Arawn knew she had to keep moving and feared what would happen to Orgetorix should she be captured. In the confusion of battle, Arawn was able to slip out of the king's gate without being noticed by the warriors fighting before the hall. A little further from the gate were two of Viridomarus' blue painted warriors stood with their backs towards the king's gate, pointing down towards the gate of Peleus. They never noticed Arawn before it was too late. Swiftly she slayed both and began making her way to the gate of Peleus, weaving around the roundhouses to remain undetected. There at the gate was a handful of the king's Companions, formed up in a shield wall defending the gate so that the people could escape. Arawn rushed over and was met by Zegofax, the Captain of Horse and friend of her husband.

"Lady Arawn I feared that you had been killed," Zegofax said, his aged face spattered with blood and tired. He was a short man with dark hair that was greying at the roots and a long moustache that was plaited and decorated with small bones from birds. "You must flee from the town lady."

"What of my husband and your prince?" Arawn asked, unwilling to leave without him. "The king?"

"I know not my lady," Zegofax replied, his weary eyes betraying his thoughts. "Nothing has come from the king's hall."

Without wasting time for thought, Arawn handed Orgetorix to one of the Companions close to Zegofax. "Take him where he will be safe, and when the time is right, he shall avenge us."

The Companion's name was Cleph, a skilled warrior that had twice carried the horse banner of the king in battle. "My lady what about you?"

"Give him this when he is of age." Arawn took off her ring of a horse that was rearing up on its back legs, a well-known ring that interlocked with the horse ring of Cingetorix. "This shall be proof of his true heritage."

"Horse!" Zegofax called, "Get me a horse!"

Moments later a Companion returned with a horse which Cleph mounted. "May the gods be with you lady."

"Go now before all is lost," Arawn said, her pale cheeks wet with tears. "Go with the blessings of the gods."

Warriors of Viridomarus massed for an attack upon the remaining Companions, and as Cleph fled with the prince wrapped under his cloak, a vicious battle was fought by the gate. The Companions honoured their oath and died to the last man, Zegofax being the final to fall. Arawn, her green dress stained with blood, was wounded by a cut to her sword arm. But defiantly she fought on, slaying three more warriors before being subdued. From the gate she was taken to the nearby mustering field where many of the people had been gathered.

There stood Viridomarus, surrounded by his blue painted warriors. "Where is the prince Orgetorix?" He asked as he strode over to Arawn, his stick clacking loudly against the slowly freezing ground.

But Arawn was defiant and would not answer, even when a sword was pressed up against her neck by the warrior holding her.

"Search every house and comb the countryside for the prince," Viridomarus ordered his warriors. He then smiled down at Arawn and said, "I am now king, and you shall be my queen."

Arawn was disgusted by the thought and was not of a yielding nature, even when faced with death. "I shall never submit to becoming your queen. You are a traitor to your people and shall one day answer for your crime to the rightful and true king of Gondolor."

These words angered Viridomarus as he needed to find the prince and end the line of Cingetorix to secure his reign. Flushed with anger he took a sword from one of his warriors and himself placed its tip against Arawn's chest. "Tell me where he is!"

Arawn smiled and answered, "The true king shall come for you." She then pushed her weight forwards onto the sword Viridomarus held, ending her own life and any hope of Viridomarus claiming her.

"Find the prince!" Viridomarus barked at his warriors, his anger hot. "Kill any that will not submit to my rule!"

But the bravery of Arawn and the Companions had not been in vain, for Cleph had used the time to escape with the prince Orgetorix. He travelled northeast across the grasslands for many days, suffering the cold and drizzling rain that followed in the days after the Hallows. In the farming village of Tamaris did his sister dwell, a kind-hearted woman with children of her own. It was the middle of the night when Cleph arrived at his sisters dwelling, banging on the locked wooden door of her roundhouse.

"Alannah," Cleph called as he banged the door. "Alannah!" The door was opened, and the shadowy figure of his sister emerged in her nightwear.

"Brother," Alannah said, sensing that there was trouble. "What is it?"

Cleph handed over Orgetorix and told Alannah of his true birth, and all that had happened on the night of the Hallows. At first Alannah had refused the child in fear for the safety of her own children. But as she looked into the kingly eyes of Orgetorix her heart was filled with pity, and so she agreed. Cleph swiftly took his leave, saying that he would search for other Companions that may have survived. Then he would go into exile in the forest of Aurum, and there stay until Orgetorix sought him out in want of answers.

So it was that Orgetorix was saved and the people of Gondolor had an ember of hope that might one day give spark to a fire. For in the days after the Hallows rumour spread of the saved prince that shall one day ride to Gondolor and reclaim his rightful throne. To quieten the talk of a returning prince, Viridomarus sought the blessings of the gods for his kingship. Gathering with his chosen warriors at the sacred grove, Viridomarus made his offerings and spoke at length of how his actions were just, and that it was his birth right to be king. But from the water came no sign of favour from the gods, still and dark did the pool remain until the chosen warriors left Viridomarus alone.

"What hatred you have shown me!" Viridomarus said aloud with scorn. "From birth you granted me lameness and watched idly as the world mocked me! Yet what words of blame did I lay upon your altar, what unworthy gifts did I offer to offend thee?"

From the water did a mist rise, condensing upon the bank into a figure of a grey lady. "You ask for blessings upon your unrightful actions, knowing in your heart that the gods will not gift you with what you seek." Her voice was soft and haunting. "Your offerings are deemed worthy and shall grant you kingship of Gondolor. For years you shall reign unchallenged and at peace; until the son of Cingetorix shall come forth and lay claim to his throne."

"The son of my brother shall never see his adulthood," Viridomarus answered, his anger growing with the knowledge that Orgetorix still lived and had escaped him. "For even now my warriors seek him out."

"Seek they may," the grey lady gave answer, "but find they shall not. For the gods have cast a shadow of protection over him. The lost prince shall come to adulthood, and he shall seek justice for your crime." With no further words to say, the grey lady disappeared, and the grove fell still and silent once more.

Thus, began the reign of Viridomarus, a reign of darkness and fear. Any that dared to speak against the king were put to death and taxes were increased to burden the people and pay for the king's mercenary warriors. Gondolor fell from pride and became lesser, many of its warriors having to turn to banditry to support their families. A time the people of Gondolor called the Tenebris, the dark.

II

The Grey Lady

Peacefully the years passed for Orgetorix, though now he was known by the name of Cronan and his true heritage kept secret from him. Growing up in the farming village of Tamaris, he had grown into a fine man, handsome and quick in understanding, being of a warrior's build like his true father and of a fiery spirit like his true mother. His hot-headedness had often led to trouble growing up, often unwilling to accept authority of men whom he deemed lesser than himself. A great frustration dwelt within Orgetorix as he felt he was worthy of more than the simple life of a farmer that fate had bestowed upon him. Many times, as a child had Orgetorix fought with other children in the village over his lofty opinion of himself, and never once letting any of them get the better of him. Indeed, much was made of his appearance as he looked nothing like his brothers, who were smaller in stature and more readily accepting of their humble status; and these rumours led to more trouble as he grew into adulthood.

It was in Orgetorix's seventeenth year that his life took a path of turmoil and woe, on a midsummer's day after the sun had sank into the west. Crops of corn were being tended in preparation for harvesting in a few weeks' time, and the day had been long. But Orgetorix had shunned his appointed duty of shovelling manure into a small handcart to spend the afternoon with the blacksmith's daughter, Roxanna, a dark-haired beauty admired and pursued by many men. After their secret liaison, Orgetorix went to the tavern known as the Torc.

The Torc was a large roundhouse close to the hall of the Thegn, built with stone in a circular plan and with a conical roof of thatch. Inside were benches placed around a fire that roared in the centre, the hot air scented by ale and smoke. It was a place where the farmers of Tamaris relaxed in an evening and spoke of hardening times over horns of dark ale.

As Orgetorix ducked through the low entrance he noticed the familiar faces sat around the fire, in each of their hands a curved horn filled with frothy ale. They were speaking of hardening times, of shortages in the winter should the Thegn agree to the tribute of corn demanded by the king of Gondolor. Though a few were of a mind that they should send nothing as they had little enough for themselves, all knew there was little choice. If the Thegn failed to send the tribute, the king of Gondolor would send his warriors to take it all, leaving them to starve come the winter.

Orgetorix, unconcerned by their talk, took up a horn and scooped himself some ale from a barrel.

"My father shares meat and ale this very night with a representative from Gondolor. He knows of our concerns and will plead our case." It was the Thegn's son that addressed the men sat around the fire, a fulsome man with a high opinion of himself. He wore fine garments of green cloth and a cloak of fur held in place by a silver brooch that marked him as a man of status. His hair was the colour of straw and tightly curled, his face slender with brown eyes set close together atop of a long nose.

"So far we are from Gondolor," one of the farmers said as he looked around the fire in search of support, "why pay homage to a distant king; better to pay a lesser tribute to Hardrada like our forefathers did."

The Thegn's son shook his head and replied, "You should choose your words with greater care, or else find them heard by the wrong ears."

"Forgive me," the farmer said, "I meant no offence."

It was now that the Thegn's son noticed Orgetorix and he stood from the bench to make his challenge. "Cronan, you enter a place where you are not welcome."

"Ceolwulf," Orgetorix mockingly smiled over at the Thegn's son and raised his horn, "I didn't recognise you dressed in women's furs."

"This is an alehouse for working men," Ceolwulf replied as he walked around the fire towards Orgetorix. "As an idle son of a whore, you are not welcome."

The men around the fire all stood, expecting trouble, but Orgetorix remained seated and finished his drink.

"I have reports that you neglected your work in the fields, and I shall personally see to it that you are whipped for your idleness." Ceolwulf said as his jabbed his finger down hard on Orgetorix's shoulder.

It was now that Orgetorix stood to face Ceolwulf, rising a full head and shoulders above him. "You have it wrong for I have worked up quite the thirst this afternoon. For pleasing Roxanna is heavy work as she is very demanding." Orgetorix knew his words would anger Ceolwulf as the Thegn was in negotiations with the blacksmith for the betrothal of his daughter to his son, and it was well-known of Ceolwulf's affection for Roxanna.

"You lie!" Ceolwulf wrapped his hand around the leather handle of his sword and pulled it free of his scabbard. "I should kill you for your dishonour!"

"Then you shall have to kill me thrice over," Orgetorix quickly responded with a smile, "for that was the number of times she demanded me."

Ceolwulf reddened with anger and went to run Orgetorix through with his sword. But Orgetorix was posed ready for such a strike and swiftly knocked the sword out of Ceolwulf's hand. With anger now blinding both to better judgement, a fight ensued. Though Ceolwulf was accustomed to violence, he was not equal to Orgetorix who swiftly beat him to the floor. Both had been long rivals to each other, yet it had never come to blows; and the Thegn would not simply ignore such a vicious assault upon his son and heir.

"Cronan stop!" One of the farmers shouted as he rushed over to stay Orgetorix's fists from beating Ceolwulf to death.

It was now that three of the Thegn's warriors rushed in to restrain Orgetorix, but even now when he was outnumbered, he would not yield. Like a savage dog backed into a corner did Orgetorix defend himself with fists alone, downing two of the warriors before fleeing out of the doorway and into the night to make good his escape. He ran swiftly to the eastern section of the palisade that ringed around the settlement. There the wood was rotten and loose, and he was able to push his body through a gap and slip out of the village.

To the northeast was a woodland, dense and ripe for concealment. There the light of the moon and stars was blotted out by a canopy of broad leaves above. Wild and unpaved was this woodland with many ancient roots twisting up out of the soil. It was on one of these roots which Orgetorix tripped, sending him crashing down to a concealed pool of still water. There from the water did a grey mist rise to condense into the figure of a grey lady, featureless apart from blue glowing eyes.

"What evil trickery is this?" Orgetorix said as he shot up onto his feet.

"I come not with intent of evil trickery," the grey lady replied in a revered voice. "But with words from the gods."

"What words would the gods have for one as lowborn as a farmer?" Orgetorix asked. "I have nothing to make offerings but my own life's blood."

"Nurtured upon the fields of corn were you," the grey lady replied. "Yet your birth and blood are that of a prince. You are Orgetorix, son of Prince Cingetorix and the most renowned shield maiden Arawn. Descendent of the last true king, Carraidin."

"I have heard much talk of the lost prince, yet I am no fool," Orgetorix replied, "and shall not fall to such ill deception."

"Search your heart Prince Orgetorix, true king of Gondolor. For there you shall find true answer to the words of the gods."

Orgetorix closed his eyes and searched his feelings, knowing that the greater part of him had never settled for the life of a humble farmer, and that he felt destined for greater things. Images of a babe in a red-haired woman's arms entered his mind, and a sweet smell of her perfume filled his nostrils. Then he knew it to be true. "What must I do?"

"The time has come forth for the lost prince to reclaim his heritage, to take back what was taken from him and restore the realm of Gondolor back to its former glory. Back into the lighter days of joy and harmony."

Orgetorix opened his eyes to find the grey lady gone. His thoughts were deeply troubled, and his heart was in torment with want of answers. For hours more did he remain hidden in the woodland, pondering over the grey lady's words, long and deep into the early hours of the morning. Then Orgetorix swiftly made his way back to Tamaris, taking great care not to cross paths with the Thegn's warriors that would surely be looking for him.

Like a child seeking comfort, Orgetorix went to the blacksmith's workshop, where he crept around to the back and knocked on the wooden shutter that he knew to be Roxanna's bedchamber.

The blacksmith had earned himself a wealthy living, and his workmanship was considered some of the finest; this reflected in his workshop which was built in stone to a rectangular plan like the Thegn's hall. To the front was his furnace and anvil, to the rear his private home.

Orgetorix had to knock three times before Roxanna opened the shutter.

"Cronan," Roxanna said with shock, "I thought that you would be locked up by now." Her dark hair hung loose at her shoulders, and even in the gloom of the early hours her brown eyes seemed to glow with desire.

"I have to speak with you," Orgetorix said in a hushed tone.

"I can't," Roxanna replied. "The Thegn has informed my father about us and put an end to my betrothal to Ceolwulf. My father beat me and has forbid me to leave the house."

"Please," Orgetorix pled. "I just need to speak with you."

"Wait there." Roxanna disappeared from the window and reappeared a few minutes later from the backdoor, dressed in a nightgown with a woollen cloak wrapped tightly around her shoulders. "The Thegn has warriors looking for you, he says that you assaulted his son."

"It is true," Orgetorix answered. Shocked by the words of the grey lady, he gave no thought to the danger of returning to the village and had acted more like a child seeking comfort from a telling-off than a rightful king. "I fled to the woodlands nearby, there I spoke with a grey lady, a messenger from the gods."

Roxanna was surprised to hear Orgetorix speak like this, for he had always scoffed at those that claimed to speak with the gods. "Cronan," she said seeing his despair, "what did they say?"

"Have you heard of the lost prince?"

Roxanna nodded her head. "We all grew up hearing the tale of the lost prince, even playing games pretending to be him."

Orgetorix revealed all what the grey lady had spoken to him, and that he somehow knew it to be true. But Roxanna was angered by her loss of a good marriage and blamed Orgetorix for her misfortune. Now her mind was crafting a way in which she could regain position and her betrothal to the Thegn's son, and now Orgetorix had given it her.

"You must go home and seek the truth from your mother," Roxanna said as she placed a cold hand against Orgetorix's cheeks. "If this is true you shall be a king and I your queen."

Orgetorix took her hand and kissed it, before turning and walking away, his heart comforted by Roxanna's promise. But unbeknown to him was that when she had returned inside, she awoke her father and told him all that Orgetorix had revealed, and together they went to the Thegn. For Roxanna disbelieved Orgetorix and her hope was that by informing on him, her betrothal would be reinstated.

The Thegn was still in talks with the representative from Gondolor when the blacksmith begged for an audience, and only granted one when the representative heard the name Orgetorix being mentioned. The representative explained that the king would reward richly any that apprehended the lost prince and would most certainly grant him whatever he asked. The Thegn, being a greedy man ever hungry for greater power, ordered his son roused and ready to arrest Orgetorix.

But for Roxanna, her hopes were not rewarded for her information, and she with her father was sent away with not a single word of gratitude. For the Thegn now had loftier ambitions than marrying his son to a blacksmith's daughter.

As for Orgetorix, he walked back home with childish images of kingship clouding his better judgement. The home that Orgetorix had been raised in was a small roundhouse on a plot of land towards the western edge of the village. All was quiet with not a sign of any warriors awaiting Orgetorix's return. Inside, sitting beside the fire was his mother, Alannah, her brow heavy with tiredness and worry.

"Cronan, where have you been," Alannah said as she saw Orgetorix enter. "Warriors came seeking you!" Her eyes were angered and yet her voice was relieved to see him safely return. "They took your father and brothers!"

"It was Ceolwulf mother, he called you a whore." Tears welled in the corner of Orgetorix's eyes as he began to explain. "He angered me, and I told him of laying with Roxanna. We fought and he lost."

"You would risk the Thegn's wrath upon us for the blacksmith's daughter?"

"No!" Orgetorix snapped back in anger. "For the honour of this family!" For a moment there was silence, but the word family stirred his emotions ever deeper in a mixed pool of hope and despair. "But they are right," he added in a calmer tone. "They were right about me."

"Right about what Cronan?"

"My true name is Orgetorix." Orgetorix slumped down on a stool by the fire, his eyes lowered to the flames. "And I am not your son."

"Who has told you this?" Alannah asked as she sat down.

Orgetorix revealed to Alannah that he had spoken with a strange entity in the woodland, a grey lady that claimed to be a messenger of the gods, and that it was she that told of his true birth.

"Then the time has come," Alannah replied. "I have feared this day since you were first brought to my door. And now that it has come, I fear losing you. For though the messenger of the gods spoke truth, in my heart you are my true son."

"And I shall always think of you as my mother, for it was you that nurtured me all these past years. But I would now like knowledge of how this path came to be."

Alannah told Orgetorix of the night her brother had come and revealed what he had told her of his true parents. The knowledge weighed heavily upon Orgetorix, for he felt that his life was a lie; and yet now he envisioned a future that he had always wanted, visions that stirred his greed.

"Nothing has to change," Alannah said, seeing the anguish upon Orgetorix's face. "You can go to the Thegn and take the punishment for your actions. He will then free your father and brothers and we can continue to keep your true birth a secret and you can remain here with us."

Though there was a part of Orgetorix which wanted all to remain as it was, his pride would not allow him to go grovelling for mercy from the Thegn, not when he was rightful king of Gondolor. "No, I have to go and claim what is rightfully mine, for if I remain here, I shall have to settle for what little I have, and I yearn for more, so much more."

Tears fell from Alannah's eyes as she knew her son was lost, lost in place of a prince seeking his crown. "Then I shall not hinder your heart with pleas to remain where you were raised but tell you that you are free to tread your own path." She stood from her stool and walked around the fire to Orgetorix, placing her hands upon the cheeks of his face. "But heed my warnings not to grow too proud, to remember always your humble upbringing. For a king should not be bound to greed and desire for more."

"I shall not forget mother," Orgetorix replied as he stood. "And I promise to come back and free my brothers and father."

"You must go to the forest of Aureum, to the White Tree, and there seek out Cleph, my brother and former member of the King's Companions. He shall guide your from there."

Through the entrance came two of the Thegn's warriors, both armed with small axes. They made straight for

Orgetorix and tried to restrain him. But Orgetorix's great strength overcome them and he killed each with his bare hands.

"Cronan you cowardly dog," the voice of Ceolwulf came from outside. "Come out! Or should I call you by your traitorous name, Orgetorix!?"

Orgetorix heart panged as he knew now that Roxanna had betrayed him. He picked up an axe from beside the body of one of the warriors and strode over to the entrance, peering out. Waiting for him was Ceolwulf and a handful of warriors.

"You cannot go that way Cronan," Alannah pled, "they will kill you." She rushed over to her bed and pushed it aside, revealing a wooden hatch. "Use this passage, it will bring you outside the village walls to the south."

"Come with me mother," Orgetorix said as he rushed over and pulled open the hatch.

"I will remain here, as is my place," Alannah replied as tears rolled down her pale cheeks. "Go now Prince Orgetorix and reclaim your throne."

Orgetorix dropped down the hidden passage and looked back up to his mother. "I'll come back mother." But then the hatch was closed, and darkness ensued.

The passage had been tunnelled during the war between Gondolor and Hardrada, a time when the village was fought over for its bountiful harvest of corn. For the most part Orgetorix had to crawl, wafting his left hand out in front of him so that he could feel his way forward. After what seemed an eon of time, a dim light grew from a shaft that led up to the fields above, there was placed a wooden ladder in need of repair. Swiftly did Orgetorix climb with many of the rungs of the ladder breaking as he climbed before he reached the top where he pushed open a half-broken hatch overgrown by long grass. The sky to the east was reddening from a rising sun, to the west still dark, and the morning air was already warm. But looking back to the north there was a pillar of smoke rising from the village, and the warm breeze carried the sound of a woman's scream, his mother's scream as she was cruelly dragged to the dungeon.

Seeing mounted warriors coming out of the village gate, Orgetorix turned to the south towards the hills where he hoped to lose any pursuer. And so, with a heavy heart he ran, swearing to one day return and avenge his mother.

III

The Pursuit of a King

The hills south of Tamaris were known as the Hills of Eros. They took their name from a giant said to have dwelt there long-ago, before the horse lords of Gondolor came to be. Eros was renowned for his deep love of jewels and his craftsmanship of fashioning the most desired trinkets. So fine was one of his pieces that it was desired by kings and gods alike. A time of turmoil followed as kings destroyed temples and forbade offerings and prayers to the heavens. The gods responded by sending floods to wash away the kings that defied them. Eros was said to be aggrieved by causing such quarrel between the gods and men, and for their actions deemed both unworthy of possession of his craftsmanship. Eros took his much sought-after amulet and cast it deep into the sea, swearing an oath never to craft such finery again. Over the passing of years, men searched the hills for Eros and his cave said to be filled with wonders. Though many expeditions had set out with good hope, none had found the cave, nor Eros himself.

It was in these hills that Orgetorix now wandered, though now he was the one being sought and not Eros. Things were desperate for Orgetorix as he had no supplies nor any hope of outrunning his pursuers. The hills were a bleak place, rocky in parts with loose stone that slid down the hillsides into deep valleys. But as difficult as it was for Orgetorix, it was twice more so for his pursuers. Their horses struggled underfoot, and the warriors were forced to dismount, slowing their pursuit. The noise of the horses echoed in the hills and alerted Orgetorix whenever they were near. One night they camped so close to Orgetorix that he was able to sneak into their camp and steal some of their supplies as they slept.

Orgetorix knew that he was going the wrong way, and that he needed to go north towards the forest of Aureum where Alannah's brother was. But that passage was dangerous as the land was flat and ideal for horses that would soon run him down. His hope was to lose them in the hills and head east towards the river Wye, where he hoped to find a place shallow enough to cross, and from there head north. But as he came to the western bank, he saw that the river was wide and far too deep to cross. It was there upon the bank that Orgetorix was caught unaware by two of the pursuing warriors.

As Orgetorix rested upon the stony bank of the Wye, two warriors walked their horses down to the water, and there stumbled across Orgetorix. Though weakened by want of food, Orgetorix was able to defeat both, taking from them their waterskins and dried, salted meat. Taking one of their horses, Orgetorix then sped south along the bank, hoping to find a crossing. For days did he travel, the horse growing more agitated the further south they went.

It was on the fifth day of riding that Orgetorix came before the Great Marsh, the horse wide-eyed and unwilling to go any further. Orgetorix dismounted and unsaddled the horse, whispering in its ear that he was now free to go where he willed.

The Great Marsh was a boggy wetland, stretching many miles south from the Hills of Eros, all the way south to the forest of Long Wood where the river Wye merges with the river Ouse. From there, the river courses to the unknown regions of the south. Vast and dull was this passage, plagued with flies and humidity that sapped further at Orgetorix's strength. For days he followed the river south in search of a crossing, days in which he became haunted by strange lights that were seemingly following him and soft voices calling out to him from the mist which concealed the ground. One night as he lay beside a pool of stagnant water, he heard a lament that drove him to despair and he plunged into a pool to end his misery. Unknown hands pulled Orgetorix out onto the muddy bank, but there was no sign or sight of any person. Then again came the sound of a woman singing.

> *O king of horse and king of men. Of*
> *humble home to silver hall, with a*
> *golden crown upon his brow. His heart*
> *doth desire his heart doth want, a*

shadow of darkness surrounds his soul.
Upon his hands are strength and doom,
a lessening will of a feeble fool. Like
the morning son shall he rise, and as
the setting sun shall he fall.

To hear such a lament reduced Orgetorix to tears and he wept long into the night, pouring out all the woe his life had bestowed upon him. The morrow then dawned, black with heavy rain driven into Orgetorix face by a shrill wind driven up from the south. All that day he wandered, losing his way as he was forced away from the river by dense thorn bushes that grew beside the riverbed. His food was now gone, and his stomach pained with hunger. Accepting his fate, Orgetorix laydown and closed his eyes, waiting for death to come and claim him. But death would not find Orgetorix this day, for the gods would not allow him to fall to such a cruel end.

For unknown hours did Orgetorix sleep, his dreams evoked with images of flamed horses carrying demon warriors with yellow eyes that were armed with spears of bone. When he awoke, Orgetorix found himself beside a fire that's flames heated a small cauldron filled with a simmering thin broth. Sitting on a stool that had half sunk into the mud, was a bearded man wearing stained robes of a crimson colour. His face and eyes had a dark hue, his voice emphasized by a strange accent that Orgetorix had never heard before.

"O, you are awake," the man said as Orgetorix groggily sat up. "I bet my wife that you were dead."

"Who are you?" Orgetorix looked around and saw that the man was alone. "And where is your wife?"

"Forgive me lord," the man replied, "for I am Eppillus and my wife, Eilis, is right here."

Sat on a small wooden chest beside a sleeping bag was a wicker doll the size of a child. It was dressed in a green dress with silver lace and its black hair hung loose around its shoulders, its eyes black glass that seemingly moved whenever one would look away from it.

"I am no lord," Orgetorix answered, feeling uncomfortable under the gaze of the doll. "I am just a humble traveller like yourself."

"Oh," Eppillus replied, wide-eyed with suspicion. "My wife said that she sees as circle of light upon your brow and a noble fire within your eyes."

Orgetorix sensed that Eppillus knew he was more than the simple traveller he claimed to be, yet he feared to say any more.

"Well it's going to be a long night, and you look like you need something warm." Eppillus took a ladle and scooped some of the thin broth into a wooden bowl. "Now eat up and rest, for on the morrow we must part ways."

Orgetorix took the offered bowl and raised it to his lips, feeling the hot liquid trickle down to his empty stomach as he took a sip. "How is it I came here?"

"We found you," Eppillus explained as he scooped himself a bowl of broth, himself taking a sip. "I had to drag you here myself." He suddenly shot up onto his feet and went over to the doll, placing the bowl at its feet. "Yes, yes, yes…you helped too."

"Where is it you come from?" Orgetorix asked, feeling unsettled by Eppillus speaking with a doll.

"What do you mean tell him? He won't tell us his true passage." Eppillus waved his hands in the air and walked back over to the fire where he slumped back down on his stool, driving it deeper into the mud. "Fine, have it your way!"

"Forgive me," Orgetorix said as he finished his broth, "I did not intend to cause argument between you and your…. wife."

"No, no, my wife wishes me to tell you so I shall." Eppillus stroked his dark beard as he began. "Once both I and my wife dwelled within the walls of Medeis. There I had been tutored since my youth at the school of Magus, learning the lore of magic. The best of my class was I, passing the trial all must complete if they were to remain at the school after boyhood. I married Eilis soon after my trial and was given a position at the school to research the essence of life itself. All was good and my work was considered the finest, but a terrible plague came and claimed my wife. Shrouded with grief, I began to search the forbidden texts for answers. Under cover of night, I began communicating with spirits upon a board of letters, learning much and being pulled ever deeper into darkness. I finally learnt how to capture a sprit, and Eilis spirit I did cast into this doll."

At this point Orgetorix looked over at the doll to see that it had moved closer to the fire, and that the bowl of broth that Eppillus had placed at its feet now lay empty. "Necromancy!" A shade of black covered his sight, like a drop of ink clouding a cup of water, and his strength lessened so that he could no longer move.

"But my work invited evil into the world, and the school was turned to turmoil by spirits that to this day haunt the halls and corridors. The people of the nearby town, learning of my misuse of magic, called for my head and I was forced to flee. So, like you I am running."

Orgetorix fell once more into a deep slumber, hearing and seeing nothing. By the time he awoke, his tiredness and hunger had disappeared along with any sign of Eppillus and Eilis. Where only the night before there had been a fire, now the ground lay clear and cold with not a trace of any camp having even been made. Orgetorix, filled with uncertainty as to what was true and what was not, rose to his feet and took flight toward the east where he once more came to the banks of the river Wye. There he found that the river was shallow and that he was able to cross.

East of the River Wye was the realm of Hardrada, a lesser state then that of Gondolor, but no less prideful and steeped in traditions. The land here was mainly flat and offered little resources other than what could be grown in its soil. The River Ouse marked Hardrada's southern border, and beyond that lay the realm of the Hill-Men, a rocky land that rose and fell from great heights. Much of Hardrada's history was plagued by the wars with the Hill-Men, who were said to be barbarians and eaters of flesh. In the long dry summer, at a time when Hardrada was at its height, the Hill-Men had crossed the shallow Ouse and raided along its banks. The warriors of Hardrada were sent south, and after a bloody battle that was said to have lasted a full day, the Hill-Men were repelled back across the river. So fearful had their raiding been, that the people of

Hardrada refused to resettle in those areas. Instead they went west where they crossed the Wye and eventually founded the settlement of Tamaris. The rich soil around Tamaris yielded bountiful crops and Hardrada grew in might. From this envy did Gondolor first go to war with Hardrada, diminishing her might by slaying many of her warriors in battle. But now, long after those events, the southern lands north of the Ouse remain empty.

Orgetorix now feared this passage and toiled with himself whether he should turn back or not. What he feared was that the horsemen pursuing him would easily see him and swiftly run him down. His hope was that he had been able to lose them in the hills and marsh. But those hopes were defeated by the sight of horsemen to the north. To the east was a woodland where Orgetorix now fled, keeping as low as he could and using whatever cover he could find. But despite his best efforts, he was seen and pursued vigorously. The ground began to vibrate as the horsemen drew near, and for a moment Orgetorix thought all was lost. Orgetorix was first to reach the woodland, and though the trees slowed the horsemen, they were able to catch-up with him. Ducking under low branches and dashing left and then right to avoid capture, Orgetorix weaved around the trees as he desperately looked for some advantage. But despite his best efforts, Orgetorix was barged into by a horseman, knocking him down a bank into the waters of a small lake.

"Cronan you dog," Ceolwulf said as he rode down the bank towards Orgetorix. "For days have you fled justice like a coward; and justice I seek to give!" He dismounted and quickly walked to the water's edge, drawing his sword.

Two other warriors dismounted and ran to take hold of Orgetorix, taking him by his arms and forcing him out of the water and on to his knees. There Orgetorix would have met his end had it not been for the timely arrival of horsemen from Hardrada. There was thirty in number, all hardened men and fresh from patrolling along the river Ouse.

"Stay your sword!" The warrior that called was the captain of the warriors of Hardrada, a burly man with a long moustache that was plaited down to his belt. Like the warriors behind him, he wore a blue cloak with a round shield covered over by a sheet of Iron that was polished to gleam like silver, hence where they took their name, the Silver Shields. "To spill blood in the Grove of Hara is a great offence to the gods and will be punished by death."

"What matter of this is yours," Ceolwulf said still holding his sword's point to Orgetorix's neck. "Begone and leave this matter to me, the son of the Thegn of Tamaris."

"I will go nowhere, for you have come into the realm of Hardrada and will obey its laws!" The Silver Shields, being greater in number and equipped with mail coats, formed up around Ceolwulf and his warriors in a semicircle. "Tell me now what offence this man has given to warrant the attention of the Thegn of Tamaris?"

"He is a coward and is wanted for his assault upon me," Ceolwulf replied as though he were the greater authority of the two.

"So cowardly that it would take eight warriors to apprehend him," the captain responded mockingly. "If you wish not to break the peace between Gondolor and

Hardrada, I bid that you relinquish your weapons and come with us to Hardrada where the king himself may pass judgement on this matter."

Ceolwulf, his anger now cooling, saw that his men were not equal to the Silver Shields, and so unwillingly dropped his sword. "Very well," Ceolwulf replied. "But my father shall not be happy with this delay and will seek recompense for this interference."

From the Grove of Hara did the company swiftly travel to the northeast towards the town of Hardrada. This passage was uninspiring for Orgetorix as his hands were bound and there was little chance to escape. All around was an endless grassland, flat and void of any dwellings or features other than grass that swayed with the breeze. After a week, the wooden palisade that protected Hardrada grew upon the horizon. They approached the town from the south where a tall gate guarded by more warriors of the Silver Shields. Suspended on chains above the gate was a skull of a dragon said to have once roamed these lands.

Orgetorix had never seen a town so large before and was awestruck as he passed through the gate. The first thing he noticed was the smell, quickly followed by the noise of blacksmiths hammers and the buzzing as the people went about their daily business. The roundhouses were much the same as in Tamaris, but the king's hall was far larger than that of the Thegn's. The townspeople stopped their activities and followed the company up to the king's hall where they gathered in great numbers, each having their opinion on what evils these men were. Orgetorix was pushed and shoved towards the double door entrance guarded by eight warriors of the Silver Shields.

The king's hall was built to the north of the town, with stone walls and a high thatched roof. The king of Hardrada's hall was of a lesser grandeur when compared to that of King Viridomarus, yet it still possessed the charm and comfort for a king. Like all kingly halls of the time, there was a fire that was kept burning day and night in the centre. Around the fire was high-backed chairs, the king's positioned closest and draped with fur skins. Hung on the walls were tapestries that depicted times when Hardrada was greater in might; and suspended from the beams of the roof were ancient shields said to have been used by the gods during the battle of Beginnings.

In his seat, mulling over a curved horn of ale, was King Eomer of Hardrada. At the time of Orgetorix's coming, he had grown plump with eyes tired and heavy with responsibility. He wore a burgundy tunic of wool and brown trousers more befitting a common man then a king. His dark beard and hair were long and speckled with grey, and upon his brow he wore a crown made of antlers from a deer.

"My king," the captain of the Silver Shields said as he bowed.

"What have we here?" King Eomer's eyes fell upon Orgetorix, and there saw recognition.

"They are warriors from Tamaris," the captain explained, "we found them about to spill blood in the Grove of Hara."

"Such a vile act is deserving of death," the King said in a serious tone.

Ceolwulf then stepped forward and knelt as was the custom when in the presence of a king. "King of Hardrada, I beg that you allow me to present my case."

King Eomer drank from his horn and nodded his agreement. "Continue and be hopeful that your words make a worthy case for me not to pass the judgement of death upon you."

"I am Ceolwulf, the son and heir to the Thegn of Tamaris." Ceolwulf rose and pointed at Orgetorix. "This man is wanted for treason against the Thegn and King of Gondolor. It is your duty to aid me in my charge of bringing him to justice."

"It is not for a lowly son of a Thegn to lecture a king on his duty!" King Eomer rose from his chair and walked around the fire to Ceolwulf. "In acknowledgment of your position I grant you safety of my hall and invite you to feast with us. But what documents do you carry to show authority to apprehend such a man?"

"My word should be sufficient, and I formally ask that you release me so that I can continue with my charge." King Eomer's eyes lingered upon Orgetorix. "I shall grant you and your warriors leave to go as you please, but this man you claim a criminal shall remain in my dungeon until I have received written word from your father for his extradition, as is the custom between our two realms."

"I fear that this judgement shall displease the Thegn." Ceolwulf's face reddened with anger as he knew some sort of game was being played. "I strongly urge that you reconsider this judgement and remember that you are a vassal to the realm of Gondolor."

"I know my place, and for the sake of my people I accept it!" King Eomer's anger now rose. He disliked Ceolwulf and would have had him flogged for his impertinence would it not cause friction on the peace treaty with Gondolor. "My judgement stands, and you can assure the Thegn of Tamaris that I shall hold this charged man until you return with the correct documentation."

Knowing that there was little else he could say to sway the mind of a king, Ceolwulf took his leave immediately. Making with all haste to Tamaris.

Orgetorix was taken to the dungeon where he was placed in a cell alongside four other men. It was late in the night when he was taken back into the hall where he was given meat and ale. After eating and drinking his fill, King Eomer joined him beside the fire.

"Tell me of whom you are," King Eomer said as he sat at his seat, wrapped in a woollen blanket to ward off the cold.

"My name is Cronan of Tamaris, a humble farmer wrongly charged," Orgetorix answered, unwilling and unsure that he should share his true heritage.

King Eomer leaned forwards in his chair and looked Orgetorix straight in his eye. "I once knew the Prince Cingetorix of Gondolor. A great warrior and the finest horsemen I have ever seen. When I received news of his murder, I wept, for such a renowned warrior to fall to betrayal from those of his own blood is unjust."

Orgetorix felt uncomfortable under the king's gaze and suspected that he knew of his true birth. "I know nothing of what you speak," he replied. "But I beg that you do not allow me to fall back into the hands of Ceolwulf."

"Tell me truthfully," King Eomer said raising a finger, "what did you do?"

"I fought with him over a woman whom he had been betrothed to," Orgetorix gave honest reply, "I beat him and the warriors that came after."

King Eomer laughed and nodded his head as if satisfied. "Good. But now let me be honest with you. Following the murder of Cingetorix, there was a story that his son had survived, a lost prince that shall one day come forth. I have cast my eyes upon Prince Cingetorix many times, and in you I see his very image."

Orgetorix sat silent, unsure of what he should say. But the King of Hardrada offered no malice towards him and had showed only kindness.

"You need not say it," King Eomer said to break the silence, "And you should know that it is out of honour for your father that I shall do my best to aid you."

"You will let me leave?" Orgetorix asked.

"No," the king replied with a smile. "For if I were to release you it would risk the peace between Hardrada and Gondolor; and my might in warriors is not great enough to challenge King Viridomarus yet."

"So out of honour for my father you would gift me to my enemies?"

"What is it you would offer Hardrada?" The king asked, knowing in his mind what he wanted. "What is it you would offer to regain your freedom?"

"I seek what is rightfully mine," Orgetorix gave answer, "and should I gain it with your friendship I shall release Hardrada from its vassalage to Gondolor."

This pleased King Eomer, for it is what both he and his people desired above all other things, to restore Hardrada to its former glory. "I cannot openly aid you for it shall mean the destruction of my people. But you shall be allowed to escape and steal all that you need."

So it was that on the very next night Orgetorix was placed in a cell with an unlocked door. He wasted no time in taking his leave of the town of Hardrada, taking with him the gifts of food, a sword and a white steed that was named Velox the Swift.

IV

The Outlaws

The passage north from Hardrada was swift and made with ease. Like the land towards the south, it was flat and ideal for horses. After three long days of riding, the golden forest of Aureum came into sight on the northern horizon. Even at a distance did the forest look endless and foreboding. To the east and west did the forest stretch for many leagues to wild and unpaved realms unknown to both Gondolor and Hardrada, its northern edge equally unknown. The trees of this forest were in an eternal state of autumn, a stillness that had lingered for an eon of time. The story was that the forest once covered the entire world and that it was men that hewn the trees back as they began building vast dwellings. It was an Imp, distraught by the loss of such greenery, which cast a spell of protection upon the forest, putting it into a tranquil state where time itself was seemingly at a standstill; and forever more were the leaves golden.

Orgetorix entered the forest and was instantly hit by the smell of age-old decay. So dense was the forest that it was in a permanent twilight as the orange and brown canopy of leaves filtered the light of the sun to give the forest a golden glow. There was no path, and the ground was broken up by ancient roots and thick undergrowth. For many days did Orgetorix wander, hopelessly losing his way, when quite by chance he came across an ancient road that was cracked and covered over in brown leaves. For a full night did Orgetorix ponder on which direction he should follow, for by his reckoning it ran from east to west to unknown regions. He believed that he was still far north of Hardrada, on the eastern side of the river Wye. So, trusting his calculations, Orgetorix turned to his left to what he believed was towards the west.

After three more days the road led Orgetorix to a small stone bridge that crossed the river Wye. Here the water ran black as night and was said to have been enchanted by some ancient sorcery that would send any that made contact with the water into a deep slumber, never to wake until the sun would rise in the west and set in the east. The bridge itself had long been forgotten and was in ill repair. With the passing of time, the stone was crumbling, and the once fine carvings of children's faces had almost eroded away to featureless ovals of stone bulging from the outer side of the bridge.

Unbeknown to Orgetorix was that the bridge was once known as the Bridge of Faces. Built by a nameless people of unknown origins. The ancient tale tells of a mischievous elf that undertook a contract to remove a fanged serpent that plagued the ancient people that dwelt in the forest. When the promised sum of silver was not paid, the elf played his panpipes to allure their children in to following him. To the river did he lead them, playing his panpipes merrily as the children cast themselves into the black waters of the Wye. It was later claimed that the architect of the bridge had seen the spirits of the children and thus carved their images into the stonework.

Orgetorix dismounted and inspected the bridge closer, hearing a faint laughter of a child seemingly echoing all around him. A section in the middle had crumbled away and large parts of the stonework were poking up though the water below. His horse could jump the gap but fear unnerved Velox and he simply refused to place a single hoof upon the bridge. After several failed attempts to persuade Velox to cross, Orgetorix slumped tiredly up against a tree to decide upon what he should now do.

Watching from the dense undergrowth were four hooded figures, each armed with bows and a quiver of sharp arrows. Silently did they move to surround Orgetorix, having it in mind to deprive him of any wealth he might be carrying. Once in place they sprang from the undergrowth and took Orgetorix by surprise.

"Turn over your horse and possessions and you may yet live to see your wife again," one of the hooded men said as he drew back on his bowstring to let loose his deadly arrow.

But the blood of Arawn and Cingetorix flowed through Orgetorix's veins, and he would not yield so easily. Pulling his sword from the leather scabbard hanging at his waist, he challenged the hooded men. Bows were considered a coward's weapon by the warriors of Gondolor and were held in distain; and Orgetorix felt no different towards them. Protected by the gods, all arrows missed Orgetorix as he swiftly rushed his attackers. Three he swiftly grounded, inflicting minor wounds upon them; but the fourth was more skilled then the other three and was able to withstand Orgetorix's assaults using his dagger. Though this man was skilled, he was no equal to Orgetorix, and was finally bested by a clumsy blow that knocked the dagger clean out of his hand.

"Mercy," the man said as he fell to his knees. "I beg mercy."

Orgetorix anger quickly cooled as he paused to draw breath. "Take me to the White Tree," he said as he sheaved his sword.

"What are you doing this deep in the forest?" the man asked as he slowly stood.

"I'm seeking a warrior, a former member of the king's Companions," Orgetorix replied. "I was told that he dwells in this forest, by the White Tree."

"If you were truly told this by friendly words, what name does this warrior go by?" The man was suspicious of Orgetorix and feared that he was a spy sent by king Viridomarus to learn of the whereabouts of the outlaw's camp.

"Cleph," Orgetorix answered. "He is brother to my mother."

By giving this name, the man was assured that Orgetorix was no foe. They spent that night beside the bridge, two of the men hunting rabbits so that they could eat. The next morning, they led Orgetorix further north where there was another bridge. This one was much narrower than the Bridge of Faces and made of wood, built by the outlaws themselves so that they could cross the Wye and enter the northern realm of Hardrada swiftly and with greater ease. After a week of traveling they came to the outlaw's camp, an austere place filled with grim men toughened by the hardship of dwelling in the forest.

The White Tree was by far the biggest tree that Orgetorix had ever seen. Its trunk and branches were wide, strong, and white in colour, its leaves a bright pink. Beside the majesty of this tree, between two great roots, was a roundhouse. It was here that the men took Orgetorix.

Inside was much the same as any roundhouse, bare earth floor with a fire in the centre and a bed and a few chairs placed around the fire.

"What evil have you brought into our layer?" Cleph looked up from the fire and stared straight at Orgetorix, recognising him instantly.

"I am Orget…."

"I know who you are," Cleph interrupted as he stood from his chair and walked around to greet Orgetorix. "For you are Prince Orgetorix, the son of Cingetorix and the renowned shield maiden Arawn, grandson to the last true king, Carraidin. I know this because it was I that was charged with absconding you to safety."

"Indebted greatly am I to you," Orgetorix said. "And you will be richly rewarded once I regain my throne."

Cleph smiled and shrugged. "Leave us," he ordered his men as he went and sat back down in his chair.

"I want to know everything," Orgetorix said as he took a seat opposite Cleph. "All of what happened that fateful night of the Hallows, my true parents, everything."

Long into the night did Cleph retell the tale of the Hallows, the fire burning low to glowing orange embers. Cleph spoke of how Viridomarus had enlisted foreign mercenaries to take the throne and subject the people of Gondolor to his will. He told Orgetorix of his father's prowess in battle, unmatched by any man, and that his only equal had been his mother Arawn. Cleph then told Orgetorix that it was during the Battle of Barley Field that the two had met. Cingetorix had charged with the Companions, riding with ease deep into the fray and wielding his axe with ease. Many had fallen to his prowess and he freely rode calling for any to dare challenge him. No warrior would as they feared his might; but from the ranks of the enemy came a red-haired beauty clad in a shirt of mail and carrying a warrior's shield and spear. She had called her challenge and Cingetorix dismounted and accepted. They fought for the remainder of that day, the warriors of both sides ceasing their killing to watch the heroic duel. Both were as swift and graceful as dancers upon ice with neither able to strike the other. Finally, both fell exhausted and Arawn proclaimed that she had now found her husband as the gods had promised. For it was believed that she swore an oath never to take a husband who was not her equal in battle.

Finally sleep took both Cleph and Orgetorix, and each dreamt that night of better times, only Cleph's was of the past, and Orgetorix's of his envisioned future of kingship.

The next few days were spent idle as Orgetorix knew not how to proceed for challenging for the throne. Cleph had made it clear that he and his fellow outlawed Companions would support him but warned that they were not numerous enough to overthrow Viridomarus. Though the outlaws numbered over one hundred men, most were simple men that had been exiled from their homes for petty crimes. They were skilled in forestry and in the use of a bow, but they were not warriors able to withstand a charge of horsemen that Viridomarus could command. But among these simple men were thirty former members of the kings Companions, each now aged and nurturing long beards. Their horses were long gone, sold so that they could buy food as they had retreated to the forest to begin their exile. Many had perished that fateful night of the Hallows, and those that were able to escape had gathered in the forest where they knew they would be safe. Their mail armour and iron helms they had stowed for long years in preparation for the coming of the lost prince; and now that Orgetorix had come fourth, they proudly donned their armour once more.

Now Orgetorix reformed the Companions, each swearing an oath of loyalty to him, and he was presented with a banner that was taken from the great hall of Gondolor to escape the carnage of the Hallows, the banner of his father and grandfather, a white horse upon a dark-green field. Cleph then presented him with a silver ring of a horse that was rearing up on its back legs, the ring of his mother, Arawn. The roundhouse beside the white tree was gifted to him by Cleph, who was given the title of Captain of the Companions and advisor to the king.

That winter was spent in many long debates over what they should now do. Orgetorix believed that he should make himself known to the people of the northern realm in the hope that they would revolt against Viridomarus. But Cleph had argued that it was foolish to believe the people would join Orgetorix, a person they did not know or love. Cleph suggested that if Orgetorix wanted the people to flock to his banner, he must first earn their love. So, it was agreed that they would adopt a guerrilla warfare tactic and target the tax collectors that travelled the old road between the villages of Arowyn and Goedwig.

Orgetorix also spent much time during the winter months in training, becoming skilled in the use of a bow and learning much in the ways of forestry. By the time spring arrived, Orgetorix was able to move swiftly and silently through the forest and was able to hunt and survive alone for a lengthy time. Many times, had he wandered deep into the forest, in search of some wisdom; and it was now that they said that Orgetorix left a boy and came back a man.

But now the man had to become a warrior, and the warrior to become a king.

V

The Battle for the North

Orgetorix now tried to be kinglier in nature, and having grown up on a farm, he knew the importance of food. So Orgetorix ordered the construction of a granary so that they could build up a surplus of food in case hard times should befall them. Next, he introduced a daily training regime to increase the fitness and skill of his warriors. But weapons were in short supply, and most were merely armed with a hunting bow and small dagger which they used for cutting meat. So Orgetorix ordered that spears be made from branches and using flint for their tips which was found in abundance further to the north where the land became steep and rocky. With the camp and men now better organised, Orgetorix took thirty men, five being from his Companions and the others being forestry men. Leaving Cleph in command of the camp, Orgetorix and his company swiftly travelled east for five days before turning to the south towards a narrow road known as the path of Eogan.

The old road was a narrow dirt track flanked by overgrown bushes that encroached over the road, narrowing its path further. It ran between the village of Arowyn in the west and Goedwig in the east, offering a shorter route than the better kept road to the south which passed the hillfort of Bryn-Duro. Midway between the two villages, the road was engulfed by a section of forest that grew further to the south than the rest. This section of the road was an ideal place to set an ambush, and all knew it. But the tax collectors were idle men who sought a swift ending to their task so that they may quickly return to their soft life; and it was well-known that they used this path. But none had dared to steal from them until now.

Close to this road did Orgetorix and his company settle, and for days after they kept a careful watch over it in hope of seeing a tax collector. It was on the sixth day that horsemen were spotted riding from the east, and Orgetorix and his men rushed to take their appointed positions. They remained hidden in the undergrowth, silently watching as the horsemen approached. There were seven horsemen in total, all wearing a black cloak that marked them as collectors for the king. The man leading them was the finest dressed of them all, wearing a black tunic with a silver badge of a horse that was a mark of his rank. Each of these men were armed with swords and rode fine bay horses that Orgetorix was in great need for.

Orgetorix had placed his men well, splitting in to two groups that hid in the undergrowth on either side of the road. When the horsemen were at their closest, Orgetorix gave his prearranged signal of a hooting and his men sprang forth, their bows at the ready. The horsemen were taken by complete surprise, and two were shot from their saddle as they tried to turn and flee, the others were overwhelmed and taken captive.

"Surrender your arms, horses and silver," Orgetorix said as he strode over to their Captain.

"An assault upon one of the king's appointed men is an assault upon the king himself," the captain of the tax collectors said as he drew his sword and pointed it towards Orgetorix. "I shall see to it that you are put to death for this!"

Orgetorix, with the swiftness of a hero, drew out his own sword and disarmed the Captain in a graceful movement that left a deep cut under the Captain's left eye. "I stand innocent of treason against the tyrant Viridomarus. For he is no king by the laws of Gondolor, nor by the laws of the Gods."

"Whom are you to say such treasons against your king whom the Gods have appointed to rule over you?"

Orgetorix held out his left hand, his smallest finger adorned with the horse ring of his mother, the sight striking shock and fear into the Captain, for that ring was known to him. "I am Orgetorix, son of Cingetorix and rightful heir to the throne of Gondolor."

"The lost prince that was foretold would come forth," the Captain spat out the words with displeasure. For under King Viridomarus he had grown wealthy and now feared to lose it all should Orgetorix take the throne.

"Yield now and I shall grant you pardon," Orgetorix said in hope that the knowledge of who he was would sway the Captain to his side.

But the Captain simply laughed and replied, "I see, nor recognise no king here, just a band of outlaws whom the king shall crush."

Knowing that the Captain, nor none of the others would yield to him, Orgetorix made them strip from their garments, stating that they were not true agents of the king. They were then given leave and forced away in their nakedness as a mark of their shame for not yielding to their true king. From them, Orgetorix had taken all, their weapons, horses, and silver that had been collected from the village of Goedwig. Orgetorix ordered seven of his men to take the horses and weapons back to their camp and told them to remain there for his return.

It was to Goedwig that Orgetorix now travelled with the remainder of his company, taking with them the two small chests of silver that they had taken from the tax collectors.

As they emerged from the forest, the village came into sight. There were no walls to protect the people from any threat, and the houses were rectangular in shape and made from wood hewn from the nearby forest of Aureum. A bell was ringing out when the company neared, and the people rushed indoors where they began barricading their doors in fear of trouble.

Orgetorix led his warriors to the centre of the village where there was a clearing used for the mustering of the villagers. He then sent out men to summon the people, assuring them that they came with no evil intent. Gradually the people gathered in the centre of the village where it was announced to them that Orgetorix was the lost prince, and by the laws of men and gods was their king. There was a great disbelief to the claim made and many shouted out their concerns. But from among their number came forth an elderly lady with white hair and a bent back, leaning heavily upon a walking stick. She had once served the lady Aoife, the queen and wife of King Carraidin, and knew well the family. One glance at Orgetorix was enough to convince her to the truth of his claim, and any that were still in disbelief were convinced when the silver ring of Arawn was held above Orgetorix's head for all to see.

All knelt and lowed their heads in a show of reverence for their true king; and Orgetorix addressed them thus, "My humble subjects, it has come to my attention that you have been wronged by a man that claims to be your king. For the law is that no taxes may be taken without consent from the king. No command did I give for such taxes to be taken from you. I therefore give back what was wrongfully stolen from you."

Each person was given three silver coins and what little remained was kept by Orgetorix for the campaign ahead. Being stowed in the chests alongside the silver were scrolls that listed debts owed to the king. These Orgetorix ordered destroyed by fire and stated that no man owed him more than their loyalty. This the people of Goedwig freely gave as they cheered their rightful king, all being swept along in the euphoria of the moment.

Orgetorix remained in the village, the best house being offered to him, where for days after he took offerings of supplies of corn salted meats and barrels of ale. The village Thegn gifted five light horses, half the number that the village held, and a fine golden torc inlaid with two emeralds. Orgetorix, with their loyalty secured, then took his leave, promising that he shall return before the passing of summer. He ordered two of his men to remain to train the men into warriors and to begin the construction of a palisade for their protection.

Orgetorix then returned to the forest, back to his camp where Cleph awaited him. Orgetorix revealed his desire to move on Tamaris, his hatred urging his return to free his family from the Thegn. But Cleph counselled against such a move as they had not the warriors to yet gain victory, and he counselled Orgetorix to look past his personal anger for the greater good of his people. Frustrated by the slowness of his progress, Orgetorix organised a tournament so that he himself could judge the valour and skill of his warriors. So, the warriors drew lots and wrestled their drawn opponent in bouts that lasted for three days, the victors being crowned with a garland of wildflowers, and the losers made to train twice as hard.

It was on completion of this tournament that Orgetorix was approached by one of the men he had left at Goedwig. From him Orgetorix learnt of a company of mounted warriors that was to escort a cart of newly forged weapons and a chest of silver from the town of Arowyn, and then escort them to the hillfort of Bryn-Duro. Swiftly, Orgetorix gathered his more skilled warriors and made forthwith all haste towards the west. They moved as swiftly as they were able, fearing that they would arrive too late and miss their opportunity. After five days with little rest, they came to a halt at the forest's edge to the north of the town of Arowyn. Under cover of night, Orgetorix sent two of his men into the town to seek any information of the escort. There they learnt that the escort had left earlier that afternoon on the road which connected Arowyn with Bryn-Duro.

Orgetorix, knowing that he could now catch up with the escort, allowed his men three hours rest before leading them back east along the forest's edge for two more days, passing across the path of Eogan and swiftly coming to the forest's most southern edge. Here the land lay flat, a vast green plain dotted with little white and yellow flowers which stretched out in all directions as far as the eye could see. Visible upon the southern horizon was the hillfort itself, its wooden walls crowning a hill that dominated the landscape.

Risking his warriors upon the open plain, Orgetorix led his company southwest towards a wide dirt road flanked by rocks that marked the edges. There they met with the Warriors escorting the cart of weapons and silver. Orgetorix had with him just thirty warriors, each armed with a bow, a spear with a flint tip, and a dagger. Whereas the mounted warriors were armed with swords and axes, each with a round shield and iron helms with a wide nose guard, their bodies protected by long padded tunics. They numbered sixty in all and formed up in a long line once they saw sight of Orgetorix and his men. Believing that they were a mere rabble of outlaws, ill armed and undisciplined, the mounted warriors took out their weapons and charged.

"Form the schiltron!" Orgetorix yelled out as the ground beneath his feet shook from the mounted warriors bearing down on them.

His warriors quickly formed a tight circle and levelled their spears, holding firm in the face of sheer terror. The mounted warriors steered their horses around the formation hoping to find some weak point. A few rode too close and were almost thrown out of their saddles as the flint tips of the spears were thrust up into the horses faces. Three of the mounted warriors received wounds to their thighs as they tried to breech the circle. But seeing the stalemate they turned their horses and rode back to the road where they reformed to charge again. Orgetorix seized this moment and ordered his warriors to drop their spears and take up their bows. Jeers and mockery came from the mounted warriors, for they held the bow in low esteem, a mere coward's weapon. But Orgetorix cared not whether he won this battle in an honourable way, just that he won. His warriors loosed off a barrage of arrows which cut deep into the lightly armoured mounted warriors. Unknowing of this kind of warfare, the mounted warriors simply carried on jeering as though their insults would stay the arrows that rained down upon them. After taking many casualties, they desperately charged once more in hope of gaining victory.

But as the mounted warriors neared, Orgetorix ordered his warriors to take back up their spears. Again, the mounted men failed to break the formation and as they retreated were shot down to the man with well-aimed arrows. The victory gained horses, weapons, and more silver for Orgetorix; and he now raced back to the White Tree before he was caught in the open by a larger force from Bryn-Duro.

Orgetorix's Companions now each had a horse and he began leading them on raids further to the south without fear. So successful were these raids that merchants and tax collectors now refused to travel, and the steady flow of silver that filled the coffers of Gondolor became a mere trickle and then ceased. But the common people suffered not as Orgetorix gifted them with the silver he took. Now the people of the north began to speak loudly of rebellious talk, and the northern Thegns were forced to act. They mustered as many warriors as they could and began searching the forest. But these warriors were of little use in the dense forestry, and Orgetorix fell back to a guerrilla warfare where he inflicted many casualties upon the northern Thegns.

The news of Orgetorix's success quickly travelled south to Gondolor, enraging King Viridomarus. He summoned his best Captain, a famed warrior called Brice the Bone Crusher, and demanded that he crush any notion of rebellion in the north. From Gondolor he led a mighty host of mounted warriors to Bryn-Duro where he took command of all the northern realm. His first act was to send out many spies to seek out any that had lent aid to Orgetorix, and soon he discovered that the village of Goedwig was supplying corn and meat to the outlaws.

Brice the Bone Crusher then rode with a host of violent men, mercenaries from the unknown regions to the south. Their horses were black and larger than those used by the Companions, their armour leather and scaled like overlapping roof tiles. Upon their heads they bore rounded helms of bronze which speckled like gold in the light of the sun. Swiftly they rode to the Village of Goedwig, burning the homes and pillaging all silver, slaughtering without trial all the males that were taller than the wheel of a cart. The women and children they cast out as outlaws and forbade their return on pain of death. But this act to outlaw them was not out of the mercy of sparing them from death, for Brice the Bone Crusher had no qualms in dealing death to all, but it was a stratagem to weaken Orgetorix.

How those women lamented as they were forced at spearpoint into the forest, each tormented by the fear of hunger and thirst that surely awaited them. Mercy and forgiveness, did they beg of Brice the Bone Crusher, but his ears were death to their pleas, and he answered only with: "You have cast your lot."

Orgetorix's scouts soon came across the women and children wandering lost in the forest, and they were led back to the camp where they spoke of the destruction of Goedwig. Orgetorix in a show of distress knelt before the women and children and asked each for their forgiveness, promising that he would honour always their men's memory.

For the remainder of that summer, Orgetorix found himself unsuccessful. Too great now was the tax collectors' protection in warriors that Orgetorix dared not risk assaulting them for fear of how many men he would lose. The north fell solemn, its hope almost lost as it was once more subjected by the fear of Brice the Bone Crusher. The towns and villages that had not so long ago welcomed Orgetorix now closed their gates to him, fearing to give him any aid. As Orgetorix and his company wandered the northern realm, a mighty host of mounted warriors discovered them near Tamaris and forced them to retreat into the forest, where Orgetorix still had success. The mercenary warriors gave chase and rode too deep into the forest where they were slain by the outlaws, their bodies stripped and then buried with the honours as befitting for a warrior.

There hidden in the forest did Orgetorix remain, the warmer weather of summer passing to a colder winter. With the camps numbers having enlarged by the women and children from Goedwig, the balance of the forest became upset. Food became low and foragers were having to wander ever deeper into the forest to find whatever food source they could. The forest game had fled further north from the camp and the once plentiful mushrooms that had grown at the base of the White Tree were now depleted. Soon arguments broke out as a few of the forestry men said that they must cast out the women and children or else all starve. But Orgetorix refused, saying: "A king should not abandon his people, nor cast them aside to save himself. Together we shall taste the sweetness of victory or the bitterness of defeat."

It was then that a forestry man named Gedorix stepped forward and said: "A kingship you claim Orgetorix, yet upon your head is no crown. Here we are all equals under the laws of the forest and therefore we should cast lots to decide upon the matter."

The camp thus split in to two factions, the forestry men siding with Gedorix and the Companions with Orgetorix. There a battle between the two sides would have been fought had it not been for Cleph's timely interjection.

"Shame upon us for what we have become!" Cleph roared as he waded in between the gathering men. "Are we men so ill that we would cast aside the helpless so that we might live? Have we become so fearful of death?"

But Gedorix was set as stone in his decision and would not yield. "Why should we suffer and slowly torment ourselves for want of food. To what end? So that we can pay for a crown with our blood?"

Orgetorix had now grown tired of Gedorix and saw him as a poison to a wound. "Let us not quarrel any longer but put to the gods this question. Let us have single combat to determine the fate of those you wish to cast out."

So, all agreed that the laws of the forest were thus so, and a circle was formed, all swearing to honour the outcome. Both Orgetorix and Gedorix were given a sword equal in length and weight, and a round shield three feet in diameter with an iron boss at the centre to protect the hand. Gedorix, though not without skill, was no match for Orgetorix's great strength. Three times did Orgetorix stay his hand from delivering the killing blow to plead with Gedorix to yield; but yield he would not and was slain by the hand of Orgetorix. There upon the spot Gedorix fell was built a small mound where his body and weapons were placed in honour; and for a full day did Orgetorix lament, praising Gedorix for the bravery of speaking his true mind, and he bid all never to turn to dishonesties and gave each man leave to speak freely with him as though they were equals.

VI

The Fall of the North

After a winter of hardship, Orgetorix and his warriors were weary. Food had been in short supply and they had been forced to kill their horses in need of meat, all except Orgetorix's horse, Velox the Swift. Along with the warmer weather of spring came the reports of a camp of warriors at the blackened ruins of Goedwig. Reports of them entering the forest, hewing the trees, and burning the undergrowth unsettled Orgetorix and he feared that they would be discovered should he not act. So Orgetorix led his Companions out of the forest and undercover of night attacked the warriors at Goedwig. Though these warriors were greater in number than the Companions, they were not their equal in skill at arms. Catching them by complete surprise, Orgetorix's victory was swift and he captured their plentiful stores and all their horses. Orgetorix had slew four warriors himself before taking another as a prisoner. From this warrior they learnt that Brice the Bone Crusher had spent the winter subjecting the people of the north, hanging any that spoke in favour of Orgetorix. Then he had issued an edict decreeing that the people had to now travel to Bryn-Duro to pay their taxes. This move frustrated Orgetorix as he knew it would stay his tactic of taking from the rich and giving back to the poor. Now there was little choice but to change strategy from a guerrilla style warfare to a more open one with pitched battles.

Knowing now that he must take the town of Bryn-Duro, but not knowing how such a feat would be achieved,

Orgetorix sent all but Cleph back into the forest. From Goedwig they rode swiftly southwest towards Bryn-Duro where they disguised themselves by covering their heads with hooded cloaks. For the next couple of days, Orgetorix and Cleph inspected the town, hoping that they might learn of some advantage they could exploit. But all was secure as they believed it would be.

The hillfort of Bryn-Duro had been built long-ago upon a rocky hilltop that commanded the grassy plains below. Once it had been a town renowned for trade, but now instead of being filled with goods and merchants, it was filled with armed warriors. About half a day's ride to the north was the forest of Aureum which would offer Orgetorix men cover as they approached. But what then? Once clear of the forest it was an open grassland and they would be seen in plenty of time for the defenders to organise a defence. The wooden palisade that protected the town was high and strong with no hope of succumbing to any assault Orgetorix could muster; and he lacked the warriors to encircle the town to slowly starve them into submission. It was much too strong to be taken.

Orgetorix retreated to the White Tree where he re-joined his men, his heart heavy and dejected by the thought of having to somehow take Bryn-Duro. For seven days he wondered alone in the forest, heading deeper than he had ever been before, searching for some answer to his predicament. It was during a violent rainstorm in which Orgetorix found his answer. Taking refuge from the rain in a small cave, Orgetorix sat watching as black ants marched in and out of a mound built against the back of the cave. The line of ants marching in were each carrying leaves and twigs, but one drew Orgetorix's attention. Hidden in the line was a red ant carrying the body of a black ant upon its back, and none of the other ants noticed until it had infiltrated the mound. Thus, a simple ant had inspired Orgetorix and he rushed back to inform Cleph of the plan that had formulated in his mind.

Cleph on hearing of Orgetorix's plan was unconvinced and spoke openly to him about the risks, once again stating that they lacked numbers. But Orgetorix's mind was as stone and he pointed out that a few of the boys from Goedwig had now come of age during the winter to swell their number. Cleph was still cautious, and made it known that these boys were ill trained, but Orgetorix would wait no longer for his return to Tamaris. He sent two forestry men to keep a careful watch over the comings and goings of Bryn-Duro. For a month they watched as warriors rode back and forth carrying supplies to feed both horses and men. Most rode east to the village of Tamaris that supplied the hillfort with corn, a journey that would take a week to get there and back again. All was reported back to Orgetorix, and he now mustered his warriors and made for Tamaris, a place he had longed to return to.

Swiftly the outlaws descended before the village of Tamaris, riding through the night and catching them by complete surprise before they could send any messengers out in plea for help. The sight of the settlement stirred emotions within Orgetorix, and his anger began to bubble up beyond his control. He had drawn up his Companions across the road before the gate and his forestry men upon his flanks, their bows strung and notched with arrows. Anger clouded his judgement and instead of offering the Thegn the chance to surrender, as was agreed with Cleph,

Orgetorix gave the order for his forestry men to loose their arrows.

Inside the wooden palisade was panic and anger. A few warriors were hit by the arrows but mostly they struck the ground harmlessly. But Orgetorix's intent was not to cause heavy casualties, but to strike at the pride of the warriors. To be attacked by such a cowardly method stirred a great anger within the warriors and they foolishly opened the gate and rushed out to attack. Orgetorix had hoped and expected for such a move and charged with his companions, slaying all that rushed out of the gate.

Many of the Thegn's warriors now dropped their weapons and fell to their knees in plea for mercy. But Orgetorix was consumed with a great anger and gave no quarter as he called out for Ceolwulf.

"Ceolwulf!" Orgetorix rode down two warriors as he approached the Thegn's hall where a group of warriors had gathered in a hasty defence. "Ceolwulf! Come out and face me!"

The doors to the hall opened and Ceolwulf came forth, clad in a shirt of mail and an iron helm with a wide nose guard and cheek plates. In his hands was a round shield and a fine axe. "So, the dog has returned to its master."

"My mother," Orgetorix replied as he dismounted, "and my father and brothers."

"Traitors that have been sent to Gondolor for questioning." Ceolwulf pushed through his warriors and stood with his feet spread wide ready for battle.

Orgetorix, needing no formal invitation, drew his sword and engaged in single combat. Ceolwulf had been well-trained and gave a good account of himself, but Orgetorix's great strength and raging anger overcame Ceolwulf's defence. There before the hall of his father did Ceolwulf's life ebb away from a mortal wound to his stomach, his blood pooling under his body.

The warriors guarding the entrance to the hall all dropped their weapons and fell to their knees, lowing their heads in a show of subjection. These men Orgetorix would have put to sword had it not been for Cleph bringing his mind back to reason. So instead of death they were offered to swear loyalty to Orgetorix and to repay his mercy by serving in his army.

Orgetorix then entered the hall to find the Thegn sitting in his seat, his eye cast down to the flames of the fire. "Your son is dead, and your village taken," he said as he approached the Thegn, blood dripping from the tip of his sword.

The Thegn then looked up, tears wetted his cheeks. "It matters no more." From the corner of his mouth dripped blood, and from his hand dropped an empty phial. Poison now consumed the Thegn and forced death upon him.

Tamaris now fell under Orgetorix's control, and this victory yielded supplies, weapons, and warriors for the campaign against Bryn-Duro. Now Orgetorix had his Companions take the garb of the fallen mercenary warriors that were from Bryn-Duro and load up a cart of supplies. His forestry men he sent into the forest, to remain hidden as they approached Bryn-Duro from the north, there they were to wait for Orgetorix and his Companions to enter the hillfort.

Disguised as mercenary warriors, clad in knee length leather jerkins and iron caps, Orgetorix led his Companions to the gate of Bryn-Duro. Seeing the approach of a supply cart, the gate was opened for Orgetorix as the warriors defending the gate knew nothing of Orgetorix's deceit. Alarm was then called out as warriors were seen rushing from the forest of Aureum to the north. Now Orgetorix seized his chance and stormed the gate, killing the warriors guarding it and securing it. His warriors now poured into the town, and a great slaughter ensued.

But Brice the Bone Crusher was himself a skilled warrior capable of inspiring men to fight to the death for him, and a valiant defence of his hall was made. The ground before the hall became strewn with bodies and blood, many of which were slew by the great axe of Brice the Bone Crusher himself. Many challenged him, and many fell to his wrath. But the greatest of warriors may be slew by simple means, and Brice the Bone Crusher was no exception. An arrow guided by unknown spirits struck down Brice the Bone Crusher, his head was then cut off and paraded through the town in a manner unjust for a hero. Now the warriors of Bryn-Duro lay down their weapons and put themselves at Orgetorix's mercy. Many were simple men that had been pressed into service of Brice the Bone Crusher, and these men were granted pardon from Orgetorix. But many more were mercenaries from the unknown region to the south, and these men would not break contract by pleading for mercy, and so they were made to kneel in a long line and were executed.

All the northern realm had now fallen under the command of Orgetorix, and his first act was to issue a pardon to all that had taken up arms against him. Next, he appointed new Thegns to organise the burhs, warriors that were loyal to him, and they at once began mustering a mighty host.

For the remainder of that year Orgetorix progressed through the north, inspecting the mustering warriors, and having a great care for their training. Wherever he went, he was met with cheers and jubilation, for the people had longed for better days and now took out their horse banners from hidden places and hung them from wherever possible. Any that still refused to believe that Orgetorix was the lost prince were soon convinced when they saw him in person and saw the horse ring of Arawn.

Under Orgetorix's careful management, the granaries were filled and his warriors each armed with a spear and shield. Each member of his Companions now had a horse, mail shirt, an iron helm, shield, and sword. Thus, with all ready, he made known that he intended on marching south in the spring. To Gondolor to reclaim his stolen throne.

VII

The Battle for Gondolor

Once the winter had passed, and the fields sown with crops, Orgetorix called on his Thegn's to muster their warriors. On the appointed day Bryn-Duro was filled with warriors, and the air rang heavy with the sound hundreds of armed men preparing their weapons. Orgetorix now donned a fine shirt of mail that glistened like silver in the light of the sun, and upon his head a helm of iron with a brass decorated face guard and a transverse plume of dark horsehair.

Mounting his noble steed, Velox the Swift, Orgetorix addressed his warriors. "Today I truly begin my reign as king. The north we have freed from the usurper Viridomarus' grasp, from his unjust taxes and terror. Now I will ride south to my birth home, to Gondolor. There I will seek justice against Viridomarus and make him answerable for his many wrongs. But I cannot do this righteous deed alone, for what rights can a king do without the love of his people? So come with me, your rightful king under the laws of the gods and men, and together we shall usher in a new age, an age of peace and prosperity for all!"

The warriors gave a mighty cheer and clashed the edge of their shields with their spears, the noise sounding as thunder and travelling a great distance. Orgetorix, at the head of his Companions, led his army south.

But king Viridomarus had not been idle. During the winter he had summoned a great host of warriors to Gondolor. From the unknown regions to the south, he had summoned up a mounted force of heavily armoured cataphracts. These men were warlike in nature and a most feared sight upon the field of battle. Their horses were as equally armoured as their riders, and each man was armed with long spears and curved swords that widened towards the tip, their banner was a black crescent moon upon an orange field. Along with these warriors came many mercenary foot soldiers that were lightly armoured in leather jerkins and caps, and each armed with spears and axes. Paying for such a grand force had emptied the coffers of Gondolor, and Viridomarus had forced the people to pay further taxes, threatening death upon those that refused to pay, and many of Gondolor's people now prayed for Orgetorix's victory.

Now Viridomarus sent north his host of mercenary warriors, instructing them to put to an end the northern rebellion. The warrior leading Viridomarus' army was Toutorix the Long Spear, famed for his skill and the length of his spear. Toutorix positioned his army to the right of the northern road, along a gentle ridge that sloped down to the north, his cataphracts lined in front of the foot soldiers; and there they waited for Orgetorix.

Orgetorix himself had rode ahead of his army to scout the land ahead. When first he saw the bright, scaled armour of the cataphracts and the strong position in which they were placed, he was dismayed. His first thoughts were to retreat and draw them away from the high ground, and himself take up a position of advantage. But then his horse stumbled as it placed a hoof in some boggy ground, a stumble in which gave him hope as a plan then quickly formulated in his mind. Rushing back to his army, he began delivering his orders.

Orgetorix split his army into four bands, two being bowmen, the biggest his foot soldiers, and the last his Companions which he was to lead himself. Cleph was given command of the centre, where the foot soldiers formed a deep line as was customary, and the left flank where there was a band of bowmen. Orgetorix himself formed up with his Companions on the right flank, on firmer grassland behind the boggy ground. But kneeling hidden behind the Companions was a band of bowmen that each was equipped with spears as well as their bows.

Knowing that it was customary for mounted warriors to fight each other in battle, and though Orgetorix doubted not the courage of his Companions, he could see that the cataphracts were more numerous and better armoured. And so, he set his trap to counter this disadvantage.

A mighty horn blast sounded from the cataphracts as they nudged their armoured steeds into a steady trot. Behind them advanced the warriors fighting on foot where Toutorix the Long Spear himself lead in the frontline. Midway down the slope the cataphracts veered towards Orgetorix's right flank and broke into a charge, aiming straight for the Companions. Orgetorix was steadfast and calmly waited for his moment. As the cataphracts neared, they levelled their spears and gave a terrifying war cry that would have panicked lesser men.

"Companions with me!" Orgetorix seized his moment and led his Companions right, towards the road. "Ride with me now to victory!"

The cataphracts did not see the boggy ground until it was too late. The momentum of their charge drove their heavily laden horses deep into the mud, causing a great turmoil as they fell and crashed into each other. Then the bowmen that the Companions had been screening rushed forward, shooting arrows at close range. But even at close range their arrows could not penetrate the cataphracts' thick armour, so they dropped their bows and took up their spears. Being much lighter armed than the cataphracts, the bowmen were more mobile in the mud and swiftly they found open joints in their overlapping armour with their spears, killing all.

Cleph, on seeing the companions ride down the road, had advanced forward with the warriors and engaged with Toutorix' warriors midway up the slope. The bowmen on the left flank had advanced with them and began shooting arrows at point-blank range, killing many and causing wounds to many more. But being fewer in number and fighting against the slope, Cleph's warriors began to edge back. But Orgetorix's plan was for his foot soldiers to act as his shield, while he and his Companions acted as the sword that would land the killing blow.

Orgetorix, seeing that his warriors were holding Toutorix's warriors in place, raised his sword and shouted: "Wheel left!"

As swiftly as a flock of birds turning in flight did the Companions wheel around to the left, lining up for the charge along the ridge where Toutorix the Long Spear had begun the battle. Now the Companions charged down the slope, gaining the advantage and striking Toutorix the Long Spear and his warriors from the rear. A great slaughter ensued and Toutorix called for his warriors to standfast, but many were not willing to die in the service of King Viridomarus and simply fled in every direction.

It was during the battle's end in which Cleph and Toutorix the Long Spear met in a duel amidst the blooded bodies of the fallen. Cleph offered Toutorix the chance to yield and to serve Orgetorix. But Toutorix would not and gave answer by slaying two warriors alongside Cleph. And so, the two heroes fought, each showing their skill and bravery. So great was the sight and sound of Axe clashing with spear that the warriors from either side ceased their fighting and gathered around to watch the duel. Toutorix had the advantage of youth and agility over Cleph, but what Cleph lacked through age he made up for in experience. Rash and violent were Toutorix's strikes in hope of quickly overcoming Cleph's defence. But each blow Cleph was able to block with his dented shield. Toutorix poised himself for a thrust when his right foot slipped on some blooded ground, sending him crashing down and breaking his spear in half, the iron spearhead piercing his mail shirt and driving into his heart. The warriors fell silent, for all had heard of the words of doom that had been spoken to Toutorix.

In his youth, Toutorix had been chosen to carry the bronze spearhead of Barca the Brave during the festival of Gondolor's founding. All that long spring day had he held aloft his head the bronze spear, fearing that his arms would grow tired and drop the spearhead. For that was the custom of the festival; a boy of promise was chosen and forced upon a raised platform where he was to hold up the spearhead from dawn to dusk. To drop such a sacred item meant a year of ill omen, that the warriors of Gondolor would not be blessed in battle. With great pain and effort, Toutorix succeeded, and as he handed back the spearhead to a priestess, he uttered the words: "One day all shall fear my spear and know the name of Toutorix."

To this the priestess answered: "Like a mighty tree you shall grow Toutorix son of Horlick. But the path of a warrior will be the path of your doom, and by your own hand shall you perish."

The death of Toutorix ended the battle that became known as the Battle of Broken Spear, named in honour of Toutorix. There Orgetorix ordered a great mound constructed to commemorate his victory. High and wide was the earth over which covered the bodies of the fallen, a labour which took many days to complete. On completion all funeral rites were observed, with Orgetorix leading a procession three times around the mound before a lament was sang of the bravery of the fallen.

When news of his army's defeat reached King Viridomarus, he was said to have turned mad, and was said to have wandered through his hall barefoot and beating his fists against the walls in a fearful rage. Now he summoned all remaining Thegns within Gondolor to his hall where he accused them of conspiring against him. Four were seized by Viridomarus' Chosen Warriors and dragged out to the mustering field where they were executed without trial. The remainder of the Thegns were uncertain of what they should now do. They had a deep dislike of Viridomarus and his reign, but all had sworn an oath of loyalty to him and knew that they risked all if they were to declare for Orgetorix and he should lose. So reluctantly they set about mustering all capable men in defence of their town. Any that refused to answer the summons was declared a traitor and named an outlaw, his property and wealth given up to the king.

Thus, Viridomarus mustered a second army, and he himself was to lead it. Unable to ride a horse due to his lameness, Viridomarus was carried in a litter and surrounded by his Chosen Warriors, his black and red spider banner held up behind him for all to see. Upon the plain, before the gate of Peleus, Viridomarus drew up his warriors ready for battle.

As Orgetorix approached he saw that he was once more outnumbered. His men were tired from the march and most were carrying small wounds. Dismayed by the sight of Viridomarus' warriors, many pled with Orgetorix to negotiate some sort of compromise so that they might live. But Orgetorix had not come this far too simply compromise to anything less than gaining his rightful crown. Thus, he drew up his warriors for battle with his foot soldiers forming the centre, his bowmen upon the left flank and the Companions upon the right.

As the two armies stood facing each other, the gods, unseen by all, descended from the heavens and began reading the hearts of Orgetorix's warriors. There they saw fear and unwillingness to fight another battle so soon after the last. Now there was division among the gods over how they should proceed. Though all agreed that Orgetorix was the true king and the greater of the two men, they were split on whether to intervene on his behalf or not. For the gods believed that they were best served when they were needed the least. But it was decided that they should act, for it was them that had set Orgetorix upon this path. So, the gods began to sing in unison, rising a thick mist that concealed all.

In the mist formed shadows which tricked Viridomarus' Thegns in to charging, believing that it was an attack by Orgetorix. Lost and confused did these mounted men become that they knew not friend from foe. Blindly did they chase after the shadows calling to them, before clashing into their own warriors and causing much panic.

"Treachery!" Came the call from the captains. "Treachery!"

Hearing battle and calls of treachery, Orgetorix held back his own warriors fearing it was some sort of trick. But then he heard a soft voice all around him, a hallowed voice urging him to charge to victory, to claim his rightful crown. Putting all into the hands of the gods, Orgetorix donned his helm and charged with his Companions, following the voice, and crashing into Viridomarus' warriors upon their left flank. Viridomarus' army broke without a fight and scattered like leaves to the wind.

King Viridomarus was quickly carried back to the safety of his hall where his Chosen Warriors barricaded the door. The people of Gondolor themselves hid indoors, fearing that their fair town would be pillaged. But the warriors that now entered Gondolor came not as raiders seeking silver, but as liberators seeking justice against the usurper Viridomarus.

Orgetorix rode his steed, Velox the Swift, up to the barred entrance of the hall. There he took off his helm so that all could see his true face and spoke with the handful of warriors that had formed up in a shield wall in front of the door.

"Brave warriors of Gondolor, why do you stand between the king and his hall?" Orgetorix dismounted and walked up before the warriors. "Do you not know me, the son of Cingetorix?"

A few of the warriors had indeed seen the face of Cingetorix and could not deny that Orgetorix was his very image. These warriors were the first to fall to their knees and lay down their weapons, the others soon following suit.

"Viridomarus!" Orgetorix now called. "Open up and yield so that you may yet be spared!"

But the doors remained barred and no answer was given. Now the Companions took axes to the doors, splitting the wood and pulling aside chairs that had been used as a hasty barricade inside. The Chosen Warriors inside valiantly defended Viridomarus, slaying four of the Companions before they were all slain. Viridomarus was sat on the throne, and when he first saw Orgetorix, he thought it was his brother Cingetorix come back from the dead.

"Justice has come for you uncle," Orgetorix said as he approached Viridomarus, his sword raised and ready to strike. But pity stayed his hand, for the sight of Viridomarus was not kingly. His face was thin, emaciated from worry, and deathly pale. His hands trembling from the constant pain in his stomach.

"Justice may seek me longer, for it shall not find me in this world." In a final act of defiance, Viridomarus drew his dagger and plunged it into his heart, robbing Orgetorix of gaining justice.

Orgetorix took off his own cloak and covered the body of Viridomarus, taking the golden horse ring that had once belonged to his father. He took off the horse ring of his mother from his own finger and placed them together as proof of his claims, silver meeting gold. The spider banners of Viridomarus were pulled down from the walls of the hall and cast into the fire. Now the horse banner once more took its rightful place, as did Orgetorix who then sat upon his throne. Orgetorix then ordered his Companions to search the dungeon for his family, seizing the warriors they found guarding it. From these warriors Orgetorix learnt of his family's fate. His father and brothers had been hung and his mother sent to the unknown regions to the south as a slave. Orgetorix wept on hearing of their fate and in a fit of anger ordered the death of any that had a hand in their deaths.

For the remainder of that day the remaining Thegns were gathered in the hall and all fell to their knees and freely begged pardon, and accepted Orgetorix as their king.

Thus, Orgetorix ascended to his rightful throne.

VIII

The Reign of Orgetorix

Later that year, on the day of the Hallows, was Orgetorix crowned king of Gondolor, some twenty years after Viridomarus had seized the throne for himself. His first act as king was to give gifts of land to all those that had supported him, and to honour the gods with a feast that lasted for twelve days. Upon a pyre were the finest of thighs and joints of meat offered, along with libations of strong ale poured out into silver bowls. Songs were sung and lamentations were given for all those that had fallen in the dark times of Viridomarus' reign. To usher in a new age, Orgetorix retracted the harsh tax laws that Viridomarus had imposed upon the realm. Now the realm of Gondolor began to prosper as it once had. But there was one promise in which Orgetorix was yet to keep.

From Hardrada came a messenger from the king. Orgetorix welcomed him and gave him leave of his hall, before granting him an audience to make known the king of Hardrada's message.

The messenger was tall and proud, long in beard and dressed in a fine woollen tunic burgundy in colour, and a dark-green cloak. He bowed and congratulated Orgetorix on his victories over Viridomarus and offered him gifts of a silver cup and bowl.

"These gifts are most worthy," Orgetorix said as he inspected the cup and bowl. "But what message do you bring from my friend King Eomer of Hardrada?"

"The King of Hardrada asks that your honour your pledge to him, that you grant Hardrada its freedom from the vassalage of Gondolor."

The Thegns that were present in the hall were shocked by the pledge Orgetorix had made. Many voiced their concerns and called for a council to be held so that they might debate the matter. Orgetorix, bending to the will of his Thegns, dismissed the messenger and held council there and then with his Thegns. For hours did Orgetorix try to persuade them to support his pledge, arguing that his word of honour was now at risk if he were not to honour the pact made. But his Thegns argued that Hardrada was the old enemy, and to grant it its freedom would allow it to grow in might and once more rival Gondolor. Furthermore, a case was made that if Orgetorix was to honour his pledge, Gondolor would be bankrupted. For a quarter of silver stowed in the coffers was from Hardrada, and to lose that steady flow would tip Gondolor into decline. These things were made known to Orgetorix, with Cleph himself agreeing with the Thegns and urging him to be a king of Gondolor, to put his realm above that of his own honour. So, with dislike of what he must do, Orgetorix summoned in the messenger.

"What reply do I take back to my king?" the messenger asked as he bowed.

"After taking counsel from my Thegns, it has been made clear to me that your king's request is not in the interest of Gondolor," Orgetorix replied. "Therefore, I must decline his request."

"Shame upon Orgetorix," the messenger answered, "for you swore a sacred oath!"

This outburst angered Orgetorix and he rose from his throne, red-faced and fists clenched. "You forget that you speak to a king! Now return to your master with my answer!"

Relations now broke down between Hardrada and Gondolor, and to the east of the river Wye Orgetorix was known as the Oath Breaker. During the summer that followed, King Eomer died and was succeeded by his son Alban the pious. Alban was young and full of ambition, driven by the firm belief that Hardrada should be free. So, on ascending to his father's throne he mustered his warriors and made war on Gondolor.

Three long years of warfare followed, with neither side able to strike a blow of victory. But in the fourth year of Orgetorix's reign, both had mustered a mighty host of warriors and met upon the banks of the river Wye, east of Tamaris where the water ran shallow. There a most violent battle was fought, a battle where many good warriors fell. Orgetorix himself was unhorsed and wounded from a blow to the head that dented his helm beyond repair; and it had been this act that had won Orgetorix a victory. His Companions believing that their king had been killed led a desperate charge straight for King Alban who was surrounded by his guards, the Silver Shields. There the Companions and Silver Shields clashed, with many warriors and horses falling, until finally the Silver Shields were routed after Alban himself was slew by a sword thrust that cut open his neck, his body mutilated beyond recognition.

As the sun set that day, the river ran slow and red from the bodies of the slain. Gondolor had emerged victorious and went on to sack the town of Hardrada. The line of kings in Hardrada thus ended and the town fell under full control of the king of Gondolor. But Orgetorix was much changed after the war. Now he complained of constant pains in his head and he grew quick in anger as if he were constantly agitated. He grew paranoid of his Thegns and often accused them of treason, of conspiring with Hardrada to secure their freedom and make themselves king. But Cleph had always been able to soothe Orgetorix anger and his reasoning kept him in check. But in Orgetorix's sixth year of kingship, Cleph was taken by a sickness that had caused large boils under his armpits. This plague swept through the realm, claiming half of the population, and demoralising the moral of those that survived. Many believed the plague to have been sent by the gods as punishment for Gondolor's annexing of Hardrada, for dishonouring its fallen king Alban the Pious.

With no restraint upon Orgetorix he grew evermore paranoid, his fits of anger becoming more frequent. At council he demanded stricter laws upon the people, who were now clamouring for more freedoms and the right to elect a person to represent them on the King's Council. But Orgetorix was outraged by such a demand and ordered the arrest and execution of any that dared to speak publicly in favour of this request. Thus, Gondolor fell in to decline, the rift between the king and his people growing ever wider.

By the tenth year of Orgetorix's reign, Gondolor was but a pale reflection of what it had once been. For though Orgetorix had been considered a great man, he was no king. He had grown as a farmer with little expectation or education other than labouring. He'd had nothing other than the clothes upon his back, and now that he was king all was at his command and he fell to the sickness of that power. Orgetorix's greed for silver finally took over his wit and he began locking himself away in the treasury, neglecting his kingly duties. Finally, the Thegns would suffer no more and took matters into their own hands. In the dead of night did they make their move, breaking down the treasury door to find Orgetorix curled up asleep on a pile of silver coins. Thus, Orgetorix came to an end, at the hands of those that had sworn loyalty to him. His body was buried with full honours in the tombs under Gondolor alongside Arawn and Cingetorix. The Thegns thus gathered in the King's hall and there decided that the kingship should now pass to the strongest amongst them, not from father to son as had long been the custom.

Thus, the realm of Gondolor fell to a string of bloody civil wars whenever a king died. These wars demised Gondolor further and led it to ruin. For kingdoms are like the sun, they both rise and fall, and Gondolor was no exception. Its end finally came some seven years after the assassination of Orgetorix. From the south came violent men, hardened warriors mounted upon black steeds with red eyes. Their armour was bronze and scaled like a dragon, their hearts full of malice and intent of subjecting the world to fire. Their leader a skilled warrior said to have been the son of

Alannah, the woman who had nurtured Orgetorix and exiled by Viridomarus.

Gondolor was pillaged by these fearsome warriors, its wealth taken, and its buildings destroyed. Now all that remains of this once mighty town is a grassy hilltop haunted by faded memories of a golden time, a time of heroes and of valiant charges by the horse lords, of great kings that graciously reigned over the plains. Yet for all the deeds done for Gondolor, it was the song of the lost prince that was heard far and wide. All those that heard the song were gifted with hope that men were not defined by their birth. But the song also served as a lesson that one should remain humble and never forget their origins like the lost prince had done, that all are defined by what lies within their hearts and strength of their will. Thus, Orgetorix's deeds shall remain with us, until time itself shall end.

The End

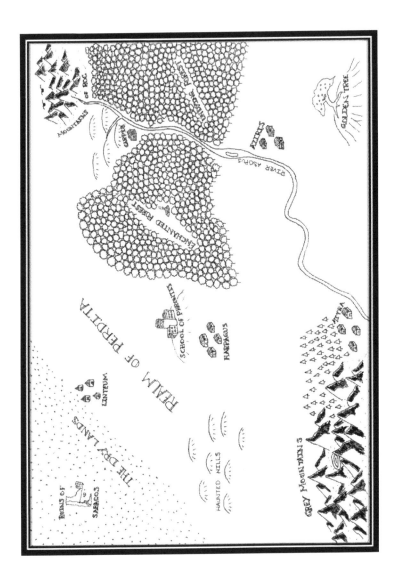

TRIALS OF A WIZARD

I

The school of Phrontis

Since the time of the beginning, the lore of magic had been practiced by many. Imps and elves had been wise and had crafted many songs and spells for the betterment of the world. But as the Age of the Beginning ended, and the Age of Heroes ascended, ambitious and greedy men began conjuring magic for their own will. So great had this peril grown that Imps and Elves began to horde their lore and would only reveal it to a select few whom they deemed worthy. Magic lessened as the years passed, and Imps and Elves began to build schools where they would teach those most worthy to use the lore of magic wisely.

One such institute was the alchemist school in the lost realm of Perdita. It had a long heritage of excellence in the fields of science, astronomy, and magic; and had been founded a hundred years ago by a scholarly Imp named Phrontis, from whom the school was named after. The buildings that made up the school were built around a courtyard with a life-size bronze statue of its founder in the centre, with an arched promenade that ringed around the courtyard. Built in dark stone to a simple rectangular plan with flat rooftops in the ancient fashion. But the central building was circular and rose higher than its flanking buildings as a giant cylinder that housed a huge telescope used to study the stars. The school had been placed upon a strategic hilltop that overlooked the Enchanted Forest to the east, and the town of Harpagus to the south, making it a more prestigious sight. Inside was a network of laboratories and workshops used for experimenting. But it was in the smaller rooms used for study that the magisters lectured their students, sharing their wisdom and knowledge in hope of inspiring a new generation of wizards.

The school had begun its life as a place where the Imp Phrontis stored all the ancient scrolls that he had collected on his travels. Quickly it became a place where men seeking knowledge would travel to study. Donations were freely given by those that visited and the school's reputation steadily grew with the passing of time. Now the school was famed throughout the realm for its excellence, a place where those families of wealth would send their children for an education. But entry as a novice, as the students were called, was not as simple as making a generous donation. It was expected that an applicant should be eight years of age and have a letter of recommendation from a person of good standing, a magister from the school or a private tutor was preferred. Once accepted as a novice, pupils were stripped of their worldly clothes and given a simple robe, grey in colour and tied in at the waist by a brown cord.

For a hundred years had the school tutored the realms finest, the pupils themselves going on to achieve many great feats. But the highest prestige was to be given a place as a magister at the school, a place only offered to one whom won the Trial, an annual event where those in their eighth year were given five tasks to complete, each being a dangerous endeavour. It was in the one-hundred and first trial in which this tale begins, in a stuffy chamber where six pupils were sat at their individual desks listening to a lecture on the different powders stored in jars on the magister's desk.

Telamon sat, hunched over his desk with his head tiredly slumped in his hands, completely oblivious to the lecture that was being given. It was all work that had been done earlier in the school year, work that Telamon had found easy, and so his concentration had strayed. He watched as a spider scuttled in and out of a crack between the wall and window next to his desk, spinning an elegant web to catch its next meal. The spider scuttled to-and-fro the stone and wooden window frame laying its faint silk threads before hiding back in the crack.

"Telamon!" The magister banged the end of his cane on his desk at the front of the class. "It is in your interests to pay attention!"

"I am Magister Xander," Telamon answered as he straightened his back, his brown eyes looking suddenly alert.

Magister Xander was tall with an aged face full of wisdom. His hair and beard were greying at the roots, his hazel eyes parted by a long slender nose. Unlike the robes of a novice, his were a dark blue with a wide grey sash at his waist. Many of the school's novices considered it an honour to have been tutored by him as he was widely accepted to become the next Peritum, or Headmaster in the common tongue. But his pupils thought he was strict with little patience for any that struggled with certain tasks. Xander himself had been a pupil at the school, and after serving as a Magister for twenty years, he had grown to dislike children. He believed that the younger generations were too easily distracted, and that they had become lesser in their will to control their urges. Many of the other magisters had said to him that he had been young once and had been just as rash. But Magister Xander knew this to be untrue, and the fear was that the future of the school rested upon these lesser students.

"Then prey tell me," Magister Xander said as he strode over to Telamon, "What my last sentence was about."

Telamon sat silent, knowing that he hadn't a clue.

"Tomorrow," Magister Xander said, holding up a finger to exclaim his point. "Tomorrow you shall begin the Trial. Five tasks that all aspiring to become a Magister at this school must complete."

Telamon felt uncomfortable and instinctively looked across to his left, towards a boy sat on the opposite side of the room. His eyes were narrow, hostile, and his face full of self-confidence as he glared over at Telamon. It was Aristides, a boy who had constantly got the highest grades and was by far the favourite to win the Trial. His father was a rival to Telamon's, so Aristides had a natural hatred of him and had bullied him since their first year.

"It is my duty," Magister Xander went on, "to ensure that you are prepared." He walked back to the front of the class, his navy-blue robe sweeping against the stone floor, and picked up two glass jars filled with powder. "Telamon, I want you to mix the right quantity of powder with water to cause enough smoke to conceal yourself."

Telamon reluctantly went to the front of the class, feeling the uncomforting eyes of his fellow pupils. He took the two jars from Magister Xander and poured a measure of both onto the desk, then mixing them together with a small wooden rod. He knew the amount of powder didn't matter, what mattered was how much water to drop on. Taking the water beaker, he hovered it over the small mound of white and grey powder. A hushed giggle made him look up, and he met the unfriendly gaze of Aristides. He was shaking his head, his face twisted in scorn. Nervousness made Telamon's hands shake and too much water poured out from the beaker. The powder hissed and fizzled frantically as a pillar of smoke quickly rose and filled the room. All were forced out into the corridor, coughing and spluttering as they went.

"Telamon you fool!" Magister Xander roared in anger, his face red and his eyebrows cast down. "Has your mind parted company with sense?"

Telamon could feel the disappointment coming from Magister Xander, and his shame would not let him look him in the eye. "Sorry Magister."

"Sorry!" Magister Xander repeated and he stooped down and jabbed the tip of his cane into Telamon's chest. "I will speak with your father about this." He then stood back upright and turned towards the other pupils who were standing around. "The rest of you may go, take the afternoon to reflect on all you have learnt over the years, for on the morrow you shall need it. But you Telamon shall fetch water and soap to clean my desk." Without another word he angrily strode off down the corridor, his slippers softly sounding against the stone floor as he went.

"You're such a failure," Aristides said with a telling smirk. "Now go fetch your bucket like a good scullery maid."

Tears welled in the corner of Telamon's eyes and he turned and fled down the corridor towards the scullery. In the years at the school, he had never fitted in with the others and had found it difficult to make friends as he was shy by nature. But where his nervousness came from was a mystery to him as his parents were the opposite. His mother was a member to the town's council in Harpagus, a strong-minded lady that had little time for fools. His father was equally as impressive as his mother and had himself studied at the school. His father had been the best in all subjects, winning every ranking contest held at the end of every year and the Trial before being offered a position of a Magister. But it was not just his father that was renowned at the school, for Telamon was a third generation to attend the school and great expectations were placed upon him, expectations he often fell short of.

"Telamon wait!" It was Calliope that called after him, a gentle girl with tanned skin and long dark hair that she twisted up into a bun and pinned in place with a long needle-like hairpin.

That afternoon, while the others studied for the looming Trial, Telamon scrubbed Magister Xander's desk, the water cooling from the length of time it took him. But Telamon had not been alone in his punishment as Calliope had remained with him, herself taking a scrubbing brush and cloth.

"One would think that it was a dragon to have scorched this," Calliope said, her sleeves rolled up to her elbows and her hands blackened. "What we need is a little magic."

"Telamon, his own sleeves rolled up, shook his head. "Magister Xander says it's forbidden to use magic unnecessarily."

"I know that," Calliope laughed, "But I won't say anything if you won't."

"We just need clean water," Telamon replied, fearing that he would get into more trouble. "I'm in enough trouble as it is."

"With your father?" Calliope asked, knowing that Telamon was ever anxious to please his father.

Telamon nodded his head. "I'm going to be the first in my family not to win the Trial and become a Magister." He had often opened-up to Calliope, feeling at ease in her company, and had found her words of encouragement soothing.

"You shouldn't worry," Calliope said as she stopped scrubbing and wiped her dampened forehead on the back of her hand, leaving a blackened trace. "You are the most skilled of our class."

Telamon smiled as he vigorously scrubbed at a black stain smeared across the desktop. "Your words are kind Calliope, yet they are not truthful. We both know Aristides will go on to win the Trial."

Calliope dropped her scrubbing brush into the bucket, dirty water sloshing over the brim and onto the floor. "That arrogant fool."

"He's won the ranking contest every year," Telamon shrugged.

"So, what!" Calliope exclaimed. "The Trial is all that matters."

"What about you?" Telamon asked. "Do you not worry about the Trial?"

Calliope shrugged and answered, "A little. But I worry about staying alive, not winning it. My parents have told me that many times." Calliope's family had moved from Linteum, a town on the borders of the Dry Lands to the northwest, when she was still in her mother's womb. Her parents had been less pressuring than what Telamon's had and had only ever told her to do her best and that they considered her returning alive from the Trial a victory.

Telamon was envious of such an easy-going home to have grown up in, and had many times wished that it were so for him. But his grandfather had set a high example of what was expected, and the very least was to win the Trial and be made a Magister.

For an hour more did they scrub the desk, much of that time silent as each thought of the Trial before Magister Xander returned and told them to go and prepare for the morrow. With his hands still blackened and seemingly mocking him of his failure, Telamon began his walk home.

A path from the school led down the hill where the town of Harpagus lay, a rich town with wide streets and buildings three stories high. So peaceful was this town that they had no walls to protect them, no warriors to defend them, and it was said that if one wanted an easy life in Harpagus, they were to join the Sheriffs whom did nothing other than walk the streets bidding people a good morrow. The buildings themselves were built from red brick and blackened beams, and the rooves were clad in overlapping slate and pierced only by chimneys which in the colder weather released a grey smog over the town. The citizens were split into two classes, the first being made up of those higher up on the social ladder. These citizens were known as the Equals, fewer in number than those of the second class, and all serving in prominent positions upon the town's council, or as Magisters at the school. The second class were known as the Dwellers and were made up of men and women of a lesser heritage and education than those of the Equals. These citizens made up the town's workforce, tending to the wheat fields and cattle, serving in the homes of the equals so that they were free to seek enlightenment in the lore of their chosen subject. Close ties with the school of Phrontis did the town have, each year donating a ten percent tithe of its annual yield in crops and money.

Telamon walked the familiar street, passing a sweeping gang whose task it was to keep the streets clean. Their foreman called a halt to their work to allow Telamon to pass unsoiled from the dry dirt that was swept up by their brooms. Telamon nodded his thanks, as was the custom, and hurried along further down the street. His family home was on the main road up to the school, a prominent place greatly desired by any moving to the town. Most of the Magisters had a home on this road, as well as all the members of the town's council. Each of the houses were three storeys high with lead framed windows. He came to a dark-blue door with brass numbers 34 screwed onto it. As Telamon entered, he was met by the sweet smell of freshly cut spring flowers and the soft humming of the maid as she brushed the corners of the reception hall with a long feather duster.

"Is mother home?" Telamon asked, interrupting the maid's humming.

"No Master Telamon?" the maid answered. She was young with golden hair tied up with a black ribbon and wore a long black dress with a white apron tied around her slender waist. "Your lady mother is at council and won't be back till late. But your father is waiting for you in his study."

"Thank you, Mildred," Telamon said as he began to climb the polished oak staircase. His father's study was on the third floor, a large room with a window that looked out into the back garden. By the time he reached the door to the study, his heart was racing. But it was not from the climbing the many stairs, but for the wrath he knew awaited him upon the other side. Taking a deep breath to calm himself, Telamon knocked.

"Enter," a gruff voice came from within.

"You wanted to see me father?" Telamon, closing the door behind him, came to a stop before his father's desk. Piles of papers littered his desktop and the room smelt of pipe tobacco. Along every wall was a bookcase filled with books and scrolls, and by the window was placed a brass telescope. Telamon's father, for a moment, never took his eyes from the scroll he was reading, before calmly placing it down and glaring up directly at Telamon. It was the calm before the storm.

"I have not long ago spoken with Magister Xander." Telamon's father was a dumpy man with short hair, dark in colour, and a close clipped beard. His eyes were brown, his eyebrows angled down in anger. "He told me that you failed with a simple calculation!"

"I know the right calculation father," Telamon quietly replied, "It was…."

"I don't care what it was!" Telamon's father slammed the palms of his hands down on his desktop and rose from his chair. "You made yourself look foolish! To have failed in such a simple task is not worthy of our family name!"

"Sorry," Telamon sullenly replied, his eyes lowered to the floor.

"Sorry!" Telamon's father repeated as he strode around his desk and grabbed him by his shoulders, shaking him as though it would release his inner foolishness. "I have just had to concede my study of the outer world to Aegeus, my life's work to be merely handed over to that arrogant man! To constantly hear that his son Aristides is by far the worthiest to win the Trial and be made a Magister! And you! You the son and grandson of former victors are unable to succeed in a simple task!"

"It's not my fault!" Telamon's outburst flared his father's anger far beyond his level of control, and he struck him clean across the face with the back of his hand.

"I will have no more of this foolish behaviour! Tomorrow you shall begin the Trial and you shall win!"

Tears rolled down Telamon's cheeks as a feeling of helplessness swept over him.

"You will win the Trial!" Telamon's father said as he released his vice-like grip. "You will win the Trial! Is that understood?"

"Yes father," Telamon cried as his hands began to shake.

"Good, for failure is not an option!" Telamon's father turned and picked up a pile of scrolls from his desk before turning back to Telamon. "Two generations of this family have become a Magister, and you shall follow in our footsteps."

"Yes father," Telamon dutifully answered.

"Good, now I must return to the school. You, however, shall go to your room and study, prepare yourself for the Trial."

Telamon dejectedly went to his room on the second floor, where he fell onto his bed and cried himself to sleep. He awoke later that afternoon and began studying maps and books on creatures which roamed in the wild. Late into the night did he ponder over what tasks might be given in the Trial, taking no food or drink, until finally slumber took him, and dark dreams troubled his mind.

II

The Beginning of the Trial

Telamon was awoken early, before the sun had risen, to bathe. For an hour he lay in a copper bathing tub filled with warm water, pondering over what lay ahead, before the housemaid called him to breakfast. So, he climbed out of the bath and patted his skin dry with a towel before dressing in a clean robe laid out for him. From the washroom he went directly to the dining hall where his mother was sat at the table's head reading the early post.

"Good morning mother," Telamon said as he sat at the place laid out for him next to her.

"You look ill," Telamon's mother said with a brief glance up from her letter.

"I'm quite well mother," Telamon replied, "A little nervous, but well."

Telamon's mother set aside the letter and picked up her china cup filled with hot tea, gently blowing on it before taking a sip. She was a strong-willed lady who knew her own mind, with little time for those who constantly made mistakes. Each morning she would rise three hours before sunrise to bathe and dress for the day, and she now wore a red dress decorated with white lace, her dark hair tucked under a red gable edged with pearls. Her face was friendly in nature, but her hazel eyes were keen and as a hawk stalking its prey. "Your father and I expect good things from you Telamon."

"I know what is expected of me mother," Telamon answered as he poured himself a glass of water from a pewter jug set out before him. "I shall win the Trial," he added unconvincingly.

"Your father cares deeply for you Telamon. He knows how skilled you are and wants you to succeed, to follow in his and your grandfather's footsteps and become a Magister."

Telamon's stomach grumbled with hunger, and yet his yearning to eat was suppressed by his growing nerves.

"Well you must eat plenty now to keep up your strength," Telamon's mother said as she rose from her chair. "For in the coming weeks there will be times when you shall have to go without."

Telamon took a sweet bun from the platter and began picking at it. "What if I fail mother?"

Telamon's mother walked around the table and kissed him on his forehead. "Worry not of failure, for in my heart I know that you shall succeed."

Telamon didn't know what he could say to make his mother understand his apprehensions, and so he simply remained silent and nodded.

"Good," Telamon's mother said with a smile. She then turned and plucked up the letter she had been reading. "Now I must go as I have many meetings to prepare for." Coldly she walked towards the door, but her maternal instincts forced her to stop and look back at Telamon. In her eyes she still saw him as the baby he had once been, not as the eighteen-year-old about to begin the Trial. She wanted nothing more than to go back over to him and embrace him in her arms, to comfort him by telling him that it didn't matter if he failed. But soon he would be exposed to the true world, and the world was a cruel place that would offer him little comforts. So out of necessity and not cruelty, she left Telamon alone.

Telamon spent another hour trying to eat in hope of steadying his churning stomach. But his efforts had the very opposite effect and he had to rush to the washroom where he vomited into the copper bathtub that had now been emptied. Feeling suddenly better, Telamon left his home, fearing that it would be the last time he saw it. He had made the journey from his home to the school many times over the last eight years, a short journey that would normally have taken him half an hour at most. But that morning, despite the cheerfulness of the weather,

Telamon's legs were unwilling to move with any haste. Partway down the road, Calliope was awaiting him as she had most days, herself wearing clean robes of a novice. Together they walked up the hill towards the school where many of the pupils had gathered at the gates. As Telamon and Calliope passed them by, a few wished them luck and others even applauded them.

The day of the Trial was unlike any other. Normal lessons were abandoned for the day in favour of joyous games, readings of previous Trials and a feast filled with exotic goods. Where this tradition came from is uncertain, but what was reckoned at the time was so that the pupils saw the Trial in a good light and not for the reckless peril it put those participating in. Indeed, if this was the strategy used, it worked, for the pupils welcomed the Trial and openly spoke of it as a prestigious event to look forward to. For it was widely acknowledged as a coming of age passage where a boy would become a man.

Telamon and Calliope were the last of their class to arrive, the first, of course, being Aristides. As was the custom, they had been made to wait in their classroom where they each sat at their desk in a nervous silence. There was six in all to take the Trial that year, Telamon, Calliope and Aristides we know, but there were three others.

On the desk behind Aristides was Dardanus, a tall and skinny youth with straw coloured hair who had showed great promise in the lore of mathematics. He was good friends with Aristides and the two were often seen together outside of their lessons. His family were noteworthy members of the school, his father being a Magister and his mother in charge of the library.

Then there was Olen the Elf, named after his great grandfather who had been an elf. He was taller than an elf, though still smaller than the average man. His ears were long and pointed, his face slender with dark eyes that saw at a great distance. His lore of the unseen force, an invisible force believed to hold the world together, was so deep that he could move objects using the power of his mind alone.

Lastly there was Solon who was deep in the lore of history. He was of average height and build with a mop of dark curly hair. His eyes were blue, and his fingertips stained from ink as he liked to write poetry in his spare time.

After waiting half an hour, Magister Xander strode in and instructed them to the storeroom where they were to take provisions and equipment for their journey. So, the pupils walked out and up a long corridor that was now empty of anyone other than them, silent other than their soft footsteps. From the storeroom they each took a hooded cloak, a backpack made of brown leather and a bedroll of woollen fleece with an outer layer of soft leather. To the sides of their packs they shared between them a rope, pans, and lanterns. Next, they began filling their packs with provisions of food, both fresh and hardened biscuits that were made to last. They then each took a tin canteen which they filled with water, which they strapped over their shoulder, and a staff to aid their walking. Once they had taken all they needed, Magister Xander led them to the Founding Hall where all the school had now been gathered. All fell silent as they entered the circular chamber.

There were seventy-four pupils, differing in ages from eight to seventeen, stood in a semicircle behind an ageing man dressed in a long red robe with a blue sash tied around his waist. Despite his age, he was taller than all in the chamber, his head bold and his face clean shaven. He watched, straight-backed with narrow eyes as if weighing up the readiness of the pupils striding towards him. He was the headmaster, a Peritum as they were called, a man deep in the lore of astrology. Telemachus was his name, a highly respected man whom many would seek wisdom from. But to the pupils he was known as the Ogre, both for his appearance and his grumpiness.

"Today," Telemachus said as the pupils came to a stop before him, "today the one hundred and first Trial shall begin. You have each been tutored to pass this trial, each has been given ample supplies to succeed." He then turned to a Magister stood to the side of him and took a scroll. "Five tasks shall judge you, five task that shall make or break you." Carefully, he unrolled the scroll. "The first of you whom brings me these items, and places them upon the founding stone, shall be named the victor. The amulet of the woodland enchantress. A tail feather from a Roc. An apple from the Golden Tree. Water from the Spring of Youth, and finally, the Heart of Sabacos."

The pupils stood behind the Peritum began to mutter of the difficulty of the Trial, and many now doubted that there would be a victor that year. Telamon himself had felt a cold shudder as he listened to the five tasks being read out. He had glance to his left to Calliope who herself was awestruck at the tasks being given, nervously smiling at the enormity of the challenge.

"You are free to choose your own path, be it alone or together," Telemachus went on, "By what means you obtain these items shall be down to your own cunning. But the use of magic is strictly forbidden, along with the slaying of your fellow pupils, nor of any persons of who you might meet. You may ask aid, but not steal; and you shall respect all laws imposed upon you."

The pupils were given a map of Perdita which showed the places of their tasks and were led out again by Xander. He took them as far as the gate where he halted and said, "I shall go no further with you and offer you only words of enlightenment. That is to trust yourself and your skills in this venture."

"It has been an honour to have been tutored by you," Aristides said, his face full of joy for the adventure to come. "And know that I shall return and become your equal."

But Xander would say no more and simply turned and walked back into the school.

And so, the six began the Trial, each being a mix of nervousness and optimism, a shrill of freedom and a sense that anything could happen. They walked the road down to the town of Harpagus, passing their homes. Telamon had an urge to return and see his mother before leaving but knew he could not. At the southern edge of the town the road then forked, its main path continuing south while a narrower path turned east. This road they took at a steady pace, the day slowly passing into the twilight hours where the land greyed and the forest upon the distance before them turned black. Behind them was the red glow of the setting sun, and Aristides said that they should make camp for the night, beside a small stream which ran parallel with the road. It was there that they decided to remain together upon the Trial, believing that it was their best chance of survival. But each knew that there could be only one victor of the Trial and argument broke out over how they were to decide amongst themselves. Finally, they agreed that none of them should decide and that they should leave it to fate by means of casting lots ones they had gathered the five required items.

That first night they ate well from their fresh provisions and they lay around a fire speaking long into the night with much excitement. But for Telamon it was anything but exciting, for upon the horizon, black against the purple starlit sky, was the Enchanted Forest. That place had been the essence of many horror stories told by generations of pupils at the school. A place of unknown evils and ancient malice, a place where none would willingly tread, a place said to be inhabited by an enchantress.

III

The Amulet of the Enchantress

Telamon awoke to a damp spring morning. The sky was almost perfectly clear, and the grassy glades were silvery with dew. The sun was still low in the east, slowly rising above the Enchanted Forest where shadows stretched out before the treeline. He was the last of their company to rise and found himself the victim of harsh words from Aristides for being so. Aching from constantly tossing and turning on a hard ground, Telamon quietly rolled up his bedroll and strapped it to the top of his pack. Looking around he noticed a change in his fellow pupils. The previous day's optimism had now dispersed, giving way to fear caused by the gravitas of the task. All were irritable and grumpily went about various tasks in preparation for continuing with their quest.

Dardanus rekindled the fire and placed a frying pan over the flames, placing in thick cuts of bacon that began to slowly sizzle and fry in their own fat. The smell was alluring and invited pangs of hunger into the pupils' stomachs. Aristides and Olen were studying the map, debating over where they believed the enchantress's dwelling was. Solon was sat alone some distance from the fire, his back to the company, staring towards the forest, deep in thought of how they could gain the amulet. Calliope, however, was concentrating on matters closer to hand. She was checking what provisions they had left, calculating how many days their rations would last.

"We've eaten too much already!" Calliope exclaimed in disbelief at what remained.

Aristides looked up from the map and glared over at Calliope. "What are you worrying about? We'll find food in the forest." He looked back down at the map and added, "Besides, we have enough of Balor's Bane to last for a month."

Balor's Bane was a hard biscuit as big as the palm of your hand and baked with a spell so that one biscuit was enough to fill the stomach. For many months could these biscuits last before they became spoiled by mould, and so hard were they that they would break teeth if one were to bite into them. In order to eat these biscuits, they would have to be covered in hot water, when the biscuit would break down to form a porridge.

"Three weeks," Calliope corrected. "And our fresh supplies are almost vanquished."

Aristides blew out a heavy breath of frustration and angrily rolled up the map. "What is it you want Calliope? For us to go hungry. You may take one sixth of what remains and go alone if you wish." He rose from the damp ground and turned to the fire to warm his back.

"My point is," Calliope went on, "is that we need to be careful with supplies and plan ahead for our own preservation."

Aristides turned back to the fire and rubbed his smooth chin. "What we need is a leader," he said after a moment's thought. "A leader to keep us on task and appoint duties."

Telamon remained quiet, knowing where this debate was leading.

"As the best amongst us," Aristides went on, "I believe that leader should be me."

Olen and Solon, who were beside the fire, nodded their approval. Dardanus, on hearing of the proposal, joined them beside the fire and gave his support of Aristides.

"Well that decides it then," Aristides said with a wide smirk of satisfaction. "I will lead, Olen will guide us and scout ahead where it is needed. Dardanus will act as my second and Solon will brief us on the lore of the places we shall visit. You, Calliope, shall keep a watch over our provisions, forage when we are short and to keep our canteens filled. Telamon will help you in this task."

Calliope felt angry and degraded by being given such a demeaning task, but knew that there was no other option, not if they wanted to remain together. So, she remained silent and took to her task, beginning to ration out what stores they had left. Telamon she tasked with refilling the canteens from the stream.

They each ate a little of the bacon with bread before packing up and continuing towards the forest, which grew menacingly closer with every step. Every now and then, one of them would glance back towards the school, which was by now but a distant smudge upon the skyline, wishing that they were once more back within their comforts. Even Aristides, despite his show of confidence, felt a yearning for home. As a result of their desire of home, their progress was slow and it took them a full day to reach the edge of the forest, a journey of little over half a day. The sun was now setting, and Aristides decided that they should spend the night there. So, they collected a pile of sticks and made a small fire to keep the growing cold of night at bay. Calliope handed out the last of their bread and gave each a morsel of cheese and cold ham, saying that they were to have no more until morning. After they ate this meagre meal, they each rolled out their bedrolls, circled around the fire, and settled in for the night.

"Solon tell us what you know about the enchantress," Aristides said as he poked the fire with a stick, sending glowing orange embers wafting up into the cool night air.

Solon leaned up on his elbow and thought. "Well," he began as he rubbed his chin with his free hand, "They say that the Enchantress was once a pupil at the school, a pupil of great promise. Thera was her true name. Her lore in the mixing of potions was deep, indeed, many of what we now use was formed by her. Yet her desire to be the greatest drove her ever closer towards what is forbidden. It was in her final year in which she crafted the amulet we must now gain, a black stone made from a molten rock and mixed with a powerful potion she had concocted. This stone was set in a golden necklace and contained the power to bend all people of a lesser force to her will. The Peritum at that time was an elf named Granicus, himself a powerful mage who could feel the presence of the forbidden arts. He challenged Thera, demanding that she relinquish the amulet. But she would not."

"Did she bend Granicus to her will?" Calliope asked, deeply enthralled by the tale.

"She tried," Solon continued, "but Granicus was too powerful for Thera. She was stripped of her place at the school and the amulet taken from her and placed in the vaults where it was never to see light of day again. But Thera was by no means defeated. From her exile in the forest, she conjured up a shadow demon from her malice and hatred. This demon she sent to the school where it obtained the amulet and murdered Granicus. That was some seventy years ago now, and Thera remains in the forest, where she stalks any brave enough to venture that passage."

"A fable told to frighten the younger pupils," Dardanus said as he lay back with his hands tucked under the back of his head. "I was told a similar tale when I first started. They told me that the Enchantress returns each night to take blood from her chosen victim. It took me near three years before I had the courage to sleep in the school's dormitory."

"A lot may be mere tale," Aristides said as he placed more sticks on to the fire. "Yet there is no smoke without fire."

Solon nodded his agreement and added, "I once looked into the records of pupils to have attended the school, and there in the very year of these events was a name barely visible for the ink which had been scored across it. Thera."

The fire spat at the sound of the name and the sky seemed to darken. Clouds had slowly gathered overhead, and the world was still and ominously quiet. The forest seemed foreboding in the dark, a black place concealing unimaginable evils. The pupils, all now heavy-eyed, lay down to sleep and one-by-one slumber found them.

Telamon was closest to the forest and he refused to sleep facing away from it. So troubled by it had he become, that he would not allow himself to close both of his eyes. While the others slept, he watched with expectations of some evil thing coming fourth to harm them. But as the night wore on, nothing did he see apart from a faint silhouette of an owl, its wide eyes unblinking, perched upon a branch watching them. Finally, he fell to his need for sleep, his dreams haunted by black shadows stroking his and his companions faces as they slept.

The night passed and Telamon was roughly awoken. "Telamon!" Calliope's voice sounded urgent. "Telamon wake up!"

Telamon was slow to wake and his body ached from tiredness. "What is it," he managed to say, his eyes still closed.

"It's morning and we need to get going."

Telamon suddenly snapped into motion and wriggled out of his bed. Despite the cool of the morning breeze, he was sweating and his face pale.

"Telamon," Calliope said with concern, "are you alright?"

"I'm... Fine," Telamon replied, his words stumbling from his mouth rather than forming a graceful flow. "I'm fine. Just a bad night that's all." It was then that he noticed the others were packed up and ready, their eyes fixed upon him with anger.

"Well we need to get going!" Calliope's face was flustered, and her abrupt manner gave clue that there had been some argument.

Telamon, sensing that his oversleeping had caused argument, quickly rolled up his bed and strapped it to the top of his pack.

"No stopping until nightfall," Aristides said as he turned and walked towards the forest. "Now let's go!"

Telamon walked at the back, his stomach grumbling for missing breakfast. Calliope walked beside him, herself quiet and gloomy. "What has happened?"

"It's you!" Calliope said with more anger than she intended. "You woke us in the early hours!"

"I did?" Telamon answered with puzzlement.

"Yes, you were sleepwalking," Calliope explained. "I awoke to find you walking towards the forest. You were shouting for Augur."

"Augur," Telamon repeated, "who or what is Augur?"

"Three times we had to fetch you back; and none of us dared to sleep after! Then you slept in as if all is merry!" Calliope knocked the yellow head from a dandelion with her staff in a show of frustration. "Aristides wanted to leave you, claiming that it was the spirit of the Enchantress to have possessed you. You can thank Solon and I for swaying his mind."

"Solon," Telamon said with surprise. He had expected Calliope to have spoken in his defence, but Solon?

"Yes, he pointed out that the Enchantress had never left the forest, so, it was therefore impossible that she had possessed you. Instead he said that your night terror had been caused by a weak character and being away from home, something Aristides believed with ease."

"Oh," Telamon replied sombrely, "sorry."

"It's fine," Calliope said as she playfully nudged into Telamon, "I expect we shall all suffer from this Trial. But promise me one thing Telamon." She stopped and looked Telamon in the eye. "No matter what, we shall stick together."

Telamon glanced over at the others, they were walking ahead and unknowing of their conversation. "I promise Calliope."

Calliope smiled; her gloom seemingly lifted. "Good, for I do not trust Aristides. He seeks to use us for his own ends and will by no means draw a lot to deem the winner of this Trial. He will take all for himself and claim all the glory."

The others came to a stop at the edge of the forest and Aristides looked back. "Come on!" he shouted.

Telamon looked towards Aristides, his face self-assured from ambition, and suspected the same conclusion as Calliope had made. For now, they were safer together, but the time would come when they would have to decide whom should win the Trial, and Aristides would never concede to anything less than his victory.

So, the pupils entered the Enchanted Forest, divided and in mistrust. But the forest seemed to lighten their mood as it was nothing like what they had expected. They had believed the forest to be dark, sinister, and unwelcoming. A place, so the tales said, full of evil spirits and strange orbs of light that danced around and sang in torment of their victims. A place of sheer fear and anguish where the bravest of the brave dare not to tread. But before them was an elegant tranquillity of which would inspire poets. The trees were prestigious and were seemingly glowing gold from the sunlight that filtered through the green canopy above. The forest floor was covered by shrubbery, which in places was difficult to pass through, and the air was pleasant on the lungs.

"Well," Aristides said as he stopped to admire the majesty of the forest, "I did not expect this."

"So, the stories were wrong," Solon said as he too halted. "I wonder if there is truly an Enchantress?"

"We would not have been sent for her amulet if she were not real," Calliope said. "It's like you said Aristides, there is no smoke without fire."

"So, where might the Enchantress's dwelling be?" Aristides said, thinking out loud.

"I doubt that she will dwell close to the fringes of the forest," Dardanus said. "It's more likely that she would dwell somewhere deeper, closer to the centre where she could remain hidden."

Aristides agreed with Dardanus and led them deeper into the forest. For a week did they wonder, losing all sense of direction and becoming hopelessly lost. Aristides had scratched a marking onto the trunk of a tree with a small pocketknife to aid them in their direction, and three times had they came back to the same marking. Tired and dejected, the company slumped down beside a small pool of murky water that had collected at the base of a boulder covered over with moss.

"It's no good," Olen moaned, "we're lost!"

"Stop your whining Olen!" Aristides slammed his staff down in a temper. "Solon, do you not know anything of the Enchantress's dwelling?"

Solon shook his head and answered, "Nothing."

"Then what use are you!" Aristides shook off his pack and climbed the boulder, hoping that being higher up might offer him some clue. But he saw nothing but endless trees in all directions, and so he dejectedly climbed back down again.

The heat had risen over the last couple of days, and the forest had become unbearably muggy with gnats irritating their faces. The heat sapped at their strength and made each irritable and quick to blame each other for their misfortune. By night they would be awoken by strange noises, wild animals that stalked them in the shadows. But what unsettled them more was the feeling of being watched. Each night they had been watched by a grey owl, silent and unflinching it perched, its black eyes watching them as they slept. Adding to their misery, their supplies had become low, having now only the hard biscuits to nourish them. Fresh water was nowhere to be found, and Calliope had the laborious task of purifying any water they came across. She now systematically began to scoop up the water from the pool with a pan and poured it through a tightly woven cloth, where it slowly dribbled down to another pan placed below. This water she then boiled and mixed with a bit of vinegar to make it safe to drink, though its taste was awful.

The forest darkened with the onset of night and they rolled out their bedrolls in a circle around the fire, each sleeping facing outwards. Like the previous nights, the forest came alive and a growl sounding close by woke them all. Aristides shot out of his bed and peered into the gloom but saw nothing, nothing other than the grey trees and the dark undergrowth that looked like a vast black mist that concealed the ground. But there high in the tree closest to them was the owl, its eyes fixed on Aristides.

"What do you want?" Aristides shouted up towards the treetops. "Are you the Enchantress come in the form of an owl?" Bending down and rummaging around on the ground, Aristides picked up a stone. "I am not afraid of you!" He threw the stone as hard as he could towards the owl, his arm pained from the effort. It struck the trunk and caused a loud *clack*, but the owl remained, unmoved and unafraid. Aristides was overcome by a sudden anger and he quickly plucked up two more stones from the ground, throwing them and shouting as though he were possessed.

"Calm yourself," Dardanus said as he grabbed hold of Aristides, "It's just an owl."

Aristides watched the owl for a moment, their eyes meeting through the gloom, before it took flight.

Weariness swept through Aristides and he collapsed and fell into a deep slumber. The others believed that he had suffered from a night terror like Telamon had before entering the forest, and so they lay him in his bed and awaited the light of a new day.

The morning after dawned, gloomy with a shade of grey. They each ate a hard biscuit and set off in an unknown direction. After a couple of hours of aimlessly wandering they halted, tiredness hampering their spirits. They each sat and drank what remained of their water, silent and in despair of death. A heavy downpour drummed against the canopy of leaves above and filtered its way down to the forest floor. The deluge caused further misery for the pupils, but it also offered them opportunity to refill their canteens. It rained for the remainder of that day and night, and they were unable to light a fire. By the morning all were wet through to the skin. The rain had now eased but they were still unable to light a fire. So, wet, and hungry they continued, each doubting that they would ever find the dwelling of the Enchantress.

After searching for hours, the morning drizzle turning back into a heavy deluge, Olen spotted smoke rising out of a chimney not too far from where they were. A debate followed over what they should now do. Aristides said that it could be the dwelling they sought, but Olen said the home did not appear to be sinister. The dwelling of the Enchantress, so they believed, was made from the bones of her victims. But Olen claimed to see nothing of the sort, so they agreed to head in that direction and gain a better view.

After half an hour's walk, they came within sight of the house. It was rectangular in shape, its walls were made of wattle and daub, and the roof was an apex covered not with slate but with grassy earth. A stone chimney rose from out of the roof, and a single wooden door was the only entrance. By the door was a barrel that collected rainwater, now filled and sloshing over the brim. Around this home was a clearing of felled trees and a patch where vegetables were grown. Disappointed that it was not the dwelling of the Enchantress, and yet relieved at the welcoming sight, they slowly approached the house.

As they neared the door opened and a woman with a blanket wrapped around her shoulders greeted them. "Well met strangers," she said with a friendly smile. "What brings you to my hearth and home?" She was young, attractive, with full lips and alluring green eyes. Her hair was long and straight, the colour of straw. A red dress clung to her slim body and adorned by a wide black belt with a brass buckle finely polished to look like gold.

"We ask shelter from the rain," Aristides answered in his finest voice. "Also, if your good nature shall allow it, a meal."

"My nature is indeed good, and I welcome you to share my warmth." The woman waved a hand, beckoning them to follow.

Aristides was the first to enter and was met by warm air scented by the herbs hanging from the ceiling. "We thank you," Aristides said as he quickly made for the fireplace to dry his dripping cloak and robe. The others quickly followed suit.

Inside was a homely home, welcoming and warm. The floor was wooden and partly covered by rugs, the walls were painted white and grubby with ware. To the right of the door, as one would enter, was a bed large enough for two people with an empty shelf above it. At the foot of the bed was a wooden ottoman where the woman stored her clothes and extra bedding. In the corner beside the ottoman was a cupboard filled with pots storing potent smelling ingredients. From the left of the door was the stone fireplace, before it an open space with two wooden armchairs.

"Take off your cloaks," the woman said as she shook off the blanket from her shoulders and placed it on a peg next to the fire. "Dry and make yourselves comfortable."

So, the pupils took off their cloaks and hung them on the wooden pegs, making themselves comfortable in front of the fire. Aristides seated himself in one of the armchairs, his eyelids becoming heavy from the warmth, and the other stretched out on the floor.

The woman then walked over to the table and poured water into a cauldron which she then placed over the fire. "Who are you? And what are six young ones doing alone in the forest?"

"We are students of the school of Phrontis and we have entered the borders of this forest for a task of our Trial." Aristides was too tired to stand, as was the custom when making introduction. "I am Aristides, the leader of our small company," he then pointed to each in turn, "this is Dardanus, my second. Olen the longsighted. Solon the learned. Calliope and Telamon." Aristides shifted in his chair to make himself more comfortable. "Now that you are acquainted with us, may we know your name and how it is you live in such a place."

"My name is Ellen," the woman replied as she began chopping herbs and mushrooms at the table. "I live here with my husband, a woodcutter. My family has lived here for three generations."

"Are there any others?" It was Calliope that spoke, herself believing that there must be a settlement close by. For most of the goods in the home were not to be found in the forest, indicating trade.

"About a day's walk west of here is a small village," Ellen answered, "my husband works at the sawmill there."

A silence fell as an aura of tiredness grew ever stronger. To all the pupils the house felt like home, nurturing and familiar as though they had been before. Each would have gladly slept, but none did.

"You said that you entered the forest for a task," Ellen said as she finished chopping the pile of mushrooms, placing them in a bowl with the chopped herbs. "What task?"

For a moment Aristides was silent, unsure if he should reveal their quest. "We are seeking out the Enchantress. We were led to believe that she dwells in this forest. Maybe you know of her?"

Ellen picked up the bowl and walked over to the cauldron hanging above the flames. The water was now simmering from the heat and she tipped in the mix of mushrooms and herbs. "I know nothing of an Enchantress, though the forest is far and wide. But my husband often spoke of an old lady dwelling alone to the north of here. He said that she spoke in a strange tongue and wore a threadbare robe like the ones you now wear."

"The Enchantress," Solon said with a raised eyebrow of suspicion. "Can you tell us the name of this woman?"

Ellen shrugged and shook her head. "My husband can tell you more when he returns, he will even guide you should you wish it." The sound of heavy rain drummed against the outside of the walls, followed by strong gusts of wind that whistled through the treetops. "This storm will keep him away for the night, you are welcome to stay until the morrow."

Hearing the deluge outside, none wanted to leave the comfort of the warm house; so, they rolled out their beds on the floor and rested, taking a meal of a mushroom and herb soup. The sense of safety and warmth they had not felt since leaving their homes relaxed them into a deep slumber. It was past midday by the time they awoke the next day, the storm still raging, and they were woken to the smell of a fresh pot of soup. All ate greedily as though they had not eaten in days and drank from a jug of water which they passed amongst themselves.

"Will your husband return today?" It was Calliope that asked, rising from her bed, and approaching Ellen who was chopping more mushrooms at the table.

Ellen stopped her chopping and looked up at Calliope. "This storm will keep him away for the night, you are welcome to stay until the morrow." She then took up her blanket, which had been scruffily placed at the table's end, and wrapped it around her head and shoulders. "I will return later."

"Where are you going?" Calliope asked.

"I must collect more mushrooms for dinner," Ellen replied. "You may rest here and await my return."

So, as the day before the pupils rested all that afternoon, quietly talking amongst themselves. The storm remained a consistent howling and drumming as rain lashed against the walls. Tiredness grew once more, and the pupils were all soon deep in sleep.

The next day they awoke at the same time as the previous day. To the same smell of freshly made mushroom soup, and to the sound of Ellen's chopping. Hunger allured the pupils to the pot of soup, which again they all greedily ate. Yet Calliope felt odd, as though all were familiar and strange at the same time.

"Didn't we do this yesterday," Calliope said, her head a haze of confusion. But none seemed to hear her, and they continued in the same pattern as they had the previous day. "When will your husband return?"

"This storm will keep him away for the night, you are welcome to stay until the morrow," Ellen replied as she took up her blanket and wrapped it about her. "I must collect more mushrooms for dinner. You may rest here and await my return."

Calliope wanted to resist whatever it was that compelled her to return to her bed, but the desire was too great. There, like the others, she fell into a deep slumber, only to awake to the same cycle. Over and over, day after day, did they repeat themselves. But Calliope, one day, refused to eat the soup and whatever spell had been cast began to lessen its hold over her.

"When will your husband be home?"

"This storm will keep him away for the night, you are welcome to stay until the morrow," Ellen replied as she had each day when asked.

"That's what you said yesterday," Calliope said with anger, "and the day before that!"

Ellen just simply smiled and replied, "You only arrived yesterday." She then left, as she had each day, to gather mushrooms.

"Telamon." Calliope rushed to where he was sleeping and shook him. "Telamon wake up!" Having no success, she tried to wake the others, but they too were deep in slumber. Fearing that they were now all trapped, she decided to lay in her bed and pretend to sleep. She lay still for hours, the fire dying down and the house darkening. From outside came strange noises, like the sound of a thousand birds flapping their wings against the walls. Then all suddenly fell deathly silent and the door opened. Calliope watched, with only one eye open, as Ellen returned. She was softly humming a haunting melody that made Calliope feel cold. She walked straight over to Olen, the skirt of her dress brushing over the floor. Ellen placed a hand upon his brow to wake him, and he slowly rose and followed her out of the door. Calliope remained still for a moment, unsure of what she should now do. Then quickly she wriggled out of her bed and rushed to the door, pulling it ajar. It was still raining heavily, distorting the grey and black silhouettes of the trees and undergrowth. Peering through the gloom, Calliope could make out two figurers heading further into the forest, then they were gone. Stepping out into the rain with the intention of following Ellen, Calliope was drawn to the treetops. Like stars coming out one by one at night, came a thousand eyes, yellow and sinister, and all glaring down at Calliope. Fear consumed her and she fled back into the house where she returned to her bed, closing her eyes. There she lay, cold, wet, and frightened, until the early hours when Ellen returned.

There was no sign of Olen, nor any clue as to his fate. Calliope watched as Ellen poured herself some water into which she mixed in a phial of blood before drinking. Then she went over to the cupboard close to her bed and placed in more blood-filled phials. Looking back over her shoulder, Ellen glanced straight toward Calliope. A frozen fear gripped Calliope, and she quickly closed her eyes. She feared that Ellen had seen her, and that she would cast some spell upon her. The door to the cupboard was gently shut, the knock sounding ominous in the dark. Footsteps followed by the ruffling of blankets and the creaking of wood. Then all was silent.

Calliope waited, laying still with her eyes shut. After what seemed an eternity, her courage grew strong enough for her to open her eyes. Ellen was laying still in her bed, softly snoring. She had to do something, or else be trapped forever more. Quietly wriggling out of her bed, she tiptoed over to the cupboard in the hope of finding something in which might aid them. As Calliope pulled open the door, she instantly recognised a few of the ingredients being kept in glass jars. There were three shelves, all crammed with glass jars and phials. As quickly and quietly as she could, Calliope rummaged through until she found a jar filled with a black liquid. Calliope pulled out the cork wedged in at the jar's neck and sniffed. Nightshade. One small drop of Nightshade was enough to send a person into a deep slumber for many days. Calliope, with a plan quickly formed, crept over to Ellen's bedside. She held her breath as she stretched her arm over Ellen's head, tipping a drop of the Nightshade into her partially open mouth. Calliope, being familiar with the liquid, knew she had dropped more than enough to have knocked out an entire town. But there was no reaction and she wondered if it had worked.

Ellen's eyes suddenly shot open, wide, and wild, she grabbed Calliope by the throat and began to softly sing. Calliope felt as though she were fading, her limbs weakening. In her hand, she still clutched the jar of Nightshade, and in an act of desperation she swung it up at Ellen's head. It shattered and the liquid seeped down Ellen's face, her grip on Calliope loosened and then let go.

"You…" Ellen cried out with pain, "You!"

"I'm sorry," Calliope cried, never intending to cause such a reaction. She turned to the table where there was a jar of water. Picking it up, Calliope turned and tossed it over Ellen, hoping that the water would wash away the Nightshade. But it made matters worse. Now Ellen's skin began to melt, like cheese bubbles and softens to the flame, and she fell back on the bed and fell silent. Calliope, exhausted and cast under a sleeping spell of song, fell to the floor, and slept.

The day after, Telamon was the first to wake. The first thing he noticed was the smell, a pungent and putrid smell that clung to the back of the throat. His stomach was uneasy, and his joints ached. "Calliope," he said as he slowly rose from his bed. It was then that he noticed Calliope lying on her side facing the door. "Calliope," he said again, rushing over and kneeling beside her.

The others began to stir, and like Telamon they were drawn to the foul smell.

"Where is Olen?" Aristides unsteadily walked over to the door, ignoring Telamon and Calliope. "That smell is…" he quickly opened the door and rushed out, vomiting.

Calliope then came around and revealed all that had happened, that they had been placed under a spell and her fight with Ellen. Together they inspected the body of Ellen and found that it had much changed. Gone was the young attractive woman in place of an old hag wearing a threadbare grey robe many years old. Her face was distorted, the skin completely gone in place to reveal bone, and around her neck was an amulet, a black stone set in a golden necklace.

"The Enchantress," Solon declared, "she was the Enchantress all along."

Aristides quickly took off the amulet and declared that he would safeguard it. Having no energy to argue otherwise, they all agreed. For the remainder of that day they did little other than rest. The body of the Enchantress they simply covered over with blankets, for none dared to touch her in fear of some curse. Once they had regained some strength, they searched the house for food, finding a hatch in the floor that led to a filled larder. From this storeroom they took the salted meats and dried fruits, and for three days they rested, making a brief search for Olen, before setting off for their second task.

IV

A Tail Feather from a Roc

For ten days did they walk northeast, seeking the end to the forest. Now their heads were clear, free from the spells of the Enchantress, and they were able to think more decisively. At regular stops, Calliope would climb a tree and peer above the treetops, making a note on the sun's position. From this information they were able to keep to their desired direction. The nights were cold and still filled with strange sounds; and like the nights before they entered the Enchantress' dwelling, came the owl, its black eyes fixed upon them.

By the end of the eleventh day, the density of the trees lessened, and the sunlight ahead of them grew brighter. They strode clear of the forest, tired and yet with renewed energy at leaving such a place, the bright sun dazzling their sensitive eyes. Aristides called a halt to determine their position on the map, believing that they had strayed too far to the north. To their left the forest swept around to the north, around into unknown realms. In front of them, at a distance, were grassy hills dotted with buttercups. To the west of these hills ran the wide and fast flowing river called the Asopus. Nestled between the hills and river was the town of Carpis, a place where Aristides hoped to find aid before traveling further north to the Mountains of Roc.

By the end of the day after, they came to the outskirts of Carpis. There they were greeted by three elves, short of stature and dressed in clothes fashioned from leaves. So alike were they, that it was almost impossible to tell one from the other.

"What brings you to our realm?" The elf that had spoken was older looking than the other two, his hair greying and his face wrinkled.

Aristides stepped forward and answered, "We are merely passing on our journey to the Mountains of Roc, and we humbly ask for your hospitality."

The elves formed a huddle and whispered amongst themselves for a moment. "I cannot grant you hospitality myself, but I can speak with the Elder on your behalf. Only he may grant what you seek."

So, on the edges of the town were the pupils made to wait. As they waited, the Elder called an emergency assembly of the elves, who gathered around a giant mushroom. As was the custom, the Elder addressed them from atop of this mushroom. For a full afternoon did they debate the arrival of the pupils, until they finally agreed that they should be given their hospitality. The pupils were led to a hall large enough for them to fit, and there they layout their bedrolls and were given a salad, fish, and bread as a meal.

The hall, like the homes, were burrowed into the earth. But to think of them as being dark and damp would be wrong. For inside was warm and comfortable. The floor was of polished wood like the walls, only they were carved to look as though there were columns of giant mushrooms holding up the roof, which was domes glass that gave the hall light. Between the wood and outer soil were stones which gave enough heat to keep the room warm, but not get hot enough to cause a fire. In the height of summer these same stones could become cool, chilling the hall. How the elves controlled the temperature of the stones is lost to us; but it was suspected that magic was involved.

Once the pupils had finished their meal, the Elder came in, flanked by two other elves. The Elder at the time of the pupils' arrival was an elf named Abydos. Like all the other elves, he wore clothes fashioned out of leaves, and small boots made from tree bark. He wore no gold or finery, nor any distinguishing mark of his rank. The only difference between the Elder and the other elves was that he had a beard, long and grey to reflect his wisdom.

"Now that you have settled," the Elder said with a courteous bow, "I hope that you might give light to how it is you came to our humble town."

Aristides rose from his bedroll and bowed. "I am Aristides, the leader of our small company," he then pointed to each of his company in turn, "this is Dardanus, my second. Solon the learned. Calliope and Telamon. We lost one of our number in the forest, Olen, a man with shared heritage with elves."

"Then truly he is lost," the Elder replied, "for that forest is haunted by the Enchantress."

"Fear no more of this Enchantress," Aristides said with a hint of arrogance. "For she is no more."

Intrigued, the Elder sat upon a stool, silent and keenly listening as Aristides revealed all. He spoke that they were students of the school of Phrontis, competing in the Trial, and of their ensnaring by the Enchantress. The news of the Enchantress' demise was pleasing to the Elder's pointed ears, for the Elves had once inhabited that forest and had been forced to flee in fear of her cruelty. Long had they desired to return to their homeland, and in a triumph of joy he leapt up off the stool and began dancing, the two other elves with him joining in.

"What a gift you have given," the elder beamed with happiness. "The thanks of my people you have, and I now gift you with the title of Friend. You may remain with us for as long as you choose, from our stores we shall feed and aid you in any way we are able." Unable to contain his joy, the Elder danced his way out of the hall, announcing to all that their homeland had been freed.

So, over the next few days, the pupils rested and took the time to better understand their hosts. The Elves of Carpis were different to any other elf that they had come across. Their skin was of a darker tone due to them not living under the shade of the forest, and their demeaner was less mischievous than most other elves. Indeed, many would be forgiven for thinking them Imps. But there were similarities also, for the Elves of Carpis had a fondness for the forest and things that grew out of the earth. They firmly believed that all elves were equal, and that no one elf should have more than his neighbour. All worked for the betterment of the community, and all crops harvested were equally shared out so that none went hungry. All were expected to take a turn at being the Elder, serving for a year at most. The way the Elder was elected was odd to outsiders, for they were not chosen by vote casting as is seen elsewhere. Instead, all over the age of thirty would pick a pebble from a sack, and the elf to pick the black stone would serve as the Elder for the next year. In this time, it was forbidden for the Elder to shave, or continue working as he had done before. The Elder's role was not to act like a king or chief, but as an overseer who ensured all had equal share. Once their term was served, they would be put to trial by the elves to ensure that their every action as Elder had been fair, and for the betterment of the community. Despite the work it took to maintain themselves, all were happy and prosperous. Their numbers had once been great, filling large parts of the Enchanted Forest. But since their exile, the populous had lessened to the extent of less than five hundred. Like other elves of the world, they were solemn when it came to religious matters. They gave thanks to the river spirits of the Asopus which nourished them with fresh fish and water. Each night all would gather on the riverbank and sing to appease the spirits. As a mark of respect, it was forbidden to wash in the river, nor was it allowed for any beast to drink from it.

For a week did the pupils regather their strength before Aristides said that it was time they continued with the Trial. All would have happily stayed in Carpis for the remainder of their days, and they were slow in gathering supplies.

The night before they departed, the pupils took a last meal with the Elder, whom they questioned about the Mountains of Roc. The Elder admitted that he had never stepped foot in that region and had only seen it from afar. But what he did know was that a mighty race of birds nested there, birds far bigger than all others and unwelcoming of outsiders. The elder pled with them not to tread that passage, but Aristides said that they needed to fetch a tail feather as an item of the Trial, and that he intended to push on come the morning. The Elder aided them as much as he could, gifting them five sleek boats, on the promise that they would return and tell all about their adventure in the mountains. Aristides agreed to return, knowing that they could resupply at Carpis before traveling further south.

The morning after, the boats were packed with supplies enough for a month, and the pupils said their farewells. From the riverbank the elves watched and waved them off, a few singing a soft song of friendship. Rooted to the bank did the Elder remain, tears falling down his reddened cheeks, until the pupils had faded from sight. That night he ordered a lament given, a woe to those that sought peril in the mountains, and the elves cried out in fear of the pupils never returning.

The River Asopus began in the Mountains of Roc, gathering in volume as it wound its way south. Fast and wide was the water, plunging deep down to unknown depths. Upon the eastern bank was another forest, far more foreboding than the Enchanted Forest. The leaves here were golden brown all year long, and it was known as the Undying Forest, a place the elves dared not to tread. Any normal boat would have struggled against the strong current of the Asopus, but the elves of Carpis had long mastered the art of boatbuilding. Though each boat was heavily laden, they rose high upon the surface, elegantly gliding as though they were on ice. As a result, the miles passed by with ease, and by the end of the second day they reached a fork where a smaller, unnamed river joined with the Asopus from the hills north of Carpis. Here they put in and rested for the night, and they discovered the ruins of an ancient temple.

The ruins were massive, far bigger than anything any of them had seen before. There was little left to gaze upon other than stone foundations with the odd bit of wall poking up through overgrown grass. But there was one feature that captivated Solon, a stone column that had long ago broken in half. Even though it was but half the size that it had once been, it stood tall, and it was hewn with straight letter runes, the runes of the Gigantes. Solon spent most of the night examining this column, and by morning he had reached a conclusion. It was a way marker built by giants that had probably left because of the great flood said to have devastated the area about a thousand years ago.

After making a note of the ruin's whereabouts on their map, the pupils took back to their boats and continued upriver. For days they journeyed on, the Undying Forest to their right and hillocks to their left. Gradually the hills and forest ended, and tall grey mountains grew ever larger on the northern horizon. The river began to narrow and the grassy ground on either bank became stony. The water shallowed and its flow lessened, the riverbed becoming more visible with each passing mile. Fearing that they would damage their boats, Aristides ordered that they should pull in and make camp. The mountains now dominated their view to the north, and the land before it was stony and grey with an odd tuff of yellowing grass. There was little shelter from the cold breeze as the land before the mountains was flat and featureless, and they all huddled around the fire as they debated their next move.

"I think that Telamon should remain with the boats." Aristides poked at the fire, sending glowing embers into the air.

"We'll have to leave some of the supplies," Dardanus added, "we won't be able to carry it all."

"Why don't you remain with the boats?" Calliope said, her anger rising. "Or is it you mean to leave Telamon here so that he finds a cruel death?"

Aristides smiled as he added a few sticks to the fire. "That is not my intention."

Telamon sat silent, feeling awkward. A part of him wanted to argue with Aristides that they would be better staying together. But another part was scared to climb into the mountains and wanted to stay with the boats, but not alone.

"My intention," Aristides went on, "is to safeguard our supplies."

"I think you mean for Telamon to find a cruel end," Calliope accused. "That you intend to be rid of us all once you have the five items of the Trial!"

Aristides' face flashed with anger, yet he remained calm. "Your callous suspicions are the only thing causing division." He paused and pointed up at the mountains. "It will be a long and difficult climb, dangerous enough on its own. And nesting there are giant birds with a dislike of men. If we should find ourselves in difficulty, we shall need a person to aid us. Adding to all that, it would be folly to leave our boats and supplies unattended, at the mercy of whatever evil dwells these plains." He then pointed across the fire at Telamon, his finger jabbing the air. "Telamon is the weakest amongst us, and it make sense to leave him in charge of the boats."

"Alone!" Calliope shook her head and shrugged. "In your opinion is Telamon the weakest, for I say that his skill surpasses yours. And as for leaving him, under the pretence of some reserve in case we should become ensnared, I say how would he know that we have become ensnared?"

"We should allocate a time," Dardanus interjected, "say that after a week or so he should come and find us."

"But how would Telamon know where to find us?" Calliope said, pointing out the obvious. "And would the threat to our supplies no longer exist?"

Long into that night did the pupils argue, until the need for sleep grew beyond measure. The next morning, they awoke refreshed and with more clear heads for thinking. As they ate a breakfast of porridge made from their hard biscuits, they decided to split into two groups and carry as much of their supplies as they could. Aristides and Dardanus would be one group, Calliope and Telamon the other. Solon was given the choice, and he choose to go with Aristides. After they had finished their breakfast, they began filling their packs with as much as they could fit in. What was left, they stowed in the boats.

With an agreement made that they should head back to the boats in four days' time, successful or not, and there wait a further four before leaving. So, at the foot of the mountains, did the two groups take their leave of each other, each in search of the nests of the Rocs.

The giant birds, known as Rocs, nested high in the mountains, and were seldom seen in the lowlands. They had once been numerous throughout the realm of Perdita, nesting far and wide, even in the lower regions. They came from unknown origins and had shared the ancient world alongside many races. But as the populous of men grew, they hunted the Rocs for meat until they declined in number. So, their hatred of men began, and they began nesting higher into the mountains where men struggled. So reclusive had the Rocs become that now many doubted their existence. But there had been a few reports over the years, reports that told of giant birds, vicious and unfriendly, attacking men as they neared their mountain dwelling. One such tale was of an expedition to map the mountain passages. It had been thirty years before when a company of ten men set out from Harpagus. They had knowledge of the Rocs but had believed them long extinct. From the ten that set out, only two returned a year later. They spoke of being constantly harassed by Rocs as they had headed further into the mountains, the other eight of their company slain by the talons of these winged terrors. So now none would travel by the way of the Mountains of Roc, for the fear of these winged terrors.

Telamon had expected the mountains to be a dull and cold place, full of razor-sharp rocks that would hinder their climb to the higher regions. But instead, the air was warm and there was a dirt path which offered them a gentle climb. The path was narrow, its soil red and the rocks to either side of it a dark grey. Tufts of dry grass grew wherever it could take hold. As the path took Telamon and Calliope higher, the air became scented by the distinctive smell of feathers.

"It smells like an aviary," Telamon said as he came to a halt.

Calliope stopped and sniffed the air. "It's cooling also."

Telamon felt a cold shudder and turn back to look at the passage they had come. The view behind them was a majestic sight, an inspiration for poets who could better describe its beauty. The land was lush and green with the Asopus flowing like a silver line tracing its way south between the two forests. The hills north of Carpis were visible and the thoughts of that comforting town stirred a longing to return. Telamon then glanced up at the mountain and could see that the path would soon come to nothing and the real climbing would begin.

"You know, my grandfather once saw a Roc," Calliope said, seeing that Telamon looked worried.

"He did?"

"Yes," Calliope smiled. "He had been exploring in the Haunted Hills, trying to determine where the green mist originates there. He claims that it had swooped down and snatched up a hare close to him."

"And you believe him?"

"Of course I believe him!" Calliope replied as though it was sacrilegious to suggest her grandfather a liar.

"Sorry," Telamon replied as he kicked a stone over the edge of the path. "What did it look like?"

"He didn't really know. It swooped down so fast that it just looked like a shadow."

"Then how did he know it was a Roc?"

"He told me that for an hour after it circled high above him, its beady eyes peering through the clouds at him. It landed close by for a moment before taking to the sky again. It was then that my grandfather managed to see enough of it through the mist to determine it was a Roc."

"And it didn't attack him?"

Calliope shook her head and answered, "No."

For a few more hours did they follow the path before the sun disappeared below the horizon to the west. Finding a small grassy patch, they rolled out their beds and took a meal of salted fish and dried fruits that they had taken from the stores at Carpis. That night passed with surprising comfort, and they both awoke refreshed and ready to continue further into the mountains. The path suddenly took a steeper incline, and their progress slowed. Both drank heavily as the day was warm, the sun's rays unhindered by any clouds. By midday they came across a rocky crag that overhung the path. Fresh water pooled here before filtering down into the mountain. Telamon and Calliope each drank deeply from this pool, refilling their empty canteens. There they rested, taking a small meal of dried apricots and nuts. Telamon would have happily remained there until the morning, but Calliope ushered him on.

By mid-afternoon, the path suddenly ended, the red soil giving way to the dark grey rocks of the mountainside. The climbing was tough, and by the time the sun sank, both Telamon and Calliope were exhausted. They both took shelter on a crag barely big enough for them both to sit on. All that night they sat, feet tucked into their chests, cold and cramped. Neither dared to sleep for fear of falling from such a great height. As the sun rose the next morning, they continued their climb, their arms and legs paining from the strain. After a couple of hours, they came to a large crag where they rested and took a small meal. After another short climb, the mountainside levelled out. Here was a spring and a small olive tree, where they rested for the night. Soundly did they sleep until they were awoken by the sound of a bird squawking. Rattled by fear, Telamon and Calliope hid as best they could under the tree. The noise echoed all around them and it was impossible to determine where it was coming from. The night air was stirred up by the beating of unseen wings, and the screeching intensified. For a few horrible minutes did the screeching continue, Telamon and Calliope having to cover their ears before the night suddenly fell silent. Fear kept them alert until the morning when they began to explore further.

The sun was warm and a southernly breeze carried the scent of spring. Telamon and Calliope trudged on, weary and in want of sleep. Their hope was that they might find a loose feather littered somewhere amongst the rocks. But no feather did they find. By mid-morning they came to another incline that rose about one hundred feet. Atop of this crag was a large nest made of young trees easily bent and glued by mud so that it resembled a wattle-and-daub wall.

"A nest," Calliope said with disbelief. All was eerily quiet with no sight nor sound of a Roc. "Let's take a look."

Telamon looked skyward, expecting to see a Roc swoop down upon them. But the sky was calmingly clear.

Calliope began to climb and was the first to reach the summit. The scene that greeted her, filled her with rage. Lying dead in the nest was a baby Roc, its brown feathers matted with drying blood. "What evil did this?" Calliope knelt beside the baby Roc and began examining it to determine the cause of death. There, in its beak was a torn piece of blooded cloth, grey in colour. "Aristides!"

"We don't know that," Telamon said as he knelt beside Calliope.

"Then how do you explain this!" She held up the blooded piece of robe, her hand shaking with anger. Calliope had a great love of animals and had studied their behaviour. So deep was this lore, that she was able to read their behaviour patterns and determine their next move. "That's what the screeching was last night!"

"Then we had better go before its parent returns," Telamon said as he stood, filled with a sudden dread.

"It will be the mother Roc," Calliope explained, "the mothers stay with their offspring until they are fully grown."

"Come on," Telamon turned and stepped over the side of the nest.

"Wait." Calliope picked up two white tail feathers that had fallen from a fully-grown Roc and handed one to Telamon. "Take this."

"Won't Aristides already have one?"

"We cannot trust Aristides," Calliope replied. "I think he means to leave us here at the mercy of the evil he has evoked."

"The boats!" Telamon was filled with the realisation that Aristides would take them all.

"Let's get going." Calliope led the way, and their passage down was hastened by urgency.

With their weariness and hunger now forgotten, they began to climb back down the way they had come. The onset of night forced them to stop, and they each took turns at keeping a watch until the morning. The mountains remained quiet and they began to think that Aristides had killed the mother Roc. After spending another full day climbing down, they found the path that would lead them down to the boats. For another night did they rest before continuing with their final leg back to the boats.

When they arrived back, Aristides was already there, his face mucky and tired. Leaning up against the side of the boat was Solon, his hands clutching at a wound to his stomach.

"What happened?" Telamon asked.

"We know what happened!" Calliope rounded on Aristides, her face red with anger. "You killed the Roc!"

"We did no such thing!" Aristides pointed towards the mountains. "The Roc was dying when we found it! But it still had the strength to attack us!"

"It's true," Dardanus said as he walked up and stood beside Aristides. His appearance was equally as shabby as Aristides', and his face was a show of horror.

A black shadow swept over them, stirring the air into a sudden gust. From the sky swooped down a Roc, a giant bird that was black and raven like in features. The pupils fled and dived out of the way of the Roc's talons. But Solon was too deeply wounded, and he was scooped up at taken back into the mountains, his moans fading as the Roc slowly squeezed the life from him.

"To the boats!" Aristides roared, "Quickly!"

The pupils scrambled into the boats and paddled like they were possessed. The Roc again descended from the mountains, its black talons dripping with blood and its eyes a black fire of hatred. Mightily it screeched as it swooped down and overturned the boat that Dardanus was in. The water was still shallow enough for him to safely wade back to the riverbank where he slid between two rocks for cover. Aristides, seeing his friend in trouble, quickly took off his travel stained cloak and set it alight with his tinder box. He stood in the boat and scooped up the burning cloak with his oar and began waving it above his head. After their ordeal with the baby Roc, they had been attacked by the mother. Solon had told them that the only thing a Roc was believed to fear, was fire.

The Roc on seeing the fire, gave another mighty screech. In horror it turned and fled back to the mountains where it vented its anger upon the poor body of Solon. Dardanus slid out from between the rocks and waded out to Aristides' boat. With all haste they paddled, the river's flow growing stronger and carrying them further to the south. Behind them the Mountains of Roc began to diminish in size, but the pupils dared not stop until they had reached the safety of Carpis.

V

A Golden Apple

Once back at Carpis, the pupils were greeted in a most welcoming manner by the elves. They were led to the hall where they had stayed before and given a meal of fresh fish with a leafy salad. After their meal, they stretched out on the floor and slept. So tired were they, that they slept for two straight days. When they awoke, and were more refreshed, the Elder came to them and asked that they make good on their promise. So, Aristides told all, of the Roc attacking them and of losing Solon, and finished by asking for further aid, saying that they now had to head south, to the place of the Golden Tree. The Elder reaffirmed that they were friends and he would grant them all that they needed. He told them that Carpis had regular trade with the town of Aziris to the south, and that they were welcome to take passage on the next trip. For the next week, the pupils rested, waiting for the preparing of the boats. In this time, a great mistrust lay between the pupils and there was a clear divide. Calliope refused to accept Aristides' version of events and would not speak a single word to him. Dardanus naturally took to Aristides' side and accused Calliope and Telamon of deliberately not coming to their aid when attacked by the Roc. Much of this time did the two factions spend apart, making their own preparations for the next task.

On the morning of the eighth day, the pupils took to the boats. There were two, each wide bottomed and laden with goods. As before, the elves sang them off, promising them a warm welcome should they ever return. So, the long journey downriver began. To either side were the dense forests known as the Enchanted Forest to their right, and the Undying Forest to their left. The Undying Forest was an unpleasant sight. Though it was spring, the leaves were a golden brown as though it were autumn, and the shape of the trees were sinisterly twisted. Upon this bank, the elves would not step foot, nor would their gaze linger upon such a place. To them it was a cursed place filled with spirits and strange orbs of light that vibrated and caused sickness. There dwells only evil, a cold malice of terror and woe.

Steadily the boats sailed, following the river Asopus as it wound its way south. Each day, when the sun reached its height, the light would glisten off the river's surface, making it look like a silver sheet that the boats glided over. At parts, it was wide enough for the boats to sail side-by-side, and so deep were the waters that not a ripple was made from its flow. The days on board were tedious for the pupils and they spent much of their time below deck in their makeshift cabins, trying not to get in the way of the elves as they went about their daily duties. Telamon, however, enjoyed sitting on the top deck, watching as the elves handled the boat. There were oars to power the ship, though they were not needed as the river's flow was strong enough to carry them south. To the back was a rudder which was kept constantly manned both day and night. So familiar with this route were they, that Telamon thought that they could have done it with their eyes closed. On board was no captain to take charge, and each elf knew their duties well enough without the need of being told. Amongst them there was no greed, or jealousy, nor any loafing so that one might have it easier. Like a colony of ants working for the common good were the elves, and Telamon felt ashamed. Like the other pupils, Telamon had urges to win the Trial for his own betterment. Indeed, he now thought the school to be wasteful, for he and his fellow pupils all had their merits and would all be fine additions to the school. But why only one? Was it to promote self-serving greed? Was it just to enhance the prestige of the school? Men were indeed darkening, Telamon thought.

It took a week before the town of Aziris came into sight, and another day before the boats docked on the wooden jetties. There the pupils were greeted by a woman, red haired with pursed lips and suspicious eyes. She was dressed in a long black dress and carried a leather-bound ledger under her arm.

"Greetings lady of Aziris." Aristides said as he bowed. "We come seeking an audience with whom commands this pleasant place."

The woman opened her ledger and took out the pencil that had been resting between the pages as a marker to her place. "Names," she ordered.

"I am Aristides, the leader of our diminished company." He then pointed to each in turn, "This is Dardanus, Calliope and Telamon."

The woman scribbled the names down. "And where is it you have come from?"

"We have just come from Carpis, as you can see," Aristides answered. "But our origins are from the School of Phrontis."

The woman raised an eyebrow as she made her notes. "What business brings you to Aziris?"

"We come with no designed malice if that is what's worrying you," Aristides said, growing impatient.

"And you want an audience with the mothers?"

"We want an audience with the leader of this town," Aristides corrected.

"No one person rules here," the woman replied, "you will do well to remember that. Here we are governed by the Council of Mothers. It is to them I shall report your arrival, and only them that can grant you an audience." The woman placed her pencil down and closed the ledger, tucking it back under her arm. "If you will follow me, I shall escort you to the Holding House."

"The Holding House?"

"Yes," the woman replied. "The Holding House is a place where all unexpected visitors must await the Mothers' blessings to enter the town. It is a comfortable place and you shall be well looked after."

"Prisoners you mean," Aristides said with distrust.

"No," the woman gave answer, "you are free to leave whenever you choose. But you may not enter Aziris or its realm without leave of the Mothers."

There was no choice for the pupils as the next task was within the territory of Aziris. So, they followed the woman to a large boarding house made of red brick with a slate roof and lead framed windows, like the homes of Harpagus. Inside was warm and elegant, the maids that worked there friendly and welcoming. They were taken to a room large enough to accommodate them all. Four beds with feathered mattresses and pillows lined against a wall of panelled dark oak. opposite was a small fire, clean and yet to be lit. The floor was polished wood and covered by red rugs, three of the four walls bare and painted white. The pupils could freely walk the grounds of the Holding House; indeed, the garden was a most pleasant walk in an evening after supper.

Calliope was most intrigued by the people of Aziris. From speaking with the maids, she had learnt that the town was greatly different to any other when it came to governance.

Unlike any other town, Aziris was ruled by women. The ruling body was made up of thirty women who were named Matres. From these thirty women, one was elected to the position of Avia, or grandmother in the ancient tongue. The Avia was appointed for life but could be removed if she abused her powers, and her task was to make final decisions on matters if the council were evenly split. This council met around a round table so that all were equal, and each member carried a golden sceptre with a red ruby attached to the top as a mark of their rank. In meetings, they had to hold their sceptre up if they wished to speak, for it was forbidden to shout and speak over each other, that was the rashness of men. Indeed, it was the men that made up their workforce; and many that had visited the town commented that it was the women which wore the trousers, and the men the dresses. But curious enough to Calliope was that they didn't seem to mind their humble position. Under the rule of the Mothers, they were well-fed and supplied with a home and comforts. Each were given ample coin and were appointed a wife after the age of twenty. The men had no choice of whom they were to marry, nor could they divorce; their duty of marriage was to solely maintain the population. They had no voting rights and were forbidden from holding any office. From the pupils, Calliope was the one whom the maids would talk to most. With the others they were more speaking through duty of their task, but with Calliope they were more freely open about sharing their customs.

For two days the pupils waited, being kept in good comfort and were well-fed, before they were summoned before the Council of Mothers. A black carriage being pulled by four white horses came to a stop outside the Holding House, waiting for them. It was being driven by a woman dressed in black trousers and a crimson tunic with a yellow sash tied around her waist. A maid from the Holding House waited by the carriage door and opened it up for the pupils as they approached. Seated inside was another woman, equally dressed as the driver.

"You are to enter the Matres' Chamber," the woman said as the pupils took a seat in the carriage. "You will answer all questions put before you and answer truthfully." A maid closed the carriage door and the driver cracked her whip over the horses' heads to get them moving.

The town of Aziris was three miles from the Holding House and the jetty, connected by a smooth road where cartloads of goods moved back and forth. To either side of this road was fertile fields where wheat was growing. In summer, these fields would ripen and turn yellow, and to outsiders Aziris was known as the place of golden fields. At the western entrance, the carriage passed under a triumphal arch of white marble. Here a gang of men worked, cleaning dirt from the carved depictions of elegant looking women in classical poses.

"Who are they?" Calliope asked, quite taken by the splendour of the arch.

"They are the sisters of liberty," the woman proudly answered. "It was these women which overthrew the reign of men in Aziris. Before them, we women were but servants chained to the scullery and at the mercy of the rashness of men. It was them that slayed the tyrant rule of kings and ended their dark age of hunger and poverty, them that brought us to light and prosperity."

Calliope gazed out of the carriage window one last time and felt a cold shudder at its marvel. It was a sight that inspired her and encouraged her confidence with the remaining tasks ahead.

As the carriage smoothly went on, it became apparent that the splendour of Aziris did not end at the arch. The streets were clean with oil lamps that would be lit at night, and there were wide spaces with greenery and flowers. There were wooden benches also in these public gardens, where women gathered to chat or sit and contemplate on important matters. Most of the building were of red brick with black beams showing as though the houses bones were on display. The carriage took a turning to the left, towards the northern part of the town. Here were the public buildings, a temple to the Mothers built in stone and painted white that shone brightly in the light of the morning. Opposite the temple was a vast colossal of a woman, her naked image captured perfectly in bronze. The carriage went past, heading straight for a two-storey building ahead of them. The House of the Mothers. In front of this building was a grand fountain of five tiers, each level getting smaller as they rose. Tall arched windows flooded the interior with light, and two women armed with spears guarded the double door entrance.

The carriage came to a stop by the entrance to the building and the driver jumped down from her cab and opened the door. The woman that had been sat inside with the pupils now led them through the double doored entrance and into a hall, where they were given a seat on a long bench with cushions for comfort. The hall was of dark, polished wood fitted with bronze busts of prominent women which lined along the walls.

In this hall they were made to wait for two hours, tediously watching as official looking women came and went. Eventually, a woman dressed in a red robe and wearing a white mask which covered her entire face, came and led them through a door and up a set of oak stairs. At the top of these stairs was another hall, though smaller than the one they had come from, but no less decorated. The masked woman knocked on a door with the tip of the staff she carried, and the door was open from the inside.

The room that the pupils had been led to, was the council chamber. It was a huge chamber with bronze statues of the same women that had been on the arch. The floor was a black granite, and the walls clad over with marble, the ceiling tall and flat, depicting the image of the day the sisters overthrew the last king of Aziris. Around a circular table sat thirty women, all wearing silver robes and holding a golden sceptre with a red ruby attached to the top. On a raised platform of red carpet was a golden throne that had once belonged to the last king. There was sat the Avia, wearing a golden robe and carrying a sceptre the same as the others.

"We bid you welcome to our town," the Avia said with an authoritative tone. "How do you find it?"

Calliope bowed and took a step forward, answering, "Like a breath of fresh air."

"Good," the Avia smiled. She was older than any other on the council, about fifty years of age, and was considered the shrewdest. "Out of friendship has this council granted you an audience, for we have had dealings with the Peritum of Phrontis on a few matters. But enlighten us now as to your coming."

Aristides then stepped forward and said, "We are participants of Phrontis' famed Trial. Two of our five tasks we have completed, but the third lies within your realm. So, we therefore ask your leave to pass unhindered."

"You speak as though authority is your own," the Avia responded with a hint of distaste. "Tell me whom you are."

"I am Aristides, the leader of our company." He then pointed to each of his company in turn. "This is Dardanus, my second. Calliope and Telamon."

"First," the Avia rose from her chair, her voice taking a stern tone, "If you want leave to pass through our realm, you must surrender your leadership to the woman amongst your company. For no man may ever take leadership within our boarders."

Aristides didn't like the thought of having to be led by Calliope, but if they wanted to complete their next task there was little other choice. "We are but guests in your realm, and we shall honour your laws."

"Good," the Avia replied with an approving nod of her head. "Now what is this task you must complete in our realm?"

"Aristides opened his mouth to speak, but Calliope stepped in front of him and answered, "We must take an apple from the Golden Tree."

A wave of shock shrilled around the table, the Matres' eyes wide with horror, their faces showing their concern. But despite their shock and uncertainty, none spoke aloud and remained seated in a calm manner, though all held up their sceptre wishing to speak.

The Avia held her sceptre horizontally, a sign for the Matres to lower theirs. "You wish to take an apple from the Golden Tree?"

"It is one of our five tasks of the Trial," Calliope answered. "We would be thankful for whatever aid you are willing to give us."

"No," the Avia said with a soft shake of her head. "I cannot send you to certain death."

"Please," Calliope begged. "We have already overcome great dangers on our journey here, to fail here where I now lead would be a shame to all women."

Now that the Avia had put Calliope in charge, she had cast a light upon all women. For if the Trial should fail here, Calliope would be blamed, and the thought of men ridiculing women's leadership stirred anger within her. But the thought of sending them to certain death also lay heavy with woe upon her.

"Please aid us," Calliope said, seeing that the Avia was divided upon the matter.

"Do you know what danger lays ahead of you?"

Calliope shook her head and answered, "No, for the member of our company that could have told us was taken by a Roc."

"Then I shall tell you, in hope of swaying your mind to turn back. The name Golden Tree has often misled those with lesser knowledge of our realm, greedily they believe that the tree is of solid gold. But any of a deeper understanding of our lore will know that it is not the tree that is gold, but the apples which grow from its branches.

"The tree had grown from the seed of an apple gifted to a woman named Mylasa. The ancient tale says that the Star God Bellus, who was considered the most handsome of all the Gods, was charged with gifting a golden apple to the most beautiful mortal woman in all the world. So, Bellus descended from the starry heavens and took the form of a crippled man bent from age. For a year did he wonder from place to place, begging for a copper coin. Most payed no heed to him, and simply passed him by without a thought or sorrow for him. Bellus then came to Aziris, which was then ruled by wicked men who made all women wear face coverings whenever walking in public. But these face coverings were no obstacle to Bellus' task, for he was a God and could see within one's heart. One woman, married to a wealthy man who was an aide to the king, made a public show of charity by donating five silver coins to Bellus. He looked into her heart and saw that her gift was not out of sorrow for him, but to aggrandize her husband's name. This woman Bellus detested, and he refused her gift. Many women came and went, but none were worthy of the golden apple. Bellus was about to give up his task and return to the heavens where he would proclaim all mortals ugly, when he was approached by another. This woman was shabbily dressed, her face covering threadbare and torn to reveal her left eye and pale cheek. She stopped upon sight of Bellus, pity and sorrow filling her heart, and there gave him a single copper coin, the only money she had.

"Bellus now chose her and revealed his true form and beauty. Mylasa fell to her knees and put her face to the ground, and it was Bellus' silver hands that stood her back up. To Mylasa he gifted the golden apple, saying that it was for her alone and no other. News of this gift soon spread and many flocked to Mylasa's home to glimpse this godly gift. Many of the wealthy men, the king included, offered great wealth for the apple; but Mylasa would not yield to this great temptation. The golden apple became a bane for Mylasa, having to keep it under careful watch from thieves and suppressing the temptation of the great riches offered for it. So distraught did she become that she cursed Bellus for gifting her with the golden apple, and she took it many leagues to the southeast where there was a flat hilltop that rose from the land around it. There she buried the apple, hoping nobody would ever find it. Overnight, a mighty tree sprang up through the soil, and over time golden apples grew from its branches. Mylasa then disappears from the pages of history, but the tree remained, and news of golden fruit growing from a tree soon spread. But Bellus would not have any who were not chosen by him to take from the tree. The property of the tree belonged to Mylasa and her bloodline, and no other was to take from it. To protect the tree for the rightful heirs, Bellus conjured a great worm, a snake with fangs of venom to guard it.

"Many over the passing of years have tried to pluck a single apple from its branches, but none have ever returned. Those that pass to the southern realms will not stray too close, for fear of the great worm is deep, and its hissing has been heard many leagues from the tree. None should go there, none but the rightful heirs of Mylasa."

"I thank you for your lore and the warnings of the danger that dwells there, but we must continue or else be shamed by failure."

"Your heart is strong Calliope, yet I fear it blinds you to better judgement. To succeed or to fail in this Trial is irrelevant. For the skills you have learnt shall never leave you. Calliope do not become clouded with desires and aspirations of what the world of men expects from you. You have strength enough to forge your own path and truly become all that you want to become."

Calliope's face reddened, feeling unsure of what to say. "Help us," she answered after a moment. "As a woman seeking aid, help us."

"What say you my ladies of the council?" There was a moment's silence in the chamber as the Matres collected their thoughts. Then one by one they rose their sceptres to show in favour of Calliope's plea. "Then it is decided," the Avia said as she stood. "You may enter our realm and tread wherever you please. Our hospitality you shall have, both bed and board. From our stores you shall have what you need to see you to the Golden Tree and back."

"You have our thanks," Calliope bowed.

After the audience with the Council of Mothers, the pupils were led to a two-storey house close to the House of the Mothers. It was a well looked after house, clean and comfortable, with carpeted floors and walls painted with rich colours. There was four bedrooms in all each distinguishable by its own colour. Calliope was given the finest room, known as the red room. Aristides was given the blue, Dardanus the yellow and Telamon the green. Six servants, all men dressed in brown tunics and trousers, tended on them, and upheld the house to a clean standard. For a week did the pupils enjoy these comforts, eating fine foods and drinking a fruity wine that contented their nerves. They had been given a map of the realm of Aziris which they would place on the table after their evening meal, plotting a course on which to take. In accordance with the map, they plotted a route which would take them from home to home, steadily to the southeast where the Golden Tree grew. In agreement with the route, they then began collecting supplies. Each was given a new cloak, red in colour, which was fastened by a silver medallion the bore the image of two women embracing each other. These cloaks entitled the wearer to the protection of the Mothers, and all citizens of Aziris were dutybound to aid them.

So, with all ready, the pupils began their journey. They took the south road which passed through another triumphal arch, like the one which they had passed through when they first entered Aziris. This road was smooth, slightly raised in the centre so that rainwater ran to the sides where there were drainage ditches to carry it off. That day, the weather was overcast, and they made good time and had travelled further than they thought they would. They came to a single storey farmstead surrounded by pastures where cattle grazed. The home was built from planked wood with a porch where an elderly woman was sat in a rocking chair.

"Friends of the Mothers I see," the old woman said as she shakily stood from her chair. "I expect that you wish to spend the night here."

"If you are agreeable," Calliope replied as they came to a stop before the porch.

"You wear the cloaks of the Mothers, and I shall grant you leave to sleep in the barn."

That night they slept amidst the cattle and were awoken the next morning by the old woman who gave them hot tea to drink and toasted bread smothered in fresh butter. After their breakfast, they parted company with the old woman and continued with their journey. The next five days were much the same, following the road south and enjoying the hospitality of the homes along the way. But on the dawning of the sixth day, a cold drizzle dampened their spirits and they passed the last house. They turned off the road and made their way across the vast grasslands, where in places the grass was waist high. This tallgrass wetted them more and slowed their progress, and by mid-afternoon the rain turned heavy and the wind whipped up to bend the grass almost flat. They came to a small hillock where they found a little cover in a grove. It took hours before they could get a fire going and night had drawn in. A little of the rain found its way through the treetops, but it was the wind which whistled through the grove which kept them awake most of that night. By morning all were groggy and cold, but through the trees shone a bright sunshine. They ate a breakfast of cold meats before they continued, and for an hour they lay out their bedrolls in the sun to dry them.

Clearly now, the hilltop of the Golden Tree was visible, and by the next day they would reach its foothill. Onwards they went, the hill ahead of them slowly rising and looking evermore foreboding. As they expected they came to the foot of the hill the day after, where they made a camp and rested, ever listening for a hissing. Here the air seemed still and was scented by an intensely musky smell. No wild creature was seen upon these slopes, not even the tiniest of ants. The night was spent in caution, speaking quietly and constantly watching the slopes in fear of the great worm.

Their hope was that their presence would go unnoticed, and that they could somehow steal an apple and begone again as quick as a flash of lightning. But as they walked the slopes, they were hindered by its steepness. From below they had looked gentle, but the grass had covered the true incline and in parts the pupils were on all fours as they climbed. At the top, the grass waned and yielded to patches of mud and stones. In the centre was a mighty apple tree, its roots ancient and deep, and its branches stretching wide with lush greenery. Hanging from the branches were many golden apples, each worth the income of an entire nation. The sun shone from the eastern sky, catching the tree's form in all its glory. So majestic was this sight, that the pupils were awestruck and for a moment could not move.

"We're all going to be rich," Dardanus said, his mouth wide open and his eyes fixated upon the golden apples. He ran over to the roots of the tree where he bent down and started picking the fallen apples. Greed blinded his better judgement and distracted his mind from the danger that guards the tree.

"Dardanus wait!" Calliope yelled. But it was too late.

The ground vibrated and the soil cracked as the great worm rose from beneath. Its scales were thick and both green and brown in colour, its forked, black tongue hissed, and its yellow eyes fixed upon Dardanus. The creature moved with surprising speed for its great size, and in the time it took for Dardanus to notice the peril he was in, it was too late. The giant snake coiled around Dardanus' body, its thick scales resilient to the strikes of his fists. Slowly the great worm crushed Dardanus' bones, squeezing until his face turned blue and then purple, and his eyes bulged from his head. But worse was yet to come for Dardanus, who was at this point still clinging to life. The giant worm opened its mouth, showing its venomous fangs as it lifted Dardanus and began swallowing him whole. Where he would slowly be broken down by acid over a slow course of days.

This grotesque sight instilled fear into the pupils, and they fled with no thought of trying to save Dardanus. The great worm ignored them and devoured its meal. Telamon lost his footing and went crashing down, hitting into Calliope and sending her crashing down. They rolled all the way to the bottom where they came to an abrupt stop. They returned to their camp where they fell to their beds, exhausted. Aristides was heartbroken for the loss of his friend, and he spoke little and ate even less. For the remainder of that day they did nothing, grief clouding their minds and rendering them useless. That night passed without incidence, though sleep was difficult as they feared that the giant snake would slither down the hill for them.

By morning their minds had come to terms with the previous day's events, though Aristides' grief was no less raw. Angrily he blamed Calliope for the loss of Dardanus, saying that she must know of some lore that could tame the creature. Calliope replied that she was no less guilty than any one of them, for all had stood terrified and frozen. It took an hour more of argument before the tempers of Aristides and Calliope calmed. After taking a breakfast of dried fruits baked into oat biscuits, and drinking warm tea, they began to speak of what they could do to obtain an apple.

"Maybe we could just run, snatch one up and be away again before the creature could sense us," Aristides suggested, himself knowing that it sounded foolish.

"You saw how fast it moved," Calliope replied, "it would catch us before we had chance to turn and flee."

Telamon sat silent, rummaging through his thoughts in search of an answer. Then it came to him. "My grandfather- "

"Your grandfather what?" Aristides interrupted.

"Quiet," Calliope hushed, "go on Telamon."

"My grandfather once travelled with the nomads that wonder in the western deserts. I remember him telling me of how they made snakes dance to music."

"What is the point in this?" Aristides scoffed. "I don't see your point."

"My point," Telamon replied, "is that they were able to control the snakes, and that we may be able to control this great worm."

"We don't have any musical instruments," Calliope said with a shake of her head.

"No," Telamon conceded, "but we have your fine singing voice."

"You want me to sing to the great worm?" Calliope's face whitened at the thought, and she stood, shaking her head. "It won't work."

"My grandfather also spoke of women singing to control the snakes," Telamon replied. "It's our only chance."

Calliope thought deeply on the matter and during her studies of animal she had heard of snakes being controlled in such a way. "Alright," she conceded. "But we'll have to do it my way."

After discussing a plan of action, they climbed to the top of the hill. It was midday by the time they reached the flat summit, and the sun was high and strong. There was no sign of the great worm, even the soil where it had ascended from below the day before was smooth and looked undisturbed. The air was stiflingly musky, a clue to the great worm's presence close by.

"Sing," Telamon said in a low tone.

Calliope began singing a song of sadness; and so fine was her voice that both Aristides and Telamon felt suddenly cold. As Calliope sang, she walked slowly towards the tree, her eyes darting left and then right in search of the great worm. Aristides and Telamon lay upon the slope, their head peering over the brow. Beside them was a small pile of stones that they planned to throw at the worm to cause a distraction should things go badly. But so far, the great worm remained hidden.

As Calliope neared the tree, the ground broke up and out slithered the great worm. Its yellow eyes fixed on Calliope, but it moved slowly and without malice. For a moment nothing happened, and both Calliope and the great worm remained staring at each other. Calliope continued singing in a lower tone, her hands shaking with fear, and the great worm's head began to gently sway from side-to-side.

"It's working," Aristides whispered to Telamon, "look."

Telamon had been watching, his stomach swelling with unease for Calliope. Fearing that all was going to well, he picked up a stone from the pile and rose to his knees in preparation.

Calliope continued her song, and the great worm's eyes began to get heavy. Calliope now filled with confidence at the sight, and she carefully stretched out her hand and began stroking its thick scales. They were deathly cold to touch, yet smooth and somewhat satisfying to feel. Calliope could sense the great worm's satisfaction as its head rested upon the ground, its yellow eyes closing. Calliope carried on singing as she steadily bent down and plucked up a golden apple. The moment her hand touched it; the great worm rose to the tree's defence. It hissed and showed its fangs, readying to strike.

Now Telamon and Aristides sprang forwards, throwing stones as hard as they could. The stones that hit caused no damage and merely bounced off the great worm's scales. But they caused a blind anger within the creature and it sprang after them. Both Aristides and Telamon threw themselves down the hill in a blind panic, crashing and rolling their way to the bottom. The great worm instantly turned back to the tree to devour Calliope. But Calliope had wasted no time in making her escape and had taken flight as soon as the great worm had slithered after the others. Unwilling to leave the tree, the great worm hissed in fury and circled around the brow of the hill in hope of the thieves return.

But the pupils had what they had come for, and they regrouped at their camp, where they packed up their things with haste and speedily headed back northwest. For the remainder of that day did they hear the sharp hissing of the great worm, a sound which drove them on. They did not stop that day until it became too dark to see, and so reluctantly they rolled out their beds and slept.

When they awoke, it was mid-morning the next day. They broke their fasts on a hearty meal of salted meats, biscuits, and fruit. They each drank heavily from their canteens, emptying them, before rolling up their bed and strapping then back on top of their packs.

"Give me the apple," Aristides demanded, his hand outstretched. "I will keep hold of it."

Calliope shook her head and replied, "No, for I do not trust you. I believe that you will simply abscond once you have all the items of the task."

"I'm the leader of this company!"

"Not here you're not," Calliope reminded Aristides. "A vote decided the fate of the first two items into your possession, and now a vote shall determine the fate of the golden apple."

Aristides scrunched his face in anger, knowing that the vote would go against him as all his supporters had now perished. "Very well, have it your way!"

The journey back was awkward and full of mistrust. Like before, they went from home to home enjoying the hospitality of the people of Aziris. There tale of their adventure for the golden apple was met with rejoice and they were offered many fine things for it. But Calliope refused all and kept the apple hidden. It took three weeks before they returned to the town of Aziris, where they were immediately summoned before the Council of Mothers.

Here Calliope retold all their journey, the highs, and lows as they had successfully completed their task. The golden apple she held for all the council to see, and to no other would she show it.

The pupils were applauded by the council, and Calliope was given the title of Honourable Sister for her leadership on this quest, alongside the gift of a splendid house and leave to take up residence there. For Aristides and Telamon they gifted only warm words, and that they would be welcomed should they ever choose to revisit their town.

For a few weeks after the pupils remained in Aziris, resting, and enjoying the lengthening days of summer. Happily, they all would have stayed, but the need arose for them to ready themselves, for there was still two more tasks yet to complete. So, they once more went before the Council of Mothers and asked for passage south on one of their boats. This the council freely gave, along with stores; and the next day the pupils took their leave of the fair town of Aziris.

VI

Water from the Spring of Youth

The journey south was a pleasant one, and their boat was grand and full of comforts. The hull was blue with a carved figurehead of a fish attached to the bow. It was a wide and long vessel with two decks. The top deck was fitted with red and purple cushions to cover most of the floor, the walls and ceiling carpeted. The captain was a woman named Belia, who oversaw a crew of five women officers, twenty women marines and forty men who rowed the boat.

The days were now long and warm, the sunlight glistening off the river Asopus as it flowed south. To either side stretched lush pastures where wild game ruled. The day after leaving Aziris, the river bent to the west where it flowed for three days before bending back south for a day, then turning back west again for another four days before finally bending back south. Here the lush grasslands became patchy with rocks and dirt, and small hillocks began to form. To the southwest there was a mountain range, grey and bleak against the near perfect sky, and at the foot of these mountains was a forest of redwood trees.

The boat continued for three more days before it put in alongside the west bank of the Asopus. The captain lowered a plank and the pupils disembarked. Beside the river they made their camp for the night, consulting with their map as to where they would find the town of Mitra.

As a new day dawned, the pupils headed directly west, towards the Grey Mountains. Just after midday, they came to the outskirts of Mitra where they were roughly stopped by four grubby men garbed in animal skins. They were short and squared in physique, with flat noses and high foreheads. Their ears were pierced with small bones and their skin was covered in thin, dark hair. Even the women were of this odd appearance, and had it not been for the men having long beards, it would be almost impossible to tell them apart.

The town itself was a mucky place, the air polluted from the furnaces which melted down iron ore which the people smelted into ingots and stored in a wooden warehouse. All the buildings were made from wood which was kept together by iron nails. Outside of each of the homes were iron rods, twisted into elegant sculptures that resembled thorn bushes. Here the people lived short lives, due mainly to their mining in the mountains for iron and copper, and they could not expect to live past forty. Their diet was mainly meat which came from deer and bores which they hunted in the forest.

The pupils were shoved into a small hovel where they were locked in. It was a rundown, drag place, damp and bare of any comforts. The floor was bare earth with wet patches that smelt like urine. From outside, children peered in through the cracks of the wall, giggling at their frail appearance.

"What should we do?" Telamon asked, looking to both Calliope and Aristides for an answer. But before either could answer, the door opened, and four men armed with iron tipped spears ushered them back out.

From the hovel they were taken past a large wooden structure covered over in wrought iron shaped into interconnecting spirals. There were many people gathered here, their wide eyes watching the frail looking men as they were shoved towards a large roundhouse which was their leaders hut. Inside, there was a fire in the centre, its flames lighting and warming the interior. The floor was raised from the earth by wood and covered in the skins of deer. There were no chairs, nor anything of value, and the pupils were shoved to the floor. After a short wait, three more men entered and sat around the fire.

"Who are you?" The man that had spoken wore a crown of antlers, the only feature to distinguish him from the others.

"We are students of the school of Phrontis," Aristides replied, "and we come with no evil thoughts towards you."

"Then why have you come?"

"We are participating in our famed Trial, and we are merely passing on our way to the Grey Mountains."

The news of their wanting to take the passage in the Grey Mountains worried the leader, and he shook his head so violently that his crown fell off his head.

"What evil possesses you to take such a path?" He picked up his crown and placed it back upon his head.

"We are tasked with taking water from the Spring of Youth," Calliope replied.

The leader's jaw almost dropped to the floor with astonishment, and he immediately began whispering with his colleagues.

"We ask for your hospitality and leave to pass through your domain," Aristides said, trying to take charge of proceedings.

"You ask much," the leader replied in an uncompromising tone. "You come here uninvited and unfriended by any in Mitra, and you presume to ask for our aid? Tell me how Mitra should benefit from aiding you so."

"You speak as though we have offered you trouble, or that we have demanded unreasonable gifts." Aristides' anger was now starting to rise, for he did not understand the problem.

The people of Mitra were a reclusive people, mistrusting of all outsiders and superstitious. Few visitors had ever visited the town as it held no finery to allure travellers. Its people were illiterate and passed their lore in an oral tradition. In the shadows of the Grey Mountains have they dwelt for an unknown time, constantly living in fear of Oxylus, the god that lives in the mountains. Some nights they hear his footsteps as he strode from one peak to another, causing loose rocks to fall and smash their way down the mountainsides. High in these mountains, the people of Mitra would not travel, nor to the spring for fear of the creatures that guard that path.

"You speak of what you don't know," the leader rebuked. "For to allow you passage into the mountains would be to invite evils upon ourselves."

"Please," Calliope pleaded, "Will you not find any mercy to aid us in any way?"

The leader whispered once more with his colleagues, taking their time in discussion and them all eventually nodding in agreement.

"This matter is too great for us alone to decide," the leader gave answer. "We shall therefor call an assembly of the people who shall vote on whether to aid you or not."

"But that will take too long," Aristides moaned.

"The choice is yours, wait to see the result of the vote, or leave immediately and never return."

Having little option, the pupils chose to wait for the vote and hope the people of Mitra decided in their favour. After the meeting, they were led back to the grubby hovel where they were made to wait, and not permitted to leave.

The leader called the people of Mitra together by the blowing of a horn, and steadily did they gather at the meeting rock outside of the town. Here the leader addressed them, relaying the reason for the coming of the pupils and asking the question on whether aid should be given. The way the people casted their vote would have been perceived as odd to any whom might have seen it. Those that were in favour of a motion would place a black voting stone against the base of the assembly rock. If the pile of stones reached the top, the motion was passed, if not then it had failed. The leader, after a silent delay to think about the matter, asked those in favour of lending the pupils aid to place their stones. Few did, and the pile did not even reach a quarter of the way up.

As soon as the vote was declared, the pupils were informed that their request had been refused by the people. By now it was growing late into the day, and sparing the pupils from wilderness at night, they could remain for the night, on the promise that they left at first light. Angrily the pupils cursed the people of Mitra and began speaking of how they could overcome this delay. As they pondered their next move, a violent storm broke out over the mountains. Thunder clattered and lightning forked across the blackened sky, yet there was no heavy downpour as expected during a thunderstorm. The people fled out of their homes and fell onto their knees, holding aloft their arms to the mountains and beseeching Oxylus for his forgiveness. Most of that night did the storm last and come the morning the people gathered once more by the assembly rock. There another vote was taken as they interpreted the storm as Oxylus' displeasure at not allowing the pupils passage into his realm. So, another vote was cast, and this time the pile reached the top of the assembly rock.

Now the pupils were honoured as the chosen and given fresh cuts of meat and fine fur cloaks and gloves which would keep them warm when higher up in the mountains. Also, they were gifted with an insulated tent for when they slept. With the leader now cooperating, the pupils soon took their leave, unwilling to remain in such a drab place. The first couple of days was an easy walk as they followed a path which the people of Mitra used to get to their mines. But at the mines did this path end and the walk became much tougher.

Unlike the Mountains of Roc, that had been warm and almost welcoming, the Grey Mountains were cruel and cold. A constant wind whistled down from the snow-capped peaks, reddening their hands and faces. The rocks were sleek with dampness and weatherworn into sharp edges that resembled spears. As the pupils steadily climbed higher, the mountain was covered in a blanket of snow that became so deep in parts that it was almost impossible to pass. The wind whipped up the snow to a fine dust and the pupils were forced to stop for the night. They set up their tent and huddled together for warmth, unbeknown to them that they were being watched.

Unknown to the pupils, was that the passage to the Spring of Youth was guarded by the Rock Golems. These creatures were of stone, short and squat in stature with long, gorilla like arms. They had no head, and their faces were on their broad chests. The origins of the Rock Golems were unknown, nor as to why they took up the protection of the mountain passage. By nature, they were hostile to all, even each other. At night they would hall huge rocks at each other, causing landslides and a noise that clattered like thunder, even at times causing sparks which resembled lightning.

From high in the mountains did the Rock Golems watch the pupils, like the pupils had studied the tiniest of creatures under the microscope. At first the Rock Golems were uncertain of how to act as the pupils didn't pose any threat. But bickering amongst them broke out and rocks began to take flight.

The noise of smashing rocks awoke the pupils and they shot out of their tent and watched in wonder as huge rocks went flying over their heads.

"What are they?" Calliope asked, her eyes fixed up on the silhouette of a stone creature holding a rock clear above where its head should have been.

Aristides shook his head and replied, "I have never seen, nor heard of such creatures before."

A rock smashed close to them, and they all rushed to gather their things. Their beds they were able to pull out from the tent before a boulder came crashing down the mountainside and barrelling over their tent, breaking it beyond repair. More rocks now fell closer to them, and in fear they fled higher into the mountains. The Rock Golems, seeing an easy victory, gave chase and continued to throw rocks.

By a stroke of luck, the Rock Golems' actions caused a landslide that fell between them and the pupils. The passage behind the pupils was now blocked, and the Golems were unable to give chase. For the remainder of that night they rested, shivering cold in their beds. Come the morning they groggily trudged on through the knee-deep snow, eating stringy cuts of meat as they went. Time was seemingly lost as the days were overcast with thick clouds which blotted out the sun. The pupils' morale dropped to new lows, and they would speak little. After a few hours more, they reached a pool of steaming water, a place known to many as the spring of Youth.

The lore of the Spring of Youth was well-known to the pupils, as it was to many throughout the realm of Perdita. The spring was said to be the tears of the Goddess Artemisia, who had wept for her lost love during the Time of the Beginning. The tale is that Artemisia was admired by all the gods, but it was the god Helios who admired her the most. Many times, Artemisia had rejected Helios' advances, saying that her heart belonged to a mortal man. So, Helios grew jealous and descended from the heavens, intent on slaying the lover of Artemisia. This he did by sending a plague, Artemisia's lover succumbing to the plague along with the entire village where he dwelt. Artemisia herself constructed his funeral pyre, the flames licking high into the sky. So distraught by the sight of his burning body, that Artemisia spirited away to the Grey Mountains where she wept. Her tears rolled down her cheeks and flowed down the mountainside, pooling beside the mountain face.

"The Spring of Youth," Calliope said with a smile.

The pupils rushed over, their troubles suddenly forgotten, and began dipping their hands in the warm water. It was soft, lacking in density to such a degree that nothing would float in it, not even a leaf; everything sank to the bottom.

"I'm going in," Calliope said as she stripped off to her undergarments.

Both Telamon and Aristides watched as Calliope carefully stepped in, the mass of her body causing ripples which distorted the mirrored image on the water's surface.

"Well?" Aristides asked, "Is it like the stories say?"

The water made Calliope feel warm and fuzzy inside. The aches and pains of her body ebbed away, and any thoughts of doom were relinquished. "Come," she said before disappearing under the water's surface.

Telamon and Aristides stripped down to their undergarments and stepped in, the warmth of the water instantly relaxing their tired muscles. For a time, they playfully splashed and joked in joy, forgetting their witnessed horrors and plight. After they climbed out, their skins glistened as though they had been massaged in oil. Darkness was now looming, and they made a small fire from the foliage they found scattered by the mountain face. After taking a meal of salted meat and hard biscuit, they rolled out their beds and slept. That night passed in deep sleep, untroubled and undisturbed. They all awoke the next morning revitalized and keen to continue with their Trial. With enthusiasm, they packed up their bedrolls and ate a small breakfast of dried fruits before discussing their next move.

The passage which they had climbed up, was now blocked from the landslide caused by the Rock Golems and was now impassable. For an hour they poured over an old map which Aristides had carried with him all the way from the school of Phrontis. It was an old map which didn't even show the town of Mitra, nor the passage which they had used to reach the spring. In accordance with this map, there was but one other passage, a path named as the Passage of

Chloris and marked to the north of the spring. So, after filling a small phial with water, they headed north.

So, refreshed by the water of the spring, that their going was quick, even when having to climb; and by nightfall that day they had reached the passage of Chloris. Beside a small pool of freshwater, they stretched out their beds and settled for the night, which passed undisturbed. By the light of the morning, the passage became clear to see. There was greenery mixed with a splash of colour from wildflowers which grew in patches either side of a rough path. From this point, it was all downhill, easy going for the first day. But the next, the passage became more disordered and broken with huge boulders now slowing their progress. It was here that the Rock Golems reappeared on the clifftops that overlooked the passage. Immediately they began to throw rocks down, and the pupils took cover as best they could in the small gaps between the boulders.

Now their peril was being entombed alive or to flee their hiding place and risk being stoned to death. Aristides, seeing the danger, collected a pile of stones which he then began to utter a spell over.

"Aristides," Calliope said with shock that he would break a rule of the Trial! "What are you doing?"

"Getting us out of here alive!" Aristides snapped back. Without saying another word, he climbed out of the gap and threw stones towards the clifftop. Most harmlessly missed and bounced off the cliff face, but a couple hit the golems, causing them to shatter as though they were glass. Seeing their fate if they remained, the Rock Golems turned and fled in a wild panic.

The pupils wasted no time in making good their escape, refusing to stop until they had reached the bottom of the passage two days later. All around them now was tall redwood trees with thick undergrowth. The sun shone through the treetops, sending in beams of white light that bathed the forest floor. Now, safe from the Rock Golems, did the pupils rest. During this time, they spoke of returning to Mitra to replenish their supplies, but none were keen to return to that drab place without good reason. So, after taking stock on what provisions they had left, it was decided that there was no need to return to Mitra, and for the next three days they walked north, foraging for food and refilling their canteens from the streams which flowed plentiful through the forest.

On the morning of the fourth day since entering the redwood forest, they came to the northern edge. Before them lay lush countryside, green with yellow buttercups. The summer was now at its height, and the days were long ang hot. As the pupils headed north, they began to miss the coldness of the mountains, a coldness which they had bemoaned while experiencing it. Sweat dampened their hair and trickled down their backs; and so, they became weary and contemplated drinking the water they had collected from the spring of Youth to revitalize them. But Calliope guarded the phial closely and would not even take it from her pack to look at it.

After two weeks of long, gruelling days walking, hills grew upon the northern horizon. Dark clouds gathered above them and a vail of green mist lingered on the ground around the hills. These hills were known as the Haunted Hills, a place seldom travelled except by those seeking spirits. Those that had visited the hill spoke of how lonely and foreboding they were, and it was not uncommon for people treading that path to become so despaired that they would commit suicide. It was a path which the pupils would not take for fear of the spirits which haunt there. As they walked on, a strong wind blew from the east, forcing them on a northwest trajectory towards the hills. But Telamon noticed this, and thus corrected their path. With the wind whistling in their ears, the pupils continued towards the north. Soon the wind died down and the Haunted Hills were a lessoning feature behind them. Ahead of them lay an endless countryside ripe for farming, yet it was empty of any homes, nor was there a road. After three more days, their supplies were gone, and they battled against hunger and thirst.

The grass now waned from heat, turning yellow and lessoning to a few patches poking up through a cracked soil with scatterings of sand dusting over it. There, like an oasis in a desert, did the town of Linteum appear on the horizon. But the pupils were exhausted and could go no further. There they lay down; each expecting death to come and claim them.

VII

The Heart of Sabacos

Hours passed, the strong sun arching down from its height and sinking in the west, where its dying rays turned the sky red. Telamon, with the last of his strength, pulled up some of the dry grass and piled it together in a small heap. Aristides and Calliope were both lying unconscious and never noticed as Telamon set alight to the heaped grass. So dry was it, that the flames instantly took hold, burning through its fuel rapidly. Telamon tried to keep the fire alive, but exhaustion overcame him, and he fell into a deep slumber.

When the pupils awoke, they were inside a pavilion of red cloth. The ground was covered with green carpets, and each of the pupils had been placed on wooden framed beds with firm mattresses and feather pillows. On a table in the centre of the pavilion was a jug of water with ice and slices of lime, beside the jug a glass bowl of dried figs. Each of the pupils drank the cold water and ate a handful of the figs. Their legs were still weakened and so they returned to their beds, feeling safe as for whoever had brought them here must be friendly or else, they would have been left to die. They slept for a while longer and were awoken by the sound of a gong.

"Are they well?" A voice asked, his accent thick in a strange dialect.

Standing by the entrance was three men, each wearing long silk robes black in colour. Their skin was dark, their eyes hazel, and atop of their heads they wore a white turban. Each of these men had beards, but above their upper lip was shaved.

Wearily, the pupils rose from their beds, and it was now discovered that their robes had been removed in place of a white gown of cotton.

"I think that they are well enough," one of the men said as he picked up the jug and inspected the amount missing. By now the ice had long melted, but the man was intelligent enough to factor that into his calculations.

"I bid thee welcome to Linteum, pupils of the School of Phrontis." The man standing closest to the entrance took a few steps closer to them and bowed, his hands almost brushing the floor as he did so. "I am Icarus chief advisor to the king."

Aristides stepped forwards and took the lead. "You have our thanks Icarus, and may you now enlighten us as to how we got here."

"You were found by our Outriders three days ago two miles from our boarders. You were all close to death and could not be roused. We have been expecting you for some time now, and you were only recognised by your robes, even though they are faded and stained."

"Expecting us?" Aristides said with an arched eyebrow of confusion. "How were you expecting us?"

"My friends, we have had many dealings with your Peritum, Telemachus. Is was by his own hand that he wrote to tell us of your Trial, and it was he who asked that we aid you in whatever way we are able."

"You know of our task?"

"Yes, my young friend," Icarus replied. "We wrote back to your Peritum, asking him to reconsider putting you at great peril. But alas, he would not as he deemed you capable of achieving possession of the Heart of Sabacos."

"Then you will help us?"

Icarus stood silent for a moment, as if considering how best to approach the matter. "Yes, and no. Firstly you are welcome to freely walk our town, and each of you are given the king's protection. You shall have all your needs catered for, food, drink, and any entertainment you might wish to partake. Further, we shall mend your robes and packs, and grant you leave to take what tools you may need when wandering the desert."

"And what is the no?" Aristides asked.

"The king shall not command any of his subjects to guard you, nor to guide you," Icarus answered. "You are permitted to seek any willing to aid you of their own freewill, but none shall be commanded to do so."

This, though it may not sound it, was a bitter blow for the pupils. For their final task, the Heart of Sabacos, lay within the ancient ruins of Sabacos. Deep in the desert known as the Dry Lands were these ruins, a passage known only to the people of Linteum and kept a closely guarded secret. Those desert dunes were a treacherous path where one could become hopelessly lost without a guide. Desert jackals were said to roam there, preying on the weak and lost. They were said to be vile creatures, with the body of a man and the head of a Jackal; creatures which gorged on flesh and drank blood. Though these Jackals were terrifying enough, worse was yet awaiting those that reached the ruins. For there, roaming amongst the partially buried ruins was a bronze monster of mechanical cogs; the guardian of the Heart of Sabacos.

"In due time," Icarus continued, "the king shall summon you to an audience. Then you will give details on when you plan to leave, providing that is, that you have found a guide."

So, for the next week the pupils rested to regain their full strength. They were well fed with fresh fruits and dishes of rice mixed with chicken and vegetables. To ease their aches and pains, they were regularly given hot willow water to drink. They began to explore the town of Linteum, gradually walking further and further from their pavilion each passing day.

The town itself was on the border of the Dry Lands and was unlike any other in appearance. There were no buildings of stone, not even where the king resided. All the homes were of cloth pavilions, differing in colour and erected in a disorderly manner where it was easy for anyone visiting to become lost. The people were all dark of skin and dressed in loose robes to keep them cool and turbans to cover their hair, which they deemed sacred and would never cut. They were a clean people, bathing every day and rubbing scented oil into their skin. Around their wrists they wore copper bands, claiming that they warded off illness. All the men over thirty had beards, but to have a moustache was a detestable thing, and so they shaved their upper lip. Here they worshiped the Goddess Harena, the Goddess of deserts, and her bronze image is kept in the grandest pavilion in the town's centre.

The king sat at the top of governance and could trace his lineage back to the days when they ruled over Sabacos. Those days were spoken of much by the people and was perceived as a golden age of which they longed to return to. By the reckoning of the scrolls kept in the king's pavilion, it had been one hundred and twenty-seven years since the great flight from Sabacos. Many expeditions had undertaken the quest to slay the bronze monster and reclaim their homeland, but all had failed with only a few returning alive to tell of their cruel tale. For that was what the people of Linteum strove for, to return to Sabacos, their ancestral home. That is why they refused to build in stone, as that would be a symbolic way of stating that they were never going to return from where they came.

The pupils asked many if they would be willing to join them on their quest to Sabacos, but none were. Each time they asked, they were given the same answer. *Though we pray that Harena both guide and protect you and wish with all our heart that you are successful; we are not foolish enough to travel that path.* Desperation to find at least one person forced the pupils to look in unsavoury places of the town. Having gained permission from Icarus, the pupils began asking those being kept prisoner. They were being held in a hole dug deep into the ground, with the only way of leaving was by a rope ladder that the guards would throw down. It was Calliope that spoke with these unworthy men, many of which refused her offer. But amongst their number was a man named Scyllias.

Scyllias had been condemned to death for the murder of his brother over the matter of inheritance, an untrustworthy man with a sly looking face. His robes were shabby and torn, his manner familiar and rude. His turban had been removed and his head clean shaven, a mark of a condemned man, and his right ear was missing.

This unsavoury man was the only person willing to guide the pupils across the desert. As payment for his courage, Scyllias was offered redemption from his death penalty, providing that he serves the pupils honestly and guides them truly. For there had once been money to be made by taking payment for guiding people across the desert on the promise of finding a city of gold, then in the dead of night slip away and leave them to the desert's mercy.

Having now secured a guide, the pupils began collecting stores for their journey. Seven camels were given to them, one equipped for carrying water, two for stores of food, and four for riding. After these provisions were secured, the pupils were given leave to use the bathhouse. Each washed their bodies and oiled their hair, Calliope taking her time. They each now looked refreshed as they donned their repaired school robes and resembled more of when they first set out from Phrontis.

Icarus then came to their pavilion and guided them to the king. His pavilion was grand, second only to the one where the bronze image of Harena was being kept. The cloth was purple with silver stars and was being held up by thick wooden poles tipped with brass snake heads that glimmered gold when they caught the light. Inside was of equal grandeur to any palace, filled with comforts and attended by servants. By the entrance, the pupils were asked to take-off their shoes, as it was forbidden to wear outdoor shoes while in the king's pavilion. But being barefoot was of no hinderance as the ground was of soft carpet, white in colour and unstained; it was as if one was treading on a cloud.

Sat on a golden throne was the king, garbed in a purple, silk robe edged with a broad strip of silver. He was a heavily set man with a stern face and dark, bushy eyebrows above which was a purple turban crowned with a golden circlet fitted with emeralds. His beard was tightly curled and beaded with jade; his upper lip, like the other men of the town, was clean shaven.

"My king," Icarus bowed as he stood before the throne. "I present to you the pupils of Phrontis."

The king frowned as he examined the three students stood before him. To his eyes they were feeble looking, a far cry from the type of heroes needed to retrieve the Heart of Sabacos. "You are most welcome in my realm," the king greeted. "I trust that you have been well kept as were my orders."

Aristides, along with Calliope and Telamon, bowed as was the custom when in the presence of a king. "We have been treated with all kindness," Aristides answered. "Your realm is most gracious."

"Good," the king nodded and smiled, "And have you all that you need for your journey to Sabacos?"

"Again," Aristides replied with all due honour, "Your realm has been most gracious."

The king then clapped his hands and a man was ushered in by two guards, both armed with spears and wore leather breastplates. "And do you wish to be guided by this man?"

Calliope recognised him as the man from the prison, though now he had been dressed in baggy trousers and sleeveless jacket, dark blue in colour. Atop of his bold head he wore a red fez, a short cylindrical hat with no peak.

"Yes, we do," Calliope said a little abruptly.

"So be it," the king said as he leaned forwards on his throne. "But know this, no command I lay upon him to go further than his courage shall take him. Though an oath he has sworn to remain loyal to you, in exchange for his life he shall guide you to the ruins of Sabacos and back, but no more."

"And we shall ask no more of him," Calliope then replied, her tone now more becoming when speaking with a king.

"Then go with the blessings of Harena and the people of Linteum." The king raised his right hand and nodded his head, a signal that the audience was now over.

Icarus bowed and led the pupils back out, the two guards escorting the prisoner. Outside the camels were waiting, lying down so that they were easier to mount. A few people had gathered to watch, a few even shouting their blessings, but none expecting the pupils to ever return. The sun was now at its full height and strength, and by the time they reached the town's border with the desert they were already weary. There, at the town's edge, Icarus bid his farewell to the pupils.

For the remainder of that day they rode west into the desert, the prisoner leading from the front. Ahead of them was an endless desert rising and falling in valleys of sand dunes. Heat distorted the distant horizon and it became abundantly clear why it was so easy to become lost. For all around them was the same, an endless ocean of sand against the backdrop of a clear blue sky. None of the pupils were used to spending lengthy periods in the saddle, and by the time they stopped for the night, their inner thighs were sore. They each dismounted, though their dismount was more of a fall, and began stretching out their bedrolls while the prisoner built a fire. They rested and ate as the sun dipped below the horizon, the clear sky turning purple and then black as one by one the stars appeared.

"What is your name?" Calliope asked the prisoner.

The prisoner tossed a few sticks from a pile of broken tumbleweeds which he had collected. "Scyllias," he replied.

"How many days until we reach the ruins?"

Scyllias squinted and nodded his head ten times as he made his calculations. "Ten or eleven days."

"And what of the desert jackals?" Aristides asked, "How are we to avoid them?"

Scyllias simply shrugged. "I've never seen one, and I've travelled this passage many times."

"You have," Calliope said with surprise, but suspected that he was exaggerating.

Scyllias nodded his head. "Me and my brother used to search the deserts for precious stones, selling anything of worth that we found on the black-market back at Linteum."

"So, there's riches to be found here," Calliope said as she glanced around.

"Yes," Scyllias toothlessly smiled, "we were like our founder, wondering in search of a worthy jewel."

The tale of the founder had been long told. It told of a desert wonderer named Sabacos who had been searching the desert for a new home. Sabacos had been part of a nomad people who had spent years wandering from place to place. But in the desert, they became hopelessly lost, the unrelenting heat and want of water dwindling their number. Soon only Sabacos remained and he was visited by the goddess Harena, who took pity upon him and led him to water. There beside the pool of the oasis she said that he would find a new homeland where he found his heart. Enthralled by the thought of founding his own town, Sabacos began searching the desert, with months passing with no joy. Then one night as he was sat beside his fire, he saw a red glimmer. Catching the light of the fire was a red ruby, partially buried in the sand. This ruby eventually became known as the Heart of Sabacos, and upon the spot where he had found it, he built a home, small at first. As time passed Sabacos' house grew in size and splendour. People began to seek out the desert man who housed the heart of a god. For that was what they believed that the ruby found by Sabacos was nonother than the heart of Harena herself.

So Sabacos became a chosen man and around his palace grew a town of sandstone. It is said that the city of Sabacos was a wonder of the world, a marvel of the ancient people with much wisdom and lore of the Age of the Beginning that is now lost to us. But as Sabacos aged, his mortal flesh becoming paler and more wrinkled, he was urged to name an heir. According to the tales of Sabacos, he was believed to have had twenty wives and countless mistresses, yet unable to sire an heir. The learned men of his court began to petition him to name a successor, but Sabacos refused as he believed that they wanted his jewel for themselves. So suspicious of these learned men did Sabacos become that he wrote to the Peritum of Phrontis, asking him for wisdom for his predicament. For a donation of exotic goods and silver, the Peritum sent a Magister, a man named Eleusis.

Eleusis was deep in the lore of mechanics and had left Phrontis with a mind to build a room with intricate locks which only Sabacos could open. But when Eleusis put this plan to Sabacos it was met with dissatisfaction. Sabacos congratulated Eleusis for his drafting of such a complicated locking system but claimed that he had underestimated the intelligence of the learned men. They would simply make a lifetime study of the locks and would one day gain the knowledge on how to open them. Eleusis then withdrew that plan and began drawing up another. His second plan was met with joy from Sabacos, who ordered Eleusis to work forthwith. So, Eleusis was given a workshop on the grounds of the palace, and for three months Eleusis worked, the doors to his workshop remaining closed. All day long came hammering and the sounds of sawing, along with the smell of heated metal. From within, Eleusis constructed a man of bronze, standing some seven feet tall with innards of pipes and cogs that were covered over with overlapping bronze plates. Its face was a silver mask with wide eyes of horror, its mouth a sinister smile. In the chest of this mechanical monster was placed the red ruby that now henceforth became known as the Heart of Sabacos. What force gave this creature life was known only to Eleusis, as was its weaknesses.

For the remainder of Sabacos' days the mechanical monster guarded the ruby and would take orders from Sabacos alone. Upon his death, the mechanical monster became distraught and would not yield the ruby. Seeing the learned men as a threat, it rampaged through the palace, killing all in its path. Those that were able to escape fled east across the desert to a place where the desert ended. There they founded the town of Linteum, a town of cloth houses and rightful heirs to Sabacos. But the mechanical monster remained close to the palace

For ten days the pupils journeyed across the desert, uneventful and tedious as they were led from one oasis to another. By the morning of the eleventh day they came before the ruins of Sabacos, still a grand sight to behold despite it being unkempt and partially buried by dunes.

"That's the place," Scyllias pointed towards the tallest and most elegant building. "The Heart of Sabacos you will find there."

"Are you not coming?" Aristides asked.

Thoughts of that place instilled fear into Scyllias, for he had once been party to a gang of thieves that had tried to take the Heart of Sabacos. He had waited outside the palace as four others had entered. The sound of their screams and of scraping and clunking of metal still haunted him; and despite the heat, he felt a very cold shudder.

"Coward!" Aristides' face twisted with anger, "Have you no bravery in you?"

Scyllias simply smiled and replied, "Bravery and foolishness often walk hand in hand. And I now remind you that I was merely to escort you to the ruins and back. And there are the ruins."

"Then what will you do?" Calliope asked, her head and face covered over by a scarf to protect her from the strong rays of the sun.

"I will camp here and await you for as long as I'm able."

With nothing left to say, the pupils took some of the supplies to last them two days and headed into the town on foot, leaving all the camels in Scyllias' care. It was difficult treading as the sand was loose and their narrow feet sank to their ankles. They clumsily climbed over a dune which completely buried many smaller buildings on the fringes of the south-eastern border. Now more of the town was clear to them. There were many small dwellings built from sandstone, each wall with a small dune piled at the base. Everywhere there was debris of tumbleweed collected by years' worth of neglect, and many roofs had long collapsed from the weight of sand. Once there had been streets with pathed sidewalks, but now they too were buried, lost beneath a layer of sand. Much was still intact and resembled a time capsule of a more enlightened time. But despite the town's splendour, it was an eerie place, silent and foreboding where the sprits of the past still lingered. Ahead of them was the palace, which was by far the biggest building. The walls were high and decorated with strange gods with animal heads; and lining a path to a double doored entrance were jackals carved from black stone with red eyes that were peering down upon the path. At their base were bronze plates with inscriptions in a dialect now lost to all but the people of Linteum.

Opposite the palace was a squared building that had once been used for storing grain. Tall like a tower it stood with thick walls which slimmed the higher up they went. The roof was still mostly intact and there were two floors each covered over with a dusting of sand. On the base floor the pupils downed their packs and rolled out their beds. They climbed the ladder which led up to the second floor, and there on all four walls was a hatch that had been used to load in or out sacks of grain from a pully system attached outside. From the hatch that looked out towards the palace, they watched for the mechanical creature that was said to roam the palace grounds. They watched until the twilight hours, seeing and hearing nothing of the creature. So, they rested for the night, taking a meal, and drinking water flavoured by fruits. The night passed uneventful and they each slept undisturbed.

The pupils awoke the next morning with optimism. From their stores they ate a hearty breakfast before making their way to the palace. As they passed the red eyed jackals, their optimism wavered. It was as though the eyes were moving with them and felt as though at any moment they might leap into life. But still as stone they remained. The double doors were covered over with a thin layer of bronze and were ajar, and Aristides peered in before he entered. Calliope looked at Telamon, her face showing her anxiety, then she too entered. Telamon felt a sickening wave sweep through his stomach and he glanced behind him at the statues of the jackals, still expecting them to move.

"Telamon," Calliope said as she poked her head back through the door, "come on."

Telamon took a breath to calm his anxiety; then he slipped through the gap and came to the entrance hall. Aristides was stood in awe at the majesty of the palace, a sight that was unrivalled by any building known to him.

The walls were painted with elegant depictions of oases, so vivid and lifelike were they that one might smell the lotus flowers and hear the warm breeze passing through the palm trees. Tall columns of white granite held up a black ceiling decorated with golden stars and the floor was of green flagstone, dusted over with sand. Between the pillars were large bowl-shaped braziers of bronze, a few of which were still standing and holding the burnt remains of coals lit long ago. To the left and right of the pupils was a set of stairs which they ignored, instead heading towards an arched doorway in front of them.

This door led them to the audience chamber, which was more splendid than the entrance hall. The walls were golden and adorned with jade stones with white arches of marble encircling around the room. The ceiling was domed and carved with faces that looked down upon a raised platform of black granite. There was a hole in the roof where a beam of sunlight flooded in to illuminate a golden throne placed in the centre of the granite platform. Over the years, sand had been blown in and the throne was mostly buried under the harsh grains.

For a moment, the pupils could do nothing other than stand in marvel at the majesty of the chamber. But from all around came a rumble, a dragging of metal and thuds of heavy footsteps. From a large door behind the throne came the mechanical creature, its heavy steps dusting up the sand and its motionless face peering straight towards the pupils. Its bronze body was rectangular in shape, its arms and legs interlocking cylinders. With surprising speed, it moved for the pupils who turned and fled back the way they had come. But Aristides was ensnared by the arms of the mechanical creature, and wildly he kicked and beat his fist in a desperate attempt to free himself. But all was in vain as strange bubbling noises came from within the creature's chest. Aristides began to scream as he was pressed into the heating plates of the creature, his robe beginning to singe. Suddenly, Aristides burst into flame and his screams became a horror in the ears of Calliope and Telamon. Dismayed they fled without any thought of rescue for Aristides.

Calliope and Telamon ran without stop until they reached the grain silo, where they fell to their knees. Telamon was distraught for the loss of Aristides, a surprise for both he and Calliope. For Aristides had never been friendly towards Telamon and had often sought him out for belittlement. But for him to have fallen to such a cruel fate seemed unjust to Telamon, a harsh punishment for his childish antics. Calliope, however, was far less dismayed by Aristides loss. She climbed the ladder and looked out of the hatch, checking for the mechanical creature. But the way to the palace lay clear.

Telamon, at that point, would have happily returned to Linteum. But Calliope refused his pleas, stating that they were so close and had been through too much to simply turn back now as failures. That word, failure, had a profound impact on Telamon. For he knew that he could never return home a failure, to be the first of his family to not claim victory in the Trial would haunt him for the remainder of his days. Against his better judgement, Telamon agreed that they should try again to find the Heart of Sabacos to finish their Trial.

So, the day after they remained in the silo, watching the palace. They discovered that the mechanical creature made regular patrols of the grounds, and they watched in hope of finding some advantage. The creature was too powerful to challenge face on, its bronze plates too strong to be pierced by any weapons they might forge. What was needed was trickery of some sort. Telamon explained that even mechanical things could break, and that there must be of some method to open the plates to make repairs. It was later that day when Telamon discovered a smaller plate on the creature's back, a plate with hinges and a handle.

Quickly a plan formulated in Telamon's mind, a plan so simple and foolish sounding that it had to work. He explained to Calliope that the creature's size and shape could be used against it. If they could trip it over and keep it down, they could maybe open it up and find some way of stopping it. They spoke long into the night, defining their plan over and over until they had convinced themselves it could work.

The morning after they headed once more into the palace, as quickly and quietly as they could. The air inside was now fouled by the burnt remains of Aristides, a stench that would linger in their nostrils for a lifetime. In the entrance hall they tied the rope around two opposite columns nearest to the door to the audience chamber. Together they then entered the audience chamber. Upon the sand strewn floor was the charred remains of Aristides, still smouldering and unrecognisable. Taking one last look at each other for comfort, Telamon and Calliope began shouting to gain the attention of the creature. They were not made to wait long, as calculated the creature came from the door behind the throne. At first sight Telamon and Calliope dashed back out of the door, ducking under their carefully placed rope. The creature gave chase and crashed through the door, its thick legs tripping over the rope. With a mighty crash that shook the palace, the creature went face down. The pillars were pulled apart by the rope and a section of ceiling came crashing down, smashing through the floor to reveal a room below. The creature pushed up on its arms trying to lift its great bulk, but Calliope had placed a pole she'd found outside and now used it to knock the creature's arms out from under it.

"Quick Telamon!" Calliope called, unsure how long she could keep up the effort needed for each swing of the pole.

Telamon, half dazed and blinded by the sand whipped up from the floor, quickly climbed on to the creature's back. To his relief the panel could be opened, and he wasted no time in twisting a brass latch and pulling up the hatch, which he had to hold open using one hand to stop it falling shut again. The creature became more frantic in its efforts, and it became clear of its design floors. Had the body been more rounded, it could have easily rolled over to protect its hatch; but instead its flat front had become a limitation to its movement.

"Telamon," Calliope cried out, "I can't go on for much longer!"

Inside the hatch was a tangle of pipes and cogs which were in motion. For a moment Telamon was unsure of what he should do. Then out of desperation he wrapped his free hand around the smallest pipe and pulled with all the strength he could muster. The pipe was hot and burnt his hand, but it came away with surprising ease. From it spewed out a black liquid, hot and steaming. For a moment it looked to have had no effect upon the creature as it continued to thrash about. Telamon, unable to keep his balance, fell and had to roll clear of the creature to avoid its thrashing arms and legs. Soon came the distinctive sound of gargling, the sound of air being sucked into the pipes. It was now that the creature waned in strength, and it fell still.

Calliope, breathing heavily, dropped the pole and climbed up onto its back. There she knelt and inspected the innards. Amidst the pipes and still cogs that were now covered with the black liquid was a glimmer of red. She carefully wriggled her hand between two pipes and pulled out a red ruby. "We have them all," Calliope proclaimed with a smile. The floor creaked and strained under the dead weight of the creature and she jumped down just before it gave way.

Telamon rose from the floor, his robe and hair covered with sand. He held his burnt hand under his arm, and he walked over to the broken edge of the floor and peered down.

"Is it dead?" Calliope asked as she walked over to Telamon.

Telamon nodded as he kept his eyes down on the cooling bronze of the creature. "You were lucky not to have fallen down with it." A strong push unbalanced him, and he tumbled down into the room below, falling awkwardly and knocking the wind out of him. Telamon rolled on to his back and looked up. There peering down at him was Calliope. "Why," he called up. But Calliope had disappeared, gone to claim victory in the Trial.

VIII

Victory in the Trial

The chamber Telamon had been pushed in was dull, with the only light coming from the hole where he'd fallen. The floor was of solid stone and he felt some relief that he had not broken a bone. The walls offered no clue as to what the room had once been used for and were bare red plaster. There were no doors that Telamon could see as he desperately ran his hands over the walls in hope of finding a secret doorway. But there was nothing and the only way out was the way he had come in, the hole above him. Still half dazed from his fall, Telamon tried to collect his thoughts on how he could escape. The mechanical monster lay motionless, face down in the debris of broken wood and green tiles. Telamon climbed up onto the back of the creature and tried to jump up and reach the ledge, but it was hopeless. Next, Telamon thought that he might be able to fashion some tool that would aid him in scaling the wall. From the mechanical creature he snapped away two pipes which he then tried to bend so that they became hooked shaped; but without heating equipment they simply snapped. Using the jagged pieces of pipe, Telamon tried to climb. The plaster broke easy and at first Telamon had some success; but as he reached halfway, a large section of the plaster crumbled away and sent him crashing back down. Under this plaster was solid stone that the jagged pipes had no hope of penetrating.

Despair took hold of Telamon and he fell to the floor and uncontrollably wept. Coldly he shuddered and troubled were his thoughts of meeting his end in this manner. Why? What had he done to deserve such an agonizing death? His coldness and tears than gave way to a hot flush of anger. No! No, he would not allow himself to suffer. Telamon snatched up one of the pipes and held its jagged end to his throat, his hands trembling. But despite his anger and fear of slowly starving to death, Telamon could not take his own life. So, upon the floor he curled up and began to weep, asking aloud for forgiveness from his father for having failed.

That night, whether by chance or by divine intervention none can now agree, came a sandstorm. Violently it whipped up a sand cloud over the western dunes and swept over the ruins. Like an hourglass turned over, sand began to trickle down through the hole, heaping below in a mound slowly widening at its base. Telamon wasted no time in climbing the growing heap, struggling at first as his hands and feet quickly became buried. Twice he had slid back down as the loose sand gave way, but a powerful want of life gave Telamon renewed strength. Upon the third attempt he was able to reach the ledge, and for a moment he simply held onto a broken wooden beam to catch his breath. Feeling that his legs were becoming buried, Telamon pulled himself up over the ledge. The double doors of the entrance hall were now wide open, blew open by the sandstorm which splintered them from their hinges. Tiny granules of sand whirled around the chamber, stinging Telamon's eyes and drying his throat. He stumbled up the stairs to his right where he found refuge in a small room still intact. There he sat with his back against the wall with his knees drawn up into his chest and waited out the storm. The sound of the wind and of sand ruffling was oddly soothing and Telamon fell into a deep sleep.

When Telamon awoke, all was quiet. The sandstorm had passed, leaving in its wake a vast amount of sand which now completely buried large parts of the ruins. As Telamon left the room, he discovered the stairs had been partially buried to the halfway point. The entrance hall was almost filled to the ceiling, the doorway almost completely blocked. Only a small gap remained between the sand and upper doorframe, and Telamon had to crawl his way out.

Outside was sunny and calm, and for moment Telamon stood and viewed the much-changed ruins. Sand now completely covered over the smaller homes further out from the palace, making the town look much smaller than it was. The path flanked by the jackals had now disappeared, and the silo where the pupils had made their camp was now buried up to the hatch on the second floor. Telamon slid down the dune sloping down from the palace entrance and made his way to the silo. Inside was free of sand, though the ground floor was buried by two feet of sand which had formed a mound by the door to completely block it. At first Telamon feared to rummage through the sand, believing that it could cause the sand to filter its way in. But he needed water, and so took his chance. To his delight, his pack and canteen was still there, and he drank heavily, swilling the grains of sand out of his mouth. The food in his pack had been spoiled by grains of sand, like all that he had stowed in there. Taking only his cloak and canteen, Telamon left the ruins of Sabacos, intent on reporting Calliope's crime.

At first Telamon returned to the outskirts where Scyllias said he would await the pupils. But gone was he, along with the supplies and camels, and any sign of Calliope. All that day Telamon walked east, keeping the sun to his right. He placed his cloak over his head to protect himself from the daytime sun and drank sparingly to conserve his supply. But by night he became bitterly cold and feared to sleep. The day after his water ran out and he ditheringly trudged on, the sun obscuring his usual sense. To his left he saw trees, trees which needed water to survive, and he ran towards them knowing that there would be water. But all he saw was a mirage, a cruel hallucination of his impending doom. There in the desert he fell and would have wept if his eyes could conjure tears. There Telamon would have found death had it not been for a small group of desert wanderers, merchants from across the deserts on their way to Linteum.

When Telamon awoke, he was greeted by a friendly smile of a woman, heavily set with a round face. She tried speaking to him, her words spoken in a harsh sounding language which Telamon had never heard before. It was then Telamon realized that he was in a bed, covered over by a canopy to shade him from the sun. The bed was fixed onto a wide platform, a sledge that was pulled by two camels. The woman shook her head at Telamon and aided him to sit up.

"Who are you?" It pained Telamon to talk as his throat was dry and his lips cracked.

"Vink," the woman answered as she placed a goatskin to Telamon's lips.

Parched, Telamon greedily drank, tasting cool milk which soothed his scratchy throat.

"Malkor." The woman took the goatskin away from Telamon's lips and stood, walking over towards the front where she then disappeared through a mesh that kept out insects, again saying, "Malkor."

Moments later appeared a man, dark-skinned with a long beard whitening at the roots, and atop of his head was a red turban. He wore a white shirt, travel stained and smelling of sweat, and red baggy trousers, his boots curled up at his toes. "Ah," he said with a smile. "You yet live."

"I do," Telamon said with confusion. "But who are you?"

"I am Malkor," the man bowed. "The greatest merchant west of the desert."

"I am Telamon, pupil of the school of Phrontis; and I thank you for your kindness."

"Thank me not my young friend," Malkor replied as he sat on the chair next to the bed. "For it was the will of Harena that we found you."

The sledge suddenly jerked as it slid over a rock and Malkor called out in a reproving tone, speaking in the strange language.

"Now my young friend," Malkor said in a more congenial tone, "may I ask what you were doing alone in such a harsh place."

Telamon retold all his tale, from the beginnings of the Trial through to the betrayal of Calliope. Malkor listened keenly, even stopping Telamon at certain points to ask questions. He spoke of how he wanted to return to the school to stop Calliope claiming the victory. After hearing of Telamon's plight, Malkor revealed that he was heading as far as Linteum, and that he was welcome to remain as his guest.

In the days after, Telamon learnt that his travel companions were a family of spice traders from across the desert. The language they spoke was known as the desert tongue, spoken only by those of the city of Vespertinus. The passage to this city was known only to the people of Vespertinus and was kept a closely guarded secret. When Telamon asked why that was, he was simply told that it was the will of Harena.

After eight days, Telamon returned to Linteum. He thanked Malkor and his family for their kindness and made with all haste for the king's pavilion, pleading with the guards for an audience. It was Icarus that recognised Telamon, though his skin was more tanned from the sun since they last met, and it was he which led Telamon in to see the king.

The king was furious to learn of Calliope's treachery and he immediately ordered the death of Scyllias, who protested his innocence. Through the king, Telamon learnt that Calliope had returned, saying that the mechanical creature had killed all but her, and that she alone had battled with it. For two days had Calliope been praised by the people of Linteum, honoured by feasts and fine gifts. The king himself had gifted Calliope with the title of Restorer, for her part in slaying the creature so that the people of Linteum could return to their homeland. Calliope had taken her leave to return to Phrontis three days ago, and the king gave a fine horse to Telamon and a company of soldiers to escort him home.

That same day did Telamon ride out, and it took just sixteen days to reach the School of Phrontis. As they rode up the main street in Harpagus, people stopped in the street to watch them pass. Gossip began to circulate immediately, causing all manner of rumours. Ignoring the calls to slowdown, Telamon rode with haste up the hill towards the school. There the ceremony had already began in the hall, and Telamon with his escort passed not a sole as they rode in through the iron gates.

The Trial would officially end when the pupil in possession of the five items had place them upon the Founding Stone. This stone was the first to have been laid by Phrontis and is believed to mark the spot where he first decided to build the school. The ceremony was a welcome break for all the pupils attending the school. The day would dawn to the smell of roasting meats, fresh bread flavoured with herbs and cooling cakes topped with honey. On top of these delights the older pupils were allowed wine. Pupils and tutors would don their finest robes and gather in the founding Hall, each wearing a laurel wreath atop of their head.

The Founding Hall itself was decorated with silk cloth, long strips hanging from ceiling to floor green and yellow in colour. The hall was circular in shape with the Founding Stone placed in the centre. The pupils were led in by their tutors and made to stand around the walls, silent with lowered heads. The Peritum was stood behind the Founding Stone, staff in hand and wearing his finest red robe with a blue sash of silk tied around his waist.

Calliope had arrived the day before and was ushered in to make her report to the Peritum. After giving her account of the quest, she was led to her own private room where she ate the finest dishes the school had to offer and drank a heavy red wine that dulled her senses. That night she slept in a large bed with silk pillows and covers; and slept well she did. The morning then dawned, and she was taken to a room where a bath had been drawn for her. For an hour Calliope relaxed in the warm water, the first time she had bathed since she had been in the Spring of Youth. Next, she dressed in a new robe, grey as she was still yet a Novice. Her hair she tied up in her usual fashion and pinned in place with a long needle-like hairpin.

As Calliope entered the Founding hall, the other pupils moved aside to make an aisle that led to the Founding

Stone. In her hand was her pack that she had carried since the beginning of the Trial. In it was the five items that had been tasked, the amulet of the enchantress, a tail feather from a Roc, a golden apple, water from the Spring of Youth and the Heart of Sabacos.

Like a wise old owl, the Peritum watched as Calliope approached the Founding stone, his grey eyes seemingly knowing. "Calliope, you come here to claim victory in the Trial?"

"I do," Calliope replied with confidence.

"Then set down your proof upon the stone."

Calliope opened her pack and pulled out the first item. "The amulet of the enchantress." She then placed it down upon the cold stone and went back into her pack, where she pulled out a large, white feather. "The tail feather of a Roc." Calliope placed the feather next to the amulet and again went into her pack, pulling out a golden apple. "An apple from the Golden Tree." The apple she placed next to the feather before once more putting her hand in her pack. From it she took out a small phial of clear water. "Water from the Spring of Youth." The phial she placed beside the golden apple before finally taking out a red ruby from her pack. "The Heart of Sabacos."

The door to the Founding Hall suddenly burst open and Telamon, along with his escort, rushed in. The pupils erupted with shock, for all had heard that Calliope was the only one to survive the Trial.

"Stop!" Telamon was confronted by pupils who tried to stop him getting near to Calliope. But as his escort drew their curves swords, they released Telamon and took a step back. "She betrayed me and tried to kill me!"

Calliope stood pale with shock, and no words could form in her mouth. She had believed that there was no way out of that room she had pushed Telamon, no chance of him surviving. It had been out of fondness that she had not simply given him a quick death, fondness, and selfishness. The thought had been with her since the beginning and she had hoped that he would have met his end by some creature or other on their quest. But irritatingly Telamon had survived to the point when she knew she would have to kill him herself. One night as he slept, she had knelt over him poised to strangle him, but she could not bring herself to do it. So, when the opportunity presented itself in the ruins of Sabacos, she had panicked, and took it.

The Peritum raised his left hand and the hall fell silent. From behind stepped forwards an imp, carrying a velvet bag concealing a heavy object. The Peritum took out from the bag a red orb, smooth and glass like. It was a seeing stone, the last of its kind. In this orb, black shadows would form to show whatever the seer desired. For the whole Trial, the Peritum had watched the pupils, judging their actions, and weighing their worthiness. Upon the founding stone he placed the red orb, which did not roll as the stone was perfectly level.

"I have seen all," the Peritum announced. "From beginning to end, I have watched. Sharing in your victories and loss. Calliope has betrayed her fellow companions, our laws of the Trial. I therefore disqualify Calliope. Now she will relinquish the Heart of Sabacos and step aside for Telamon."

But Calliope would not yield the ruby and began to utter words in the forbidden tongue, words never spoken inside the school before. A shade of darkness swept over the hall and all felt the presence of evil. A dark figure with glowing green eyes formed beside Calliope and she commanded it to slay all.

Though the Peritum was aged and not physically strong, his lore in magic was deep. From his staff he Conjured a white spirit with glowing eyes the colour of ice. Thus, the battle between light and dark began. All watched the battle in fear of their lives and for their school. The hall lit up with flashes of light as the two spirits clashed above the pupils' heads. Panic ensued as both students and tutors ducked to take cover, many lying on the floor covering their heads with their arms. The black spirit gave a mighty screech which whipped up a force of wind which tore down a few strips of cloth hanging from the walls. The blast of air struck the white spirit and sent it crashing back where it suddenly vanished as smoke disperses with the wind.

"Azen morelek zonu valore!" The words of the forbidden tongue turned Calliope's eyes red, wicked with malice. She raised her hands, her right hand still clutching the ruby, and all the candles in the hall were blown out. The black spirit grabbed the closest pupil to it, a boy in his second year, and placed its vile mouth over his face. The life was sucked out of the boy, whose body shuddered and withered up to resemble more of a dried-up piece of fruit than of a human boy. The green eyes of the spirit glowed with a ferocious intensity that any it looked upon would freeze with fear.

But the Peritum was not defeated yet. *"Mirrornor belnig vomor!"* The white spirit reformed and took up the battle once more, its eyes blazing blue with resolve. It grappled with the dark spirit, and for a time none could say which would gain the victory. Three times the spirits circled above the heads of the pupils, their battling giving off a grey light which briefly lit the hall.

Calliope's strength began to wane as the duel went on, as the magic it took to conjure such creatures took a heavy toll. Though her knowledge in the forbidden lore was deep, it was but a mere drop in an ocean when compared to the Peritum.

Though aged, the Peritum's understanding was far superior to that of Calliope's. He knew he had only to wait while the dark powers sapped her strength. Finally, Calliope fell to the floor, exhausted, and defeated. The dark spirit evaporated in a sudden puff of black smoke and Calliope was apprehended by the soldiers from Linteum. The Heart of Sabacos fell from her hand and went rolling across the stone floor.

"Telamon," the Peritum spoke, "take up the heart and place it upon the stone."

Telamon did as he was bid, and it was then he noticed his father standing close to the Peritum, his eyes filled with tears of joy. Thus, Telamon won the Trial and was hailed as an unlikely hero.

As for Calliope, she was banished from the school and branded with runes on her hands to limit her power. To the Enchanted Forest she fled, taking residence in the dwelling of the enchantress. Thus, she became the second enchantress. For years after she reigned over that wicked place, her want for revenge souring the water and withering the growth of life.

For fifty years did Telamon serve the School of Phrontis, growing his understanding of the world and expanding the prestige of the school. In his last seven years, he served as the school's Peritum, years that are now referred to as the golden years. But as all things must end, so too does this tale. The school went on for years after Telamon, slowly diminishing in its lore. Magic faded and was believed to be no more than a fable from a less enlightened time, a time of people searching for the truth of the world. Thus, came the end of magic, and along with it passed the Age of Heroes.

The End

APPENDIX

Men: Humankind have inhabited the island of Valhanor for thousands of years. It remains lost in time as to when men first arrived on the island, and as to where it was they came from. An ancient tale told of a lonely giant that carved a smaller image of himself and of his recently deceased wife from a single block of stone. It was said that the Star Gods took pity on his loneliness and gave life to the carvings, thus mankind came to be. Later scholars dismissed the tale as myth, unreliable folklore from a long-lost age. Over the centuries, men lived alongside other races of the island, learning to build and govern over themselves without the aid of giants or imps watching over them. They built vast stone cities with huge step pyramids that they dedicated to the Star Gods. Each city-state had its own king and laws, unique to their own culture and traditions. Trade flourished and the ancient cities prospered with peace and wealth.

Then came the Darkness.

Nobody knows what the Darkness is, or from where it came. Wise men said that it was sent by the Star Gods to test men's loyalty to righteousness. The Darkness corrupted men's souls, and greed and power took the place of the needs of the people. Kings began to close their city gates to all but their own citizens and began to distrust their neighbours. Over the passing years, men became lesser and fell from righteousness, desiring greater wealth and power for themselves. The city-states of Dimon Dor and Balharoth grew to their heights of power, conquering nearby towns and villages to bring them greater wealth and power. The wise men of the island searched for a cure to the darkness that had corrupted men. They searched for many years before an answer was found.

After years of traveling from city to city, and reading countless old scrolls, a wise man named Adullam believed that he had found the answer. He united the ancient kingdoms and races together in a great council, in the hope of restoring the diminishing righteousness that had once thrived throughout the island. The great council agreed to the creation of a blessed chalice so that all races could gain a true knowledge to vanquish the darkness. The great kings of Balharoth and Dimon Dor, along with the other members of the great council went atop mount Gannim where the Craft Master of the Gigantes called down a star from the night sky, splitting in two as it fell. From the sea a young boy was found washed up on the shore. Adullam proclaimed the boy of heavenly descent, and that he had been sent by the gods to lead mankind back into the light. But another wise man named Baal disagreed and demanded that they continue with their plan of crafting a magical chalice from the star rock. The chalice of knowledge was thus crafted, and an ancient spell of knowledge placed upon it. All kings drank from the chalice, but it carried the curse of too much knowledge. Men became evermore greedy for power, and now understood how to gain it.

Adullam took the young boy found washed up on the shoreline and took him as his apprentice, naming him Elnar. Elnar grew up in the chalice temple built in the mountains to the southeast of the island, where the chalice of knowledge was supposed to have been safeguarded. But the chalice never made it there. The war for the chalice erupted and the kingdom of Balharoth fell to ruin. After the death of Adullam, Elnar was forced to flee west where many people believed in his divinity.

After gathering support, Elnar raised an army and marched on Dimon Dor, who now held the chalice. The two armies met on the Plains of Pendor and Elnar's forces were able to deal the forces of Dimon Dor a crushing defeat. The city of Dimon Dor was cursed and fell to ruin.

Elnar took the chalice of knowledge and founded the Order of the Star to safeguard it, ordering that no one should ever consume from it again. The city of Elnaria was founded in his name and soon the western part of the island came under Elnar's control. With the war won, the kingdom of Elnaria flourished as peace was restored to the island. The remaining city-states in the east continued with their traditions and grew in power. Many spoke of uniting the eastern kingdoms to rival that of Elnaria, but no king was able to unite them. Soon the eastern kingdoms abandoned kings in favour of electing the strongest citizen to lead them, giving them the title of satrap. The eastern city-states went on independently from the kingdom of Elnaria and refused to believe in Elnar's divinity.

The kingdom of Elnaria declared a new age, the Age of the Chalice, and began counting the years from the coronation of Elnar and labelled it AC, for after the chalice was reclaimed. Elnar commissioned the construction of the great library in Elnaria and appointed an army of scribes to record the history of the kingdom. Much of what is now known of the island comes from those old scrolls.

Blessed with long life Elnar reined for many years, but in 84AC Elnar the great came to pass. His dying words were of a fading light within his bloodline and the hope of one whom the gods shall choose to come forward and bring light back to the kingdom.

The line of kings lessened as the centuries passed, and kings became less pious and more tainted by the darkness. The kingdom of Elnaria became structured so that those at the top reaped all the wealth for themselves, and those at the bottom were no better than slaves to their lords. Thus, the kingdom remained until the coming of the one who would bring the kingdom back to the light, and to a new age.

Gigantes: The Gigantes were giants, famous for their size and strength. They stood between 9 – 13 feet tall and had the strength of twenty men. As a race, the Gigantes were generally righteous characters and lived in peace alongside the other races on the island for many years. Though a cattle farmer from Attaroth once claimed that a giant had stolen two of his cows by running past and picking them up (one under each arm) without stopping. They resided mainly in rocky hills or the mountains where they honed their skill in the crafting of metal tools and carving of stonework, which was the finest on the island.

It is generally believed that the Gigantes were the first race on the island and were believed to have built The Great Mountains to the east of the island. Nothing is known of their origin as they never kept any written records of their own, and what little is known, was written by various scribes that lived centuries after men first settled on the island. One scribe said that the Gigantes were gods cast out of the heavens for their yearning to build a paradise of their own. Another wrote that they were the gods' first creation. Another that they were mere slaves, created to shape the world. The truth may never be known as the Gigantes were secretive and kept much of their knowledge to themselves. They did have a written language, straight lined runes that they carved into stone. But only a handful of men were ever able to read them.

Unlike men, the Gigantes were not led by a king to rule over the race, instead they were mostly left to make decisions for themselves. The giant they considered to have the most knowledge in craftwork was given the title of Craft Master, who gave wisdom to any giant seeking it. Over the passing centuries, they built huge stone circles, for what purpose nobody knows for sure, though it was widely believed that they were used to map the stars. As the population of men began to rise the Gigantes began to teach them how to build but kept their greater knowledge for themselves.

By the time the darkness came to the island, their numbers had begun to dwindle. Where once there had been elegant halls carved under a mountain that were filled with generations of families, were now left abandoned. Nobody really knows as to why their numbers declined, though one scribe later recorded that it was because they were so deeply engrossed with their craftwork, that they had simply forgot to reproduce. A later scribe dismissed that claim and wrote that the Gigantes simply left the island to find a new home across the Sea of Rune. Over time, as the kingdoms of men grew, sightings of the Gigantes lessened.

After the creation of the chalice of knowledge, Craft Master Norlag urged men to come to peaceful terms with each other, to stop the bloody war that had erupted amongst men, but they did not heed his wisdom. Nothing after the war is known as the Gigantes had little more dealings with men. There were a few remote sightings and one woman called Eleanor claimed that she had become friends with a giant who lived in the hills near to Heath Hollow. In the years that passed, the Gigantes passed into legend, myths and stories told to children by the fireside. But their stonework remained, and their finely crafted swords and daggers became highly sought after. Much of their craftwork and knowledge remains hidden and awaits discovery in their long-abandoned caves.

Imps: Imps were a small, lesser folk then the Gigantes, and stood no bigger than a child. They had little love for the hot furnaces used for the smelting of metals like the Gigantes did. Instead they had a fondness for the growing of trees. A scribe recorded that when the races of Imps and Gigantes first met, it was agreed that they would share the island. The Imps grew many woodlands where they joyfully dwelt for centuries. Like the Gigantes, they kept no written records, but had an oral tradition that they passed down from generation to generation.

Over the centuries they built villages, little mud huts with thatched roofs, deep in the forests where they honed their skills in the lore of magic and of healing potions. At the coming of spring every year all Imps from across the island would travel to the northern most forest where they had planted their first tree. For three days they would drink potions that made them hallucinate and chant a magical spell which brought the trees around them to life. The trees would then pick out an Imp they deemed worthy and named him as Grand Imp.

When the darkness descended upon the island, men began to take Imps and keep them against their will to try and harness their lore of magic. This resulted in many Imps becoming mischievous and distrusting of men. Over time the Imps became mysterious and placed powerful spells upon the woods in which they dwelt to keep men away from their villages. At first, they refused to help in the crafting of the chalice of knowledge, preferring to stay hidden deep in the woods. Norlag the Craft Master of the Gigantes was able to persuade the Grand Imp Georus otherwise, saying that their lore of magic was greatly needed to repel the darkness.

Georus the Grand Imp reluctantly agreed and took the chalice deep into the woods, where the Imps placed a powerful spell of knowledge upon it. In the war that broke out after, the Imps were blamed for it. The kings of men accused the Imps of placing a curse on the chalice that made men evermore ambitious and distrusting of each other.

In the years that followed, many Imps left the island. Nobody knows as to how many remain on the island, if any. But their powerful spells on the woodlands remains strong. One such spell can be seen at the ruins of Balharoth, which was cursed to be barren by the Imps. To this day it remains an eerie place where not even a weed will grow in its memory.

Elves: Elves were often mistaken for Imps because of their similar size and appearance. Like the Imps they too had a love for the woods and dwelt alongside the Imps for centuries before men appeared on the island. Elves, however, were generally more mischievous then Imps. When men first built small dwellings, intrigued by them, they often snuck in while the inhabitants were out and stacked all their belongings into a pile in the middle of the room. An early recording told of an Elf that had terrorised a family for years, each night he came, constantly knocking on the door and running away. Then he would sit on a tree stump outside of the house, menacingly laughing until dawn.

The Elves had no king or chieftain who ruled over them. A scribe that lived long ago recorded that they were a nomadic race that travelled from forest to forest, ever searching for a paradise they would never find. They had a lore of magic, though not as great as that of the Imps. Instead they became the masters of trickery and curses. They would shoot their cursed arrows at any who walked the woods where they dwelt and watched as their victim fell to madness.

Little more is known of them and many believe that they no longer dwell on the island. Though there were still a few reports, from people traveling through woods, of hearing sniggering as stones are thrown at them. But over the years these reports lessened to where, eventually, only a handful of villages claimed that Elves still inhabited the nearby woods.

Star Gods: The Star Gods are a deity that the ancient people of Valhanor worshiped. Before the age of the chalice (what is often called the Dark Age) the many city-states dotted all over the island built vast temples to honour the Star Gods. The temple at Lhanwick was the grandest, and it was believed to be the place where the Star Gods first came to the island and where their spirit speaks with the oracle.

An ancient scroll, written by an unknown scribe, recorded that the Star Gods rode on stars across the sky a millennia before men came to be, and that it was they who created mankind at the dawning of the world. For centuries many believed this, and the old scrolls from Dimon Dor claimed that the Star Gods would descend from the sky and give them light (knowledge). The ancient scrolls describe them as tall, thin with elongated heads and large, dark eyes that could read a man's thoughts. Then one year, as the people of Dimon Dor stood ready to receive them, they never returned, and the darkness came.

Many learned men later discredited the ancient scrolls and claimed that there was no evidence to support their theory, saying that gods could not simply disappear. Though many still believed in them. The east and west divided over Elnar, as the east did not believe in his divinity and continued with their worship of the Star Gods. The western kingdom's beliefs in the Star Gods faded over the passing centuries. Many of its people still believed in them and in became customary for the king to uphold certain traditions (like seeking light from the oracle at Lhanwick).

The centuries passed and the eastern city-states still hold firm that the Star Gods will one day return, but to this day all that remains of them is the ruined temples and the crumbling statues in the ruins of Dimon Dor and the sunken images in the swamps of Balharoth.

Age of the Beginnings:

The Age of Beginnings, or more commonly known as the First Age, was a time long before the events set out in the Tales of Valhanor series. The First Age is said to have begun with the Battle of Stars, a battle fought between the Star Gods; and it was the bodies of the fallen which formed the world. The beginning of this age was ruled over by dragons and the world was a scorching furnace. After the reign of the dragons came the Gigantes, a race of giants with a fondness for crafting. From the smouldering ruins of the world they forged great mountains where they took residence. Next came the Imps and Elves who began singing life into the soil and up sprang the forests and greenery of the world. Magic was at its height during this time, and it was believed to be when the Star Gods were most willing to visit the world. It was during this age that men first came, themselves practicing magic and building grand states. But these early men grew in envy of the Gigantes' craftmanship and grew in longing for their stowed treasures. Thus, men seeking fame and fortune began to rise, and the states of men prided themselves on might of arms over the enlightenment of magic. The Age of Beginnings thus ended with the founding of the city of Balharoth.

Age of Heroes:

The Age of Heroes was known as the Second Age, a time when the race of men was at their height. During this age, the domain of men grew into a collection of powerful city states which competed for prestige. It was also a time of mythical creatures and of valiant deeds performed by men, men which were known as Heroes. It was from this age that the earliest tales come from, tales that inspired later generations. Giants, Imps and Elves were still numerous during this age, though now they were growing reclusive. The Imps kept mainly to the forests and schools where they tutored in the lore of magic. The giants remaining in the hills and mountains where they began to horde great treasures and lore of the First Age. The Elves, however, were intrigued by men and would often watch over their towns and villages. It was believed that elves were first to see the true destructive nature of men during this age, and they began to mischievously torment their homes. As the years passed, Heroes became lesser in their deeds and the once proud city states waned in power and grew in a deep mistrust of each other. Constant wars broke out between the states of men, and giants, imps and elves became lesser in their dealings with them. The Age of Heroes was said to have ended when the school of Phrontis was abandoned.

The Dark Age:

The Dark Age was known as the Third Age and was a time of turmoil and woe. The city states of men were now lesser in their lore and sought only riches and power. The great cities of Balharoth and Dimon Dor were now at their height, and their rivalry caused much friction throughout Valhanor. Little survives from this age as many of the schools founded by the Imps had been burned, their libraries that stowed ancient scrolls of recorded history used for kindling. A sickness rose from the unknown, tainting men further to vile deeds. The Darkness was this sickness called, a black plague which infected all the kingdoms of men. From this age comes little in enlightenment to the advancement of civilisation. It was towards the end of this age that all the races of Valhanor came together to combat the Darkness. From the sky they summoned a star from which they crafted a chalice blessed with a potion of knowledge. During this time Elnar the Great came to ascendancy, uniting the western city states and defeating the city of Dimon Dor. With Elnar's victory in the war for the chalice, he declared a new age, the Age of the Chalice. The Elnarians began counting the years from the coronation of Elnar and labelled it AC, for after the chalice was reclaimed. The years before were labelled BC, for before the chalice was reclaimed.

The Age of the Chalice:
The Age of the Chalice was known as the Fourth Age, a time in which the events of the Tales of Valhanor are set. Imps and Elves had long dispersed from Valhanor, and those that remained were few and seldom seen away from the forests. The Gigantes had too disappeared, their caves stowed with treasures remaining hidden. During this age, the Kingdom of Elnaria was prominent in the west, while the east remained a collection of city states. After the death of Elnar the Great in 84AC, his realm began to decline, and the line of kings lessened in wisdom. Upon the death of

King Edward V in 611AC, the kings of Elnaria were no longer in control of the Order of the Star, the Order founder by Elnar the Great to safeguard the Chalice of Knowledge. The first Grandmaster, Everard of Beolog, hid the chalice deep in the ruins of Dimon Dor where it remained undiscovered until 1089AC. Civil war broke out that same year and the kingdom of Elnaria was thrown into turmoil. From the chaos of war rose an unlikely hero, a chosen one that was claimed to one day restore the realm to light and end the Darkness.

Printed in Poland
by Amazon Fulfillment
Poland Sp. z o.o., Wrocław

64018235R00193